KICKING FIFTY

KICKING FIFTY

LISA APPIGNANESI

McArthur & Company
TORONTO

Published in Canada in 2003
By McArthur & Company
322 King St. West, Suite 402
Toronto, Ontario
M5V 1J2

NATIONAL LIBRARY OF CANADA CATALOGUING IN PUBLICATION

Appignanesi, Lisa
    Kicking fifty/ Lisa Appignanesi.

ISBN 1-55278-378-2

I. Title.

PS8551.P656K52 2003   C813'.54   C2003-904009-7

Cover and Text Design by Tania Craan
Cover Photo Credit: © Helen Ashford/Workbook Stock
Printed in Canada by: Friesens

The publisher would like to acknowledge the financial support of the
Government of Canada through the Book Publishing Industry Development
Program, the Canada Council, and the Ontario Arts Council for our publishing
activities. We also acknowledge the Government of Ontario through the Ontario
Media Development Corporation Ontario Book Initiative.

10 9 8 7 6 5 4 3 2 1

PART ONE

I started writing to Celia when my first lover died. He had been a mutual one, so it seemed like the right thing to do. Deaths, like natural disasters, have a way of making you want to reach out for your nearest and dearest of whatever epoch, just to make sure that they're still here with you, still encased in a vulnerable body on this vulnerable planet.

Once I started writing, it became a little like smoking. I couldn't give it up. Not that I posted the letters right away. I don't know quite what stopped me from posting them, unless it was that Celia and I hadn't parted on altogether the best of terms. Some twenty years have passed since she left for Vancouver.

It wasn't only the matter of Patrick's death that made me think of her, I realized. Hanker after her, if the truth be known. There was something else, something deeper. Like some teenage

sweetheart, Celia seemed to hold the keys to an earlier, untram-
melled version of myself. The time had come for me to find that
woman again. In fact, the time had almost passed. A woman
who could dare and soar, who could fly unhindered. Certainly
not a woman who needed fifty a day to keep her buoyant.

    Celia and I had been best friends for a single year when we
were ten. The period remains the only memorable one of my
childhood. Even now, when I climb a steep incline and feel my
heart begin to pound and my cheeks turn pink, I sense Celia at
my side, and I can smell the inviting coolness of the copse at the
top of the hill where we flopped down on dappled ground and
told each other the most secret of secrets.

    Celia was living with her grandmother then, almost next
door to the local school. I first became intensely aware of her not
in class, but in a playtime game of hide-and-seek. When it came
her turn to hide, none of us could find her. Not anywhere. Not
in any of the usual hiding places, nor in the unusual ones
behind the bins, where the smell was so bad. Then, just as we
were about to give up, she jumped out to startle us from the shed
where we had looked once already. I think she must have
stopped breathing.

    Celia was good at hiding. It wasn't that she didn't want to be
found, but she didn't want to be found anywhere that we might
expect and before we had all but given up the search. Once we
were in that fractious state composed partly of worry, partly of
irritation, she would beam out at us, triumphant in her self-
revelation.

    By mid-term, we were best friends. Most afternoons we'd
take off on our bikes and cycle to my house, which was a mile or

so outside town. Celia was already worldly-wise. She'd lived abroad, as far away as Iran. She had seen kohl-eyed women covered in veils. She had seen scorpions three inches long. She had ridden bareback on Arab stallions. She knew what men and women did with each other after that kiss which was all the cinema then showed. When she vanished abroad again at the end of that year, our little sphere dimmed. Life felt sadly diminished.

It wasn't that Celia herself did anything particularly wild. In fact, she was mostly rather quiet, a shy, large-eyed girl with a geometrically cut fringe. But her presence had an electricity to it. Within its field I inhabited an expanded self. I read more and worked harder. I championed causes. I was bold. On a barely expressed whim of Celia's, I pinched my mother's lipstick and eye makeup so that we could masquerade as women. I, who had never purchased anything more than jelly babies on my own, covertly took a bus into Littlehampton and bought us matching striped scarves with my savings. I even managed to grow three inches. All, I think, for Celia.

Except for a single postcard, Celia didn't write to me from wherever it was her parents had then taken her. But, utterly by chance, we found each other again at university and stepped right back into that girlhood intimacy. Once more, in Celia's presence I grew daring, adventurous. I was someone quite other than the utterly practical, hideously responsible woman that life has since turned me into. It lasted through the period we spent living together in London and continued with a charged correspondence during Celia's Paris years. Really it went on until she settled down with Jim.

And now, now that life is distinctly slipping into its final lap, I feel in need of Celia's presence again. I miss her. With her I sense I can become a desiring being again. And she can help me make sense of where I've got to. Translate me to myself. A diary wouldn't be the same. There would be only me listening, and Celia's listening was always better. Sharper.

So I started to write to Celia. Addictive as it was, it wasn't altogether easy at first. Have I remembered to say that Celia had not only a watchful eye but, when she broke her silence, a withering tongue?

LONDON, 2 MARCH

Dear Celia,
Yes, it has been a long time. Longer than either of us probably like to count anymore. But I thought the news might not have reached you across the distance of an ocean and a continent. And I know you'd want to know . . .

Patrick — our mutual lover all those eons ago, when the world was young and thirty seemed mature, forty past it, fifty ancient and sixty positively prehistoric — has, sadly, snuffed it. Kicked the bucket. Gone the way of all flesh — and he had rather a lot of it to protect him when I last saw him some eight months ago now, at a friend's fiftieth. (Do you understand why people insist on these public rites of passage? Is there really anything to celebrate about turning fifty — apart from the fact that one has endured, is still alive to drink, though less and less, and in dread of the morning after, let alone the gaffs of the night before?)

Patrick, to give the old rascal his due, was well past his Big 5-0. But he clung to that aura of celebration. It's probably what killed him. A riotous night and no morning after.

The papers said it was sudden. Unexpected. They were full of him. The way we used to be.

It all made me reach for the cigarettes, just when I was poised to kick the habit. Again. We did it together once, remember? When I was staying with you in Paris. We patrolled each other, sucked pens or countless sweets. You conquered the dreaded weed before I did, probably because I used to cheat and race down to the café as soon as you went off to work.

Funny. I never read obits in the old days. Did you? It's crept up on me gradually, like moss on an ageing wall. Don't know if it's a touch of "there but for the grace . . ." Patrick would undoubtedly have called it *Schadenfreude* — "So pleased that the Grim Reaper got you instead of me, dear."

Or maybe I just read them because the obits are the only place the press can ever bring itself to say a kind word about anyone. Sometimes I get hungry for a little gentleness with my morning coffee. Something far from the acid and the braying and the more righteous than thou and the noisy trumpeting of opinions. Well, they were gentle with Patrick. They didn't mention the acrimony of the three divorces, nor print a list of the briefly loved and more briefly fucked, which would have taken far more space, I imagine, than the eulogy to his broadcasting genius and political nous and golden tongue. They didn't mention his early radical stands either, the protests against the college's investment policy, the eulogies to Ho Chi Minh. But then all that now seems as remote and incomprehensible as histories of Cromwell, and even more ancient than my face. Time has made fools of our earnest passions.

Do you remember Patrick back then, Celia? With his dirty golden locks, his knee-high boots, that suasive Irish lilt which made disquisitions on the history of irrigation more riveting than Heather's purple hot pants?

Oh well. I probably only remember 'cause he was my first. And it might as well have been him as any other, whatever more recent decades of political correctness have now decreed. At least he had some experience. Lots of experience.

You know, writing to you makes me realize I miss you, Celia. Miss you very much. I really am sorry we grew apart. Life picks you up and puts you down in such odd places without ever asking.

Whoops. Have to go, Celia. More later. Meanwhile, tears for Patrick. A lot of them.

LONDON, 3 MARCH

So sorry, Celia,
Have only just managed to get back to you after yesterday's interruption. The customers pile in at the end of the school day — because of the coffee shop. Free espresso with any book over five pounds. Cappuccinos or lattes over six. The kids adore it. To be fair they'd probably come in just for the coffee, since it's the best in the area — which also houses a sixth-form college. But this way, I inflict an occasional book on them, too.

It occurs to me that none of this will make any sense to you. When we last saw each other, I was on my way to being a star literary agent, flitting about town and gorging myself on hype and deals and gossip. But after Robert upped and left me (did news of that reach you, or were you spared?), I turned a leave of absence from the agency into permanent leave. Presto — metamorphosis. From sparkling butterfly to creeping caterpillar, and halfway back into the cocoon.

My choice, no one else's. I simply couldn't bear the tongues whisking through my faults and my life as if I were so much offal to be dished up by the new British cuisine. I couldn't bear the compassionate smiles masking triumph. Nor was it much fun recognizing that no way could I face the prospect of selling a book to anyone in the firm at which Robert was then editorial director.

So I legged it. Got a job managing a bookshop for a small chain instead. You rarely get to see any of the publishers I know in a bookshop, let alone in this northern outpost of London. When the chain folded, I managed to find some backing from a wholesaler and bought the shop, which was doing well enough on its own and is now, since the facelift (the shop's, not mine), doing modestly better.

It's all a far cry from the cut and thrust and glam of yesteryear, but neither my appetites nor ambitions are what they used to be. In fact I've found that the only thing that grows with age — apart from the layers around shoulders and waist and tum — is envy. Nasty, petty beast that he is. Yaps at your heels in reproach wherever you go. Has he taken up a permanent seat at your feet yet, Celia? Has your husband, too, shed you like an unnecessary skin?

Who would have thought that sensible, sensitive, hard-working Robert — who managed not to bolt during those difficult first years of Nell's toddlerhood — would have been capable of it? Robert with his New England morality and his well-fed cheeks. He used so to depend on me — or that's what I thought. And it wasn't a bad marriage as marriages go. But I guess, as marriages go, it went — out to pasture. Little sex, needless to say. It was far more exciting (and restful after a hard day at office and book launches) to put one's feet up and watch a video. Our bonds were so comfortable, they were invisible. So you'd think I wouldn't have noticed when he left. But I did. And shame covered me, like some ghostly Halloween sheet to trip over at every step.

Why do we women feel shame at such moments? It's not as if we were the ones to have done anything worthy of censure — whatever the mothers may say. (I could hear mine tsking beneath her breath. "Always knew she couldn't keep her man.") I was the innocent party, after all. Betrayed. Abandoned. And yet I felt ashamed. As if I had lost out in some race for perfect womanhood and been deemed a failure. As if I were the reprobate. Maybe that's what those cuckolds felt in those old French plays; why I always imagined their faces with two perfect circles of bright pink on the cheeks.

The shame brought on my first hot flush. Really, it did. Right in the midst of a meeting with a big honcho I was trying to squeeze a little more of an advance out of for my kiss-and-tell ex-minister client.

The misery of it. There I am, two days after Robert scuttles off with his single suitcase, saying he'll come back for the rest in a couple of weeks. I'm sitting in an office which is all cool glass and stainless steel and no books. I'm in my best suit of soft dove-grey, a spotless white shirt, a cerise silk scarf artfully tied round my neck, and I get up to pace a little for effect and make a point. And suddenly my head starts pounding with a rush of heat so intense it's as if I've walked into a raging bonfire and I'm being liquefied, brain and all.

I have no idea why I'm standing up, who I'm with, let alone where. All I know is that my underarms are dripping straight through shirt and jacket, that my chest is steaming, that I have to pull this damned scarf from my throat, which is hot enough to fry an egg, while my cheeks could boil the water which should be evaporating from my forehead, but isn't. The only other thing that's clear is that it's all Robert's fault.

When I get home that evening, Nell is in the tub, and in the way she'd just begun to take on then — having reached that delicious little 12-year-old state of perversity called pubescence — she shrieks at me not to come in. Without bothering to say hello first, of course. The shriek mingles command and panic in equal measure. It's as if one little look from mother-recently-become Medusa, and her sweet little boobs will turn to stone and drop off. So I shrug and rue the cuddles of yesteryear and take myself off to the shower.

By the time I come out, she's sitting in front of the telly, though she hasn't bothered to switch it on. Her hand is clasped over her stomach. Her forehead puckers in a manner that is inescapably her father's. This has a touch of melodrama about it, so I never quite know whether to console or laugh whatever it is away.

Tonight, I tread carefully. Her father has after all just bolted, in the process leaving not only me, but less willingly her, and she has every reason to take on a tragic mien.

"How was school, Nell?" I open softly.

No answer.

"Did Ms. Dibbs like your history essay?"

Still no answer.

"Shall I make us some pasta?" This usually gets a response, since pasta in whatever shape and with whatever dollops of sauce or cream is Nell's favourite, and means we can slob in front of *EastEnders* rather than sit upright at table, knife in hand.

Still no answer.

I make a move for the kitchen and wonder whether perhaps Robert has phoned and said something which has upset her even more than she was upset the previous evening. I stub my toe on a terracotta pot and I have an all but irresistible urge to fling it at the conservatory window so that we can have some real drama, and slabs and slivers of glass and hunks of earth to hobble around in while we scream with primal gusto. But no, no. I'm the mother around here, reasonable despite my Medusa powers.

And then I hear Nell's voice quivering behind me. "It's come."

"What's come?" I veer round. She's hunched over now, her face stricken as she gives me an accusing stare. But she also looks all of five, her cheeks glistening with that delicious sheen that only a childhood layer of pudge can accomplish, and I move towards her to protect her from whatever bogey may be at hand. No matter how I may sometimes complain, I adore my daughter.

"What is it, hon bun? What's come?"

She hides her face and blurts out, "The bleeding."

I sigh in relief, hug her and welcome her to womanhood with a smile which is only a little exaggerated. I tell her she has joined the ranks of the most productive (and certainly reproductive) sex. I tell her that the curse is a great provider of excuses, let alone future glories. That it need hardly ever cause more than a little discomfort. I yammer on in the way that our generation learned from all those books about our bodies and ourselves until I have Nell giggling in complicity.

All the time I'm thinking to myself that if that God I don't believe in is really after all up there, he's gotta be male, because only a man would think of a joke bad enough to usher me into menopause and my daughter into menarche on the same day. While I rush down to the corner shop for some extra pads, I also think that forever after Nell will subliminally link her passage into womanhood with her father's departure. The first will somehow have sparked the second. She'll hate herself, her female body — unlovely, unlovable.

But never as much or as passionately, I hope, as I hate Robert now.

When I stopped hating Robert, I realized I missed him. Him. Not the salivating, hair-obsessed adolescent he'd morphed into while I wasn't watching. But the him he was. It took about four years. Until just a few months ago, really.

Nell, meanwhile, found a reasonable solution to the problem of self-hatred. She decided to blame it — and everything else in the world, including Dad's bolting — on mother. She tempered her dislike of her own body by hating her mother's instead — which is at least something we have in common.

But I'm rambling, the way I used to do when you were living in Paris and I wrote you these endless epistles from London — more diary than letters really. Yes, you were my diary then and I could tell you anything and everything. How did we ever manage to lose each other, Celia?

Enough. It was Patrick I really wanted to tell you about now. There were more obits in the Sunday papers. It turns out he was writing a memoir — had just about finished when he popped it. Clever old Patrick. His sense of timing was always good. Go before the reviews come. And the libel suits. I wonder whether we'll have our moments on his stage. Or you at least — since your moment was so much longer.

Oh damn. Customers. I'd better finish, for now at least.
*Yours, as ever**
Jude

*Not quite as ever, to be accurate. There are a few more wrinkles (thirty-eight, in fact, but that's only what I can see without the benefit of the magnifying mirror), and pouches and a little embonpoint, but who's looking? . . . It's why the eyes go, isn't it? So that you don't have to be confronted by the full horror of your face in the mirror.

LONDON, 6 MARCH

So much to tell you, Celia, I'll never get through. Never mind, I'll just collect all these sheets and eventually put them into one envelope, the way we both used to do at the height of our letter-writing. Twenty-five years ago! Gasp. It's hard to believe.

You know, I did think of going modern and trying to hunt down an e-mail address for you — I imagine you have one — but then decided against it. Even if you've moved from your last really existing Vancouver address, I'm sure you left a forwarding one. (When was it that the annual Christmas cards stopped? Ten years ago? More? . . . And I can't remember who stopped. Probably me. I gave up on cards. Could never get them done in time.)

As for e-mail and the WWW, I confess there's something about it I don't altogether trust. It always feels like a slippery, seething, corrupt kind of space, peopled by demon pae-dophiles, pornographers, child abductors and the loucher sort of thrusting businessperson. Well, seventy per cent of its busi-ness is porn, after all. And nothing is private. Not really. I imagine all those mad chat room fantasists hacking into our delicate and ever-so-personal correspondence with their machete-like wizardry. It's a far cry from mum surreptitious-ly steaming open the envelopes.

Paper's more like you and me. You can touch it, smell it. It takes a physical effort to cast it into the bin, if content offends. None of that easy deleting into a virtual rubbish tip or click-ing on "send" before you're really ready. So letters it is. I'll be ready to send soon, Celia.

Speaking of deleting, I ended up going to Patrick's funeral. Didn't intend to, but a friend rang and said I should. Patrick would like it. The more, the merrier was always his credo. Then, too, he is the first of "mine" to go.

It was ghastly, though everyone kept congratulating every-one else on what a wonderful funeral it was. I guess they were really applauding the feat of being out of the coffin rather than in.

Patrick was temporarily between wives. I don't think it was the hiatus that killed him, since he was camping out with the second when it happened. So the honours of the ceremony fell to her. Sarah Payne — remember? She was a year behind us at Cambridge — in fact, now that I think of it, she may have succeeded you as his favourite. They had a child together. I was introduced to the child at the funeral. It gave me a bout of vertigo. There stood Patrick, aged thirty, but with his hair dyed black and a little less heft. And carrying a toddler in his arms.

I hadn't realized Patrick was a grandfather. My knees grew weak. With the weight of the years on our shoulders, you understand, not with remembered passion. The tug of gravity is so strong these days. I can see it in our contemporaries' faces — when I recognize them, that is, behind new rotundities or hollows. Those drooping lips and lids, the sagging pouches beneath the eyes, never mind the pudding bosoms or trailing derrières. We're being pulled earthwards. Verily.

But no worms for Patrick. Not him. He always did have a soft spot for Joan of Arc, with her fetching little-boy hairdo, not to mention the institution of the *auto-da-fé*. So, after a series of speeches, one wittier than the next, some choice poems, and an aria from *Don Giovanni* (that must have been chosen by Sarah), off he went in a burst of flame. No, it wasn't the Commendatore's basso which dragged him towards the inferno, but a chorus of "Luck Be a Lady." In execrable taste, I agree, though it always was one of his favourite numbers — whether because he fancied himself as Marlon Brando or because he bet on the ladies and won, I don't know.

I have to confess I was in tears. And I wasn't the only one. Didn't know I still had a soft spot for the old rake. A soft spot for those youthful days buried within us, too.

I couldn't go back to work after that, so I rang the shop and went along to the wake instead. At Sarah's house in Primrose

Hill. Her husband turns out to be a sweet old stick, who didn't mind having Patrick there at all. I guess in the way the boys tally these things, he'd won out. He had Sarah and the house and indeed the pleasures of the grandchild . . . And Patrick — well, Patrick had only the basement, and now, death.

Do you know who I bumped into? Heather Glover. She of the purple hot pants. It was a relief. Her legs are still good. Well, a kind of relief. In fact, that nasty critter who's always at my toes yapped once or twice. The last time I tried to go out in a shortish skirt, Nell gave me one of her critical looks, that kind of hard, impervious peering which only her sullen lot can get away with.

"No, Mum," she said, "I don't think so."

"Think what so?" I'm instantly on the defensive.

"You can't go out in that skirt."

"Why not? My legs aren't bad."

"Like . . . it's not your legs, Mum."

"What is it then?"

"It's your face."

She says it to me with aplomb and turns away, and I rush to the mirror and you know what? She's right. My skirt is too young for my face. Never can get anything sorted these days.

I tell you, Celia, those three periods of hormonal uproar in a woman's life are exacerbated by the fact that you just can't dress for them.

Anyhow, Heather's face was older than her skirt, but she looked pretty good to me. Her hair had fetching blonde streaks in it which obliterated the grey. She looked wonderful, in fact. And I told her so, while I kicked that envious beast away from my feet. I hate him. Why is he always there? Why do I envy women for being more beautiful (viz. younger), more successful, more married; but also for being less beautiful (viz. older, but beautifully resigned to their impending hagdom), less successful and therefore at peace with their gardens, and less married (that is, with no husbands to blot their past)? I don't, of course, envy men. They're too different. And none of us envy the dead. Which is probably why everyone seemed to be having such a good time at Patrick's funeral.

Heather and I left together, decided to have coffee, which turned into a drink, which turned into several, not to mention several hundred cigarettes and tapas. And I've just got home.

Heather works at the British Museum in the Greek section. Ancient Greek. The good thing about this curatorial neck of the woods, and probably about the civil service as a whole, is that you can still be over forty and considered a functioning member of the human species. Knowledge means something other than being able to name the presenters on breakfast television, and intelligence doesn't entail recognizing this week's celebrities. So I managed a whole evening without once feeling like a space cadet. Or suffering from the kind of senior moment which isn't quite in the rank of the thankfully transcended flushes, but is still calculated to make any thoughts of the future as bleak as a stretch of February days in Grimsby. So sad they haven't invented replacement therapy for memory cells yet, though once they do I tremble to think what bits of you it'll swell out of all recognition.

Strangely enough, Heather and I had no trouble at all remembering the smallest detail of our Cambridge days. Which was mostly what we talked about. It turns out that

Patrick slept with her too, before either of us. She thinks he seduced anyone who caught his eye during his lectures, fucked them for a term, then abandoned them the next. True, in those prehistoric days, there weren't that many of our gender around. We were a prized species, outnumbered four to one. None the less, it's a good thing Patrick left Cambridge not so long after we did, or he would have left either on a stretcher or with a harassment suit on his hands, and not just one of those linen numbers he liked to wear in spring term.

I recount all this not to lessen the sense of the unique space you (and I, and all the others) held in his life. But to tell you that you really needn't feel bad — if you still ever do — about the coincidence of his divorce with your affair. Heather thinks his first wife was set to leave him well before any of us came on the scene. It just happened while he was with you. His first wife, incidentally — she of the fishnet stockings and leather skirts — didn't make an appearance at the funeral. Heather didn't know whether it was a signal of continuing rancour or just a matter of distance. Apparently she moved to Florence way back then and still lives there.

Heather, too, briefly had a foreign marriage. With a Greek. She spent five years in Athens and then came home with her small son. Her husband, she had learned, preferred boys. She hasn't remarried and her son is now off at university.

I can hear Nell's key in the lock, so I'd better sign off. My darling almost-sixteen-year-old is having one of her sweet days. She left me a pot half-full of Bolognese, with a note telling me to heat up and eat up. I think the idea of my going to a funeral scared the poor thing. Not enough to keep her home and away from her friends, of course, but enough for her to leave me a solicitous message telling me when to expect her and to ring her on her mobile if necessary.

How's your Thomas? Did you have any more after we lost touch?
Bye for now,
Jude

LONDON, 9 MARCH

Dear Celia,
I still haven't posted your letters. Maybe courage fails me. Then, too, the last few days have just been too busy. And there's still so much to catch up on. Do you know, I suspect I've reached that terrible point in life I never thought I'd reach. Not me — the Jude who never looked back, the Jude who didn't believe in regrets . . .

Well, I've arrived. I've reached the epoch of the class reunion — those preposterous years when you're suddenly curious about the friends you've lost touch with, schoolmates, university mates, toddlers who according to your mum showed you their bottoms. So you can measure the distance you've travelled against them, the pits you have or haven't fallen in to. In the past year, I've had three missives from pre-historic (or at least pre-university) friends, all of them gently enquiring as to what I'd become.

I didn't feel strong enough actually to meet up with any of them. But I responded in chirpy tones — except to the one who so blatantly vaunted her success that I knew she only wanted to score points. But then I put off the coffee dates. And put them off again, until it seemed clear on all sides that it wasn't going to happen. Afraid, I guess. There's nothing so ghastly as finding that it takes only ten minutes to sum up all those years — and having done so, to find that there's nothing left to say. Which is why it's so nice to write to you, Celia. Somehow you give me more fluency than I ever had — even with a diary. It's because I can feel you listening in that attentive way of yours. With your head slightly tilted, your chin resting on one hand, your eyes growing wide if I say something outlandish.

Patrick and I talked about you, you know, when we last met properly. Some four years ago now, funeral apart, though I guess you can't altogether call that a meeting. It was just after the debacle with Robert. I had dragged myself to one of my author's launch parties, since it would have been too rude and too cowardly to stay away, and there was Patrick, larger than life. Well, larger than he was on the politics programme he then hosted for Sky, and certainly larger than when I'd last bumped into him.

I don't know why, but it felt so comforting to see him and smell the whisky on his breath that we arranged to have dinner together. Dinner, I'm half ashamed to say, led to bed. I was so thrilled to have anyone at all want to lead me to one that I proceeded with all the alacrity that the amount of wine I'd drunk would permit. Not much wine, you understand. Two glasses, maybe. But even before the dreaded flushes began, a single glass would have me babbling away at the velocity of the high-speed trains they keep promising us and never deliver. The tilt was probably about the same, too.

I think at that point Patrick was still married to wife number three, but she evidently lived in the country, and he had his *garçonnière* (his word, not mine) in trendy loftland in the midst of Clerkenwell. Far too young for him, but then he was far too young for himself. Except in one department.

Don't blush, Celia. Or at least not on my behalf. This wasn't the priapic Patrick of yore. This one needed a helping hand, but don't we all these days. Lifts for bosoms and cocks. And it was such a feat accomplishing the act that enjoying it had far more to do with the cigarette or three afterwards, the reward for a mountain scaled, than anything that had come before.

It was then that we chatted about you. Do you think that's the one thing that doesn't change with age, Celia? The conversations lovers have after the animal act. Those wonderful whirling conversations, two parts reminiscence of past loves to one part revelation, but all in that lovely, easy tone, a free association without the bother of the therapist's presence and with no goal except its own companionable pleasure. I'd forgotten about that with Robert. And Patrick reminded me. Maybe that's really what one wants lovers for.

I'm digressing.

Patrick was sweet about you. He remembered you with wonderful accuracy, down to the cut of your fringe and your doe eyes and that revolting orange top you wore beneath the ragged, moth-eaten £1-market fur. He said the warmth of your listening, your sweet serenity was everything a man could want. The right man. And he was the wrong man. Always the wrong man, though he held in there with you for longer than he should have. He was a bastard, he said. I wondered when that realization hit him and why it hadn't knocked him over, and I was about to ask, but I think it was at that point that I got caught in a flush which had me running for the shower, trying to hide the blotchy thighs as I did so, not to mention the saggy butt, all wrapped Venus-like in a sheet which I kept tripping over. Madness.

Why do we care? I'll never be Julie Christie again, if ever I was; and Tina Turner and Cher and all the other granny pin-ups, with their personal trainers and cosmetic surgeons, have nothing to worry about from me.

Isn't life strange. When I was in my teens and early twenties, in bad moments I sometimes used to dream about reaching my fifties — being old, by which I meant being contained, tranquil, beyond passion, beyond appetite, beyond desire. I pictured myself like one of those academic women, the mistress of Girton, say, with my greying hair impeccably tied back in a bun, my downy cheeks slightly flushed from cycling, my kohl-less eyes directed only at a beyond of peaceful and fructifying knowledge. How wonderful to be like her, to be old, not to have to worry about men and spots and whether to go back on the pill and gain a stone or stay on the diaphragm and be ever-anxious about that monthly flow. Age seemed so restful, so superior a state.

And now that I'm here? Well, I'm back on the pill and have succumbed to that extra stone and I worry about getting rid of that monthly flow, which isn't one at all, not really, and I assiduously eradicate the grey from my hair and the kohl is still there and the fructifying knowledge is scoffed at by my daughter. On top of it all, there are those things the mistress of Girton didn't divulge in the purity of her smile — the thrice-nightly visits to the loo 'cause time must have done something unspeakable to my bladder, the mornings where you feel steamrollered by some vehicle you can't remember having met or lain under, and worst of all, Appetite. It's still there, the bugger. It even follows you to the oldest people's home. But I can't trouble you with stories of my mum and all that now.

I have to pick Nell up from school today. Her birthday's around the corner and I promised her a shopping spree. Shopping with Nell means donning a muzzle. I'm barred from so much as a murmur. No "That's nice, darling," let alone "Those trousers must be subsidized by the council, darling. They trail after you and sweep the streets with wondrous efficiency." I'm only unleashed when it's time for the till and the credit card.

There may not be much to say for single teenage mum-hood, but being the single mum of a teenager leaves some-thing to be desired as well . . .

My love,

Jude

13 MARCH

My dear, dear Celia,

I've just had the strangest evening and you're the only one I can tell about it.

There was a reading in the bookshop tonight, upstairs where the coffee bar is. I have them about twice a month. It helps to build up the clientele and keep the punters loyal — and to tell you the truth, I enjoy having the authors in . . . a little like the old days, though I've mostly kept away from any of the writers who were once in my stable.

Tonight it was the turn of youthful Melanie Boyd, not one

28

of the chick-lit brigade, but a Zadie Smith write-alike, or at least that's what the double spread in *The Bookseller* said way back when. In fact, it's not quite like, though the writing is razor sharp and urban and the characters suitably hybrid. What I hadn't known, and perhaps the publishers didn't either, is that two days ago, Melanie Boyd — who is big and raunchy and as sassy as they come — appeared on some radio programme and did a hip hop number with a singer famous to all and sundry except those over twenty-one.

Well! I guessed something was up before Melanie arrived, because there was a queue for tickets (£1 or £1 off the book) and no one in the queue was using dye for covering up those old fading roots. No, there were dreads and spikes and tails and knots of flamingo pink and turquoise and emerald, but not a single muted and carefully coiffed blue-grey and only a few tastefully auburn hennas. I caught the eye of Kate, my lovely chief assistant, and she shrugged and mimed astonishment. These were my sixth-formers and their mates, I guess, though I recognized only a handful. My usual lot don't normally hang about for readings by the ladies and gents of the literary world.

This, however, wasn't the literary world as I know it. There were more punters than there were chairs, and they kept on crowding in, sitting on the floor, clustered around the coffee counter, until we had to stop them. The overflow waited outside happily enough until Melanie Boyd arrived, when they besieged her for autographs. We had a celebrity on our hands. Odd what makes celebrity these days. A writer with a dozen fine books behind him draws a respectful audience of twenty-five, and young Melanie . . . well . . .

I have to say she handled herself magnificently. She reads with the panache of a Maya Angelou and the confidence of a Salman Rushdie. And she's all of twenty-four . . . Then, too, the audience couldn't have thought the book was written in the rhyming couplets of hip-hoppese, but they bought it anyway and everyone hung around forever, even after Melanie and her minder had left. I finally urged the last ones away around eleven.

What an evening for my little bookshop!

But that isn't really what I wanted to tell you about. Though from fiction to music and back again makes an interesting and novel celebrity circuit. Who knows, we may be in on the beginning of a trend — rather better than the last one, which had bad novels ghosted for long-legged celebrities without a sentence in their heads, let alone a paragraph.

Heather stayed on after the last stragglers had gone. Did I tell you she was here? She was curious about the shop, so I'd invited her round for the reading and we intended to go out for dinner together afterwards. But it was already so late that we just sat down for a chat by the bar and asked Toni to make us a couple of lattes.

Have I mentioned Toni before? Toni is Italian and works in the café. Actually, he more or less runs it now, even though, technically, he's only part-time. He's here four afternoons a week and does the evening reading shift sometimes as well. He's been with me for about six months. No one can create froth on your cappuccino like Toni. He looks the part, too. He's like one of those dreamy, imperturbable youths in a Pasolini film — pale greeny hazel-flecked eyes against matte tawny skin in a perfect face. I hired him for his eyes and kept him on for his calm. Toni never flaps, not even when the sixth-formers perform their impatient antics. He has a kind of patrician composure about him. I suspect it's because his English is strictly limited. As Nell might say, he's cool. But without being sullen. His smile comes in a flash of glistening teeth and is then slow and steady, with a hint of shyness.

Where was I? Oh yes. Well, Heather and I are perching at the counter with our coffees and I'm babbling away about something when I notice that Heather's attention is certainly not on me. She's watching Toni, who's clearing away chairs, putting the round café tables back in their places and tidying up generally. She's watching him with the air of a bird of prey who's about to pounce. And indeed, when he looks towards us, she waves him over, ogles him and all but licks her lips as she murmurs something about another coffee. Ten minutes later, she's asking him whether he'd like a lift home.

Toni looks at her, then looks at me. There's a question in his eyes, as if he wants me to tell him that it's okay to say yes. I don't. And he shakes his head and turns his back on us to do something at the bar. I walk Heather downstairs and unlock the front door for her.

"Where did you find him?" she asks me, without waiting for an answer. "He's gorgeous. I'll have to come back soon." And with that she's off and I'm staring after her, my mouth flapping like one of the mentally challenged.

When I go back upstairs, Toni has already got his coat on and is about to switch off the lights.

"I'm sorry, Toni," I say. "I didn't realize you were almost done. And now you've missed the chance of a lift. I haven't brought the car in today."

"That's okay," he says, and gives me a long, slow look of the kind I haven't felt for eons at least. It makes me blush, though any kind of rising heat these days is subject to misinterpretation. Then he switches off the upstairs lights and he's standing beside me and saying something about how much prettier I am than my friend and how he admires me and he'll walk me home if I like and his fingers are brushing my cheek and his lips are on mine and I'm trembling, then shivering, because suddenly I have an image of Nell. Nell sitting in front of the telly. Nell who is closer to his age than I am. Nell who would sink through the floor and gladly pull me along with her before admitting that sex could ever, not in a million trillion years, have anything to do with her mother. The disgust of it. The horror. Never.

Such a wonderful and powerful emotion, disgust. It brings everything down with it. So even as I stand there, wanting nothing more than Toni in my bed, I'm already trapped in the whirlpool of Nell's disgust and sinking quickly.

"Sorry, Toni," I murmur and pull away. "I can't."

By the time we reach the front door, he looks so dejected and vulnerable, despite his youth, that I find myself placing a light kiss on his lips and adding a "not tonight" as I wave him away.

The sweet firmness of his lips, I have to confess, is still with me.

What do you feel about all this business, Celia? Do you think it's undignified to desire at our ripe age? To desire the inconveniently young? Or is dignity just an idealized trap to make us put up with a mere iota of what we might otherwise have?

Are you out there with the viragos of our youth championing the Wife of Bath — gap-toothed icon of mature but undiminished appetites?

The trouble is, when your conscience is embodied in a teenage daughter, it's hard to stand up for appetite. Sometimes I think Nell is more of a moral force than my mother ever was and I'll have to rebel twice as hard to go half the distance. I run so much more slowly these days.

Do you know that in all the four-and-a-bit years since Robert left, I have never, not once, brought a man home while she was there? No, it's not that I think they'll inevitably and secretly start panting after her rather than me. Nor even that she'll stomp in and make a scene and say who is that hideous bogey you've brought into OUR house. Or give me a larger than usual dose of cold shoulder and bad temper.

It's just that with her there, I'm unwomanned — if one can say such a thing. Daughters. They run off with your sexiness and leave you with only maternity. You may fight it. But secretly you know it's the case.

I can hear you protesting. Patrick, you say, throwing the only one I really shouldn't have mentioned in my face in repayment for my bitchy mentioning of him. You went to bed with Patrick after Robert had left you. Well, yes. But it was always at his place, far from Nell's eyes, so I could pretend to be what I'm mostly not.

My two other feeble and short-term efforts at relationship are hardly worth recounting. And yes, whatever we did was always done at the man's place, though with the second one we used to resort to hotels and occasional trips. I think he felt about his sons as I feel about my daughter. They unmanned him.

Ridiculous to be entering into this complaint. You're not an agony aunt. It's just that I get prickles in my spine thinking of Toni. Italians are supposed to like older women, aren't they? They like flesh. Ripe figs. Like those Renaissance paintings. And then there are all those stories about initiation rites. An experienced older woman always stars, doesn't she? Though perhaps not as old as I am. Not that I probably know very much, certainly no more than Toni. Still . . . I'm not going to let Heather get her clutches into him.

Yours,

Jude

14 MARCH

Dear Celia,

Today dawned with a soft golden glow. This can only mean that spring, which the daffs were alone in celebrating, has now at last arrived for the rest of us. I put on my new trouser suit of celandine linen and a modish striped T-shirt. Nell looked at this get-up over breakfast with lowered eyes and a little twist of the lips, signalling that I'd been shopping in the wrong shops again. But she stayed mute and even pecked me on the cheek before rushing off to school. Something must be up.

I was looking through the HarperCollins catalogue with one of our regulars — on old tweedy gent who likes to keep up with history and biography — when Toni came in. He gave me a sidelong glance and what I think was a smile of approval and then took the stairs two at a time. I had to claw my eyes away, and my poor dear gent must have thought I was succumbing to an early bout of Alzheimer's. Churchill's letters had bounced definitively from my mind.

I didn't allow myself to go up to the café until the last of the lunch-hour stragglers had left. Kate was up there with Toni. Have I told you that Kate is almost six feet tall and has hair down to her waist and parents from Bombay who've endowed her with the most gorgeous skin? She could have been a model except that she prefers books to clothes, and indeed her husband to the catwalk, as well as, for the moment, to a legal career, which is where she was heading before she joined me. And now she's three months pregnant.

I urged Kate downstairs while I perched on a stool. I don't think I've yet mentioned just how stylish the café is. I'm really proud of it — the stainless steel counter with its espresso machine and rows of white cups and opaque polished mirror, the two sofas and the glistening round tables and wire chairs, mostly clustered towards the back of the room, which is all glass, and when it's warm enough opens up onto a small terrace overlooking a garden dominated by a cherry tree not yet in flower. The walls on the left are in pale elm, because they're not really walls, but extra stock-space behind rolling doors. And here, in rather muted classical style, I've hung large portraits of authors, culled from various publishers. The far wall is a lush fuchsia pink, the kind of deep, luminous colour you want to lick or plunge into.

Where was I? Oh yes, Toni was looking into my eyes and seemed poised to say something — something that would propel us towards uncharted terrain from which there would be no return, when we were interrupted by footsteps. Footsteps whose Nike rhythm of squeak and shuffle I recognized as they raced upstairs. All too well. I moved backwards as if I'd been caught in a clinch. My bar stool tottered towards a fall and I only just grabbed it in time.

"Hey there, Mum." Nell stared at me accusingly, all the while greeting Toni with a nonchalant wave. "You've forgotten. I don't believe it. I get here in record time, skipped prep so we can visit Gran. As per your instructions. And you've forgotten."

Nell stands over me like a minor fury. She is, by the way, a little taller than me and a good stone slimmer and all legs, though they're hidden in trousers which might as well be rubbish bags, given their general shapelessness. Her top matches. The only distinctive thing about it is the writing, which advertises some band or other. Bar the clothes, Nell looks not unlike me at her age, though she's learned how to be blonder (and on occasion purpler or bluer), and her hair is tied up in back in a stylish spiky knot, when she's not throwing it about like some lustrous net to tangle men up in. Who am I kidding? In fact, she's much prettier than I ever was and her skin is a perfect blush, and there's a lot of her father in her. Really, I do adore my daughter.

"No, I haven't forgotten," I lie. "I was just taking a break. And I thought you might like a hot chocolate before heading off."

Toni is already heating the milk and heaping chocolate into a mug. We both watch his easy movements as if they deserve the concentration of one of Hamlet's soliloquies.

"Okay," says Nell, easing herself onto a stool. "If you think there's time."

"Make it a quickie," I say. My choice of words leaves me just a little queasy.

You remember my mother, Celia. You probably still imagine her as she was during our Cambridge years when you came to stay – a bony, forceful woman who looked as if she had organized the WACs single-handedly while helping Turing crack Enigma on the side. Somehow I always associated her with the war, because she never really changed her hairdo — all those sausage curls. I used to think she kept the style for my father, who was nothing if not conservative in his tastes, but she clung on to her curls well after his death.

My mother lives in a home now. Not her home in the country, you understand. A home. A residential home (as if there were other things one did with a home apart from taking up residence in it). Couldn't be helped. Well, she thought it could be. When she decided the moment had come to shed the big and rather isolated family house, she wanted to move in with us. But that would probably have put an end to my life and *my* home — let alone my marriage, even before it did come to an end — so I put my foot down. Instead, at first, she found (with Robert's and my help) a maisonette with a large enough garden, not too far away from us. It really makes sense for the old to live in the city at a walking distance from what they need and from other people. I convinced her of that.

My mother was sensible enough to agree. That good sense, I'm afraid, went quickly. She had barely lived in her new place for two years when she started to behave quite uncharacteristically — unless that other character had been hidden there for a long time and was only now beginning to peek through. She had, to tell the truth, always been a little suspicious of anyone who came in to help, but now she accused a whole estate of cleaning women of stealing her gloves, her necklaces and bracelets and earrings, in short all and any of her precious possessions . . . even her teeth. Accused them so forcefully that, even when I found the missing items, she would insist they had been stolen only to be replaced, and the stigma of theft still attached itself to the person, who had then to be got rid of . . .

She had an expedient way of doing this as well. She simply didn't let the person into the house. Soon she was letting no one in except one friend and us lot. A slew of carers and social workers and psychiatric nurses, not to mention cleaners, were sent away. The little trickle of paranoia had sprouted into a waterfall. Within a few months, she was ringing the police on repeated occasions to complain of break-ins, usually by the upstairs or next-door neighbours, though on one occasion the person described sounded very like Robert. Maybe just a little fiercer. Her emotional antennae were obviously alert. She just didn't make the sanest possible deductions from the information received. I suspect she turned into a thief anyone who didn't pay her due respect or the kind of attention she craved. She had always had an exaggerated sense of who her enemies were.

Needless to say, this was not a situation which could go on. Between the police, irate council carers and disgruntled neighbours, something had to be done. My wits, too, I hasten to add, were at a low ebb. Oh, the joys of middle age. It really is one of life's less palatable ironies that your parents' deterioration takes on the speed of a Ferrari just as you begin to note the first signs of your own and are trying to balance job and kids and husband and whatever else besides. So you're stuck there trying to jack up the family Volvo as their Ferrari races down the incline, altogether out of control. And secretly you're loathe to chase after them, 'cause you can see the valley of gloom that awaits, with its "no exit" signs on all sides. But you have to.

Dementia, I'm convinced, is contagious.

I kept dreaming that I was turning into my mother. Hardly unusual in and of itself. But the mother I was turning into wasn't the powerful and controlling maternal figure of yore, the one we all refused in our feminist heyday, but an old bat who was patently off her rocker. Being off one's rocker isn't unusual either, of course. Apparently it's a fate that awaits most of us come a certain age. Women, in particular, though the scientists — when they aren't contradicting each other about the condition itself — don't seem to know whether it hits more women 'cause the men have already died off or whether it gets the women 'cause hormonally they've already been a lost cause for years. It also seems particularly to hit the widowed, or hits them earlier — though I don't think that fact figures in the technical literature. It's just a personal observation.

I imagine it'll hit me earlier than most, given my unmarried state.

The modish name for my mother's condition is, as you've probably already guessed, Alzheimer's. The German nomenclature looks good on grant applications to the Medical Research Council. But really it's just early-onset dying. The hormones pack up; the synapses calcify — use up all the stuff that's meant to be in your bones, which turn brittle for lack while those little neurotransmission devices get caked up instead and refuse to do their job. So you forget everything — like where you put your necklace, or your tea, or your husband, and someone's gotta be to blame for the fact that you're lost in the world and frail and can't really find your feet in the morning, let alone your knickers. Oh, oh dear.

Anyhow, one day I dropped round at my mother's maisonette to deliver the groceries and no one answered. I couldn't believe that she'd gone out when I had specifically told her I'd be coming, so I rang again, mentally adding deafness to her other problems. Still no response. After the third ring I decided she'd forgotten, and was about to leave, when I remembered that a few weeks earlier I had taken her spare key with me and, yes, there it was in my bag. So I let myself in, slightly worried that this time she'd have good reason to ring the police. At least today's burglar was leaving the groceries instead of taking anything away.

Then I saw her coat on the chair. She wouldn't go out without a coat. It was December, after all.

The house suddenly took on a hollow murmuring. There was someone there, I knew it. Someone who had conked my mother over the head. Someone who was carrying out the very burglaries she had so insistently fantasized.

I crept upstairs, my feet like lead, their weight muffled by the carpet. I peered into the bedroom. Nothing. The bathroom door was ominously ajar. But a swift glance revealed no one hiding behind the shower curtain. Which left only the little study, where she spent much of her time. I inched open the door. The curtains were drawn. It took me a moment to make out the figure on the carpet.

A small moaning sound came from her lips, a drool, too, but there was no visible blood. She was wrapped in her old dressing gown, and it occurred to me that she might have rolled off the sofa, which was littered with an assortment of bedclothes. She looked unconscious, so frail and waxen that if it hadn't been for the slight rattle of breath, I would have assumed the worst, though this seemed quite bad enough. I forced myself into action, calling her name over and over, and simultaneously reached for the telephone. Her eyes popped open just as I was punching out the last 9.

"Hello, dear," she said, as if she were greeting me at the door. She seemed utterly unaware of her supine condition.

I hesitated, then put the phone down. "I was . . . I was just ringing your doctor."

"Nice young man," said my mother.

"How do you feel, Mum?"

"Thirsty."

She gave me a half-smile, but still didn't move.

"Shall I help you up?"

She raised her head slightly and then, as if it were the most ordinary thing in the world to be found unconscious on the floor, stretched her hand towards me. "Please."

I propped her up on the sofa and rushed downstairs to put the kettle on and to telephone, this time, her doctor. Miraculously I got through to him, but predictably he couldn't make a home visit. He suggested tea with plenty of sugar and a visit to Emergency — no, not by ambulance, just told me to get her there in the car. "Carry her?" I muttered, but he talked right over me.

I sometimes suspect British GPs would be only too happy

if we got rid of the elderly rather sooner than we manage to at the moment. (One of them notoriously attempted to, of course; murdered some hundred of the old biddies we're going to become, and strangely, no one noticed for years.)

Well, I did manage to get my mum to the hospital. She was a little brighter after two cups of tea barely visible above the sugar, and her old chequered dressing gown made quite a fashion statement worn nonchalantly beneath her winter coat. Though I suspect Madonna would have got through the queue at Accident and Emergency with a little more panache. We, on the other hand, waited for a mere fourteen hours for a bed. My protests had no effect. A visible gush of blood would have had more. At some point in those hours, I all but wished that the poor old dear had been coshed.

Anyhow, to cut a very long story short, the upshot of the various tests was that she was fine. True, she was frail, confused, didn't have a clue as to where she was, but that was all but par for the course at her age — or so the nurse suggested to me. And yes, she was a little anemic and needed some feeding up and rest and looking after — definitely feeding and looking after — which I could do far better (this with a pointed stare at yours truly) than the hospital.

It was early December. Nell and I had just moved out of the family home, which Robert had generously (he thought) said I could have if we could forego endless lawyerly bartering. I forewent, since I didn't have the stamina for a mega New York–style divorce, and I sold the house to free up enough capital to take over the bookshop and convert it. We were now living on the top two floors of a nice enough, but hardly enormous house, recently converted. The spare room, which doubled as my office, was effectively the attic. The rest of the attic, needless to say, belonged to Nell and her music.

All right. So I'm overplaying the details. My guilt is showing. But I do want you to understand there was no way my mum could possibly have stayed on and on.

We got through a slightly bleak Christmas and New Year's together. Even managed to get her dressed on a couple of occasions. Dressing your mother is something else. It breaks all those deeply engrained habits which linger on from toddlerhood. Never mind Lear on his blasted heath. Dressing your mother is really what reverses and disrupts the order of the universe. Well, I didn't take to it much . . . And the indignity! But dignity doesn't really have a look-in once age comes to stay.

And then miraculously a room came free in a rather nice home, not too far from us. I think Christmas probably did away with a fair proportion not only of inmates but of waiting list. So my mum moved in.

The weird thing is that in the month or so she was with us, she never once mentioned her own maisonette. It was as if it had vanished off the face of the earth and from the recesses of her mind. Even when I asked her what she would like to have from it, she pretended not to hear me.

She moved into the home docilely enough. All her earlier protests about not needing help had vanished into an unspoken agreement that she did — as long as one said nothing about it. Maybe the not saying, the overlooking, is the last small corner where dignity can reside. It took me a while to grasp that.

My love,
Jude

By way of P.S.

I got so tired and tearful writing to you last night that I altogether forgot the point of my letter. Which was in part to tell you what Nell said on our way to her granny's.

She flounced her hair back and like some budding Athena gave me a regal, stony stare. "Yuck, Mum, the way that greasy Toni ogles you . . . I don't know how you can allow it. He's like some slobbering dog. He's like one of those ski instructors on our last school trip. Remember I told you? The ones who gave the beginners' group their intermediate badges, even though they no way deserved them. Ugh. You shouldn't allow it."

I pooh-pooh her little speech with a "Don't be silly, darling." At the same time, something in me started to sing, whether with joy or just vanity isn't quite clear.

The singing was reduced to a mere internal hum as we opened the door to the home. It's a nice door, a deep, ripe red. In fact the house itself is nice enough — all Victorian brick sprawling over two capacious bay windows, and some mock Gothic turrets. From the side you can see a more recent and utilitarian extension cutting a T through tree-clad grounds, now festooned with daffs. It's when you open the door that the word "nice" doesn't feel altogether apropos. We're in the world of fifties bed and breakfasts with a pervasive smell of stew and a hodgepodge of charmless furniture — unpolished oak, fake leather, floral wingbacks. But it's what sits or slumps or dozes in the chairs which is the real problem.

The first few times I came here, the shock was visceral. All the inhabitants of the home had the look of hollow-eyed hags in the Grim Reaper's retinue. One figure was more ghastly than the next. I just couldn't focus on them long enough to tell them apart, even though they were hardly engaged in a riotous *danse macabre* of the Zimmer frames. It was my eyes that raced over them, to come up with an amorphous, caricatural representative of AGE — sans eyes, sans teeth, sans anything, as the old bard so aptly put it in the words of one of his more melancholy creations.

I think they must shock each other at first, too. My mother used to keep her eyes glued to the floor, except when the staff addressed her. Then, gradually, we both got used to this unnatural world, so unlike the outside, where old people hardly travel in gangs. Once that happened, the inhabitants took on individual properties and characters again, became . . . well, ordinary people, though a little old, a little strange.

When she first arrived, my mother was arrogant, if not altogether outwardly hostile, towards her peers. She'd never been to boarding school, you see, and had no experience of that kind of life. Then, too, her paranoia about neighbours and burglars was transferred wholesale to the staff. Whatever their pleas and attempts at reason, she kept the door of her room angrily locked. She refused their help in bathing or dressing. The first had become irrelevant. The second she could now do, since the regular institutional meals had made her stronger and a good deal plumper. The staff, she claimed, stole. They stole her handbags and shoes and dresses and jewellery, not to mention her keys.

The one thing they probably did steal was her will. They did it when I wasn't looking. Or maybe it was the implacable progress of the disease. After some eight months in the home, my mother became more docile. She allowed herself to be washed and dressed. Her perpetual anxiety about the whereabouts of her keys vanished. As finally did the keys themselves.

With her keys went her anger. It was probably what had distinguished her. Now she began to look like all the other residents. She turned into a generic granny. She grew progressively more listless, had flecks of food on her cardy, sat immobile for long stretches of time staring into space or some dim interior, or turned towards the television, where images I don't think she took in flickered and dashed. Sometimes I'd come to visit and couldn't find her — though in fact I simply didn't immediately recognize her, until my eyes, still used to her old, erect self, took in who she was now — a ghostly mirror image of what time would soon enough do to all of us.

Yesterday she was sitting near the door, which is mostly where she likes to sit now. It's as if she's always waiting for us to arrive. She doesn't smile much. Her smile muscles have gone lax. (You wouldn't think it took muscle to smile, but it does, and lips lose it, just like tums.) But her eyes light up, perhaps with the effort of focus, and she gives us a little wave. She's touchingly grateful to see us. In the old days, the days before she went into the home, she would complain whenever Nell and I appeared. There was always a sting to her comments, which implied that our attentions were unsatisfactory; indeed, that our lives left a lot to be desired. Now she pays us a flurry of compliments about how well we look.

And, I guess, compared to the people around her, we do . . .

Nell is wonderful with her granny. She doesn't wait for her to make no sense, or pays little attention if she does. She launches into an account of her school day, or her French class or anything at all, and while she chats, she lets her granny hold her hand. My mother always comments on the warmth or coldness of hands. We are an animal comfort to her. The content of what we say, however, is irrelevant. If we mention that an old friend has rung or sent greetings or even died, she looks up at us with a "who?" The same matter can be conveyed a dozen times and is always fresh — which at least makes for no lack of conversational gambits.

Little lodges itself in my mother's brain anymore. I used to think it was her mind's revenge on her for having so long denied the reality in front of her. But it's quite clear that she's left the realm of psychology for that of neurology. Those little grey cells simply don't function as they used to, or aren't there for the functioning. Though you can never be altogether sure which bits of the circuitry have gone.

A couple of weeks ago I had to take her to the hospital where they monitor her anemia. The journey distressed her, as did the place itself. She just couldn't settle or wait her turn in the queue. When we finally got to see the doctor, she was in a state of high anxiety and talking gibberish. The doctor, a nice Bombay gent, addressed her by name, looked her in the eyes and, holding her gaze, asked for her hands. She gave them to him. After a moment, she fluttered her lashes and her face took on a forgotten aspect. Her voice emerged with unquestionable flirtatiousness. "What lovely warm hands you have," my mother said, with all the force of her one-time charm.

Perhaps prehistoric habits, old gestures are still there, buried under cold stone. A random application of heat and they stir into life.

All the time that we sat by Mother's side yesterday, a woman new to the home moaned from behind us. She had wispy mouse hair. A single tooth protruded from her lower jaw. Beneath her brown sweater rose a decided hump. Her hand flailed at the air as she swayed back and forth, back and forth.

"Help me, help me." She repeated the words over and over at rhythmic intervals. It wasn't quite a shriek, but it had a kind of insidious intensity — yet none of the staff appeared. Finally I couldn't stand it anymore and I went over to her.

"How can I help you?" I asked.

Like a bird, she rotated her head to an angle so that she could look up at me. She did so slowly, and when her face turned towards me it had a quizzical air. She didn't speak at once, just stared. She was taking me in. At last she said, "Over there." And pointed.

"Over there" was the next room, which gave on to the garden, so I helped her up and, her arm gripping mine, we proceeded in the direction of her point. She was tiny and her steps were a slippered, limping shuffle. It took an eternity to cross one room and arrive at the other. When we had and I'd lowered her into another chair, she sank back into leatherette cushions. I think I expected some gesture of gratitude. Instead she looked at me uncomprehendingly and started to sway again. With the sway came the moan. "Help me, help me."

A woman at the side gave me a sly grin. "Nothing helps," she said. "Nothing."

Why am I going on like this, Celia? It's the last thing you want to hear about. Tales from the old people's home. I think I'm turning as batty as they are. I'll sign off now. Reliving this has sapped my strength. Patrick did the right thing in going sooner rather than later. Age wouldn't have become him. I don't think it'll become me.

I think I'm finally going to post this ongoing letter to you . . . Apart from anything else, I want you to chastise me for my smoking. I'm a binge smoker, I've decided. I stop for days at a time with no trouble. In fact, it's easy to stop when you've done it as often as I have — almost as easy as starting again.
Love,
Jude

MONDAY, 19 MARCH

Dear Celia,
It's happened. I feel strange. As if I'd committed an illicit act. Which is probably why it was all so exciting. I still can't quite believe it. Though I imagine you would have done the same, in the old days at least, and then with more panache. That was always your way. None of us ever believed half the things you got up to — you looked like such a calm, sweet thing. Do you remember how you disappeared after the May Ball and we found out only after a week that you'd gone off with the guitarist in the rock band? Whereas, based on appearances, everyone thought I was the wild one . . . Well, this week, I was . . .

It all started on Friday evening, really. Francesca came around. I don't think you ever met her. She joined the foreign rights section of the agency after you had already left for Canada. We overlapped for about three years but we've only become good friends over the last few. Funny, that. It's as if one's friendships, some of them at least, blossom depending on whether one is coupled or single. Or, indeed, whether the children are compatible ages.

When Robert and I parted, the coupled friends gradually began to drop off. I suddenly presented a threat to coupledom, it seems. I hadn't grown devil's horns or a cleft foot or anything. I didn't have a new wipe-your-hard-disk-forever system. Nor had my boobs blossomed — well, except when the pills kicked in, of course, but then so did the rest of me.

In fact, several of the male halves of the couples astonished me by offering comfort. And one female half. I was so surprised, I didn't accept. I can't tell whether that made things worse or better. Worse probably.

Other friends, who had hung up their matchmaker's shingle, gave up on me after the third dinner party where the male invited just for yours truly turned out to be not quite to my taste. I don't think I was being particularly choosy. Retired serial killers and ancient, rubber-loving alcoholics in need of an agile nurse are just not up my street. But when the coupling didn't happen, the dinner invitations dropped off.

The curious thing is that my best single friend abandoned me, too. I couldn't work it out. We had been so close. Over the years she had come to a hundred dinners, Christmases, birthday parties. But then it occurred to me that our closeness was based on my having a family, which was her surrogate one, like the maiden aunts in Victorian novels.

My two friendships with gays petered out as well. Partly because I had become boring. I had no fresh gossip to recount after I left the agency. Running a bookshop simply isn't as glamorous. But I also secretly suspect that they had always liked me because of Robert. I was a kind of conduit to the world of straight men.

Ah well. And on top of all that, I stopped lunching and gave fewer and fewer dinner parties. Society, at our age, is a complicated and reciprocal business. Not like when we were young. Then we didn't see each other just because it was in the diary, but 'cause we felt like it. Now. Tonight.

It's a bit like that with Francesca. She lives nearby and more or less on her own, so she often pops in for a drink or a snack and a good old gossip about the rises and falls in the literary hierarchy. Or forces me off to the movies with her. She's tiny and vivacious and not quite forty and has never lived with a man for more than three years. Fiery impatience and low bullshit tolerance, I suspect, won't allow it. Anyhow, on Friday evening she came around to have a moan. She's been having an affair with a married man and the weekend in the country was postponed — hardly for the first time.

"I should never have broken my own rules," Francesca sighs. "But what are they for, if not to be broken?"

Francesca had promised herself never to have an affair with a married man. Out of solidarity for women. With the years, the promise slipped a little. It became never have an affair with a married man who has small children. More slippage took place in subsequent years over the definition of "small." Now it's under five, because her latest has one of seven and one of nine. I don't blame Francesca — though of course I would have while I was married. One of the things I've realized since I've been uncoupled is that there are very few eligible free men out there over a certain age. For one thing, they all leave their

51

wives when they already have another woman at the ready, so that there's no intervening period during which they might have to do something for themselves. For another, if they're not slightly unhinged, they're busy pretending they're at least twenty years younger and carousing with their would-be daughters.

So, over wine and mussels, Francesca and I had a bit of a female plaint. We didn't go on too long. There's no point succumbing to bitterness. After all, it's easy enough to do without men these days. On the other hand, we really do rather like them and agree that, bar a few eccentricities, bad manners and thoughtlessness, they're probably part of the same species. And would be even closer kin if in childhood, rather than let them chase balls across fields or missiles across screens, we forced them to read fiction in which the adventures had nothing to do with the former and everything to do with the life of the emotions.

Having arrived at this partial solution to the world's ills, Francesca dumped the keys to her country house on my table. "Here, you deserve a day or two off. Go down there. Take a friend. Or Nell. The fridge is full. There's a stew waiting to be warmed. The sheets are on the bed. No." She put out a staying hand and stopped my question. "Don't ask me to come with you. It'll just put me into a worse pig of a mood. I'm going to work. Read that backlog of manuscripts. And draft yet another ad for the personal columns. This time I'm going to advertise for a man who fancies himself as a father. And I'm going to send it off."

Francesca is always threatening to advertise for a man. I don't think she's done it yet. But she may. She's bold. And she wants a child. The old biological clock story again. I half suggested to her that she should just cheat and have one with her married lover. The perfect moment for child-bearing, after all, rarely manifests itself as perfect. It's either the wrong time or the wrong man or the wrong job. First it's too soon and then it's too late. All these efficient means of contraception put too much of a decision-making strain on us. Luckily, Nell was an accident. I kind of wish I'd had another one.

After Francesca went, I sat at the kitchen table and fingered her house keys. The next morning they were once more in my hands. I held them while I punched out Robert's number.

Nell was off to spend the weekend with him, her schoolbooks and pyjamas and a change of clothes tucked into her rucksack. She's taken to spending time with her father again, after a period of cold-shouldering. I don't know quite why. Nell doesn't tell tales or carry information, much as I sometimes hanker after it. (What sane woman wouldn't want to know a few details about her estranged husband-of-fifteen-years' intimate life with a bimbette?)

But Nell was like that from the beginning. Discreet. Even when I asked her a direct question about Robert's new household, she managed to find a way of telling me nothing that I didn't already know. And she's always refused to be drawn into a conversation which might minimize her father in any way. At the beginning, I can tell you, I was no saint, and I certainly tried to illustrate fully to her what an infantile creep her beloved dad was. I seethed with resentment and suspicion every time she went off with him and home to that underage slut he had taken up with. Gradually, through the black clouds of spite and rancour, it dawned on me that this was hardly calculated to help Nell through the situation. I could never take away the fact that Robert was her dad. The best I could do was to help her come to terms with it all. So I began to temper my emotions and pay more heed to hers.

Now my curiosity only rarely gets the best of me. And Nell is still as mute as ever. From the occasional indirect comment she lets slip, I might interpret something about the state of Robert's life. But not much. She won't even be drawn into a conversation about the woman's mag Robert's Emma works for. I imagine Nell is as discreet at the other end.

So if Robert and I want to know anything about each other, we have to ring and ask. Of late, he asks more than I do. And out of some slightly anachronistic anxiety, we keep up the habit of phoning to announce Nell's departure from our respective addresses. Today his answering machine is on, so it saves me the need of a conversation I was beginning to feel slightly nervous about. Stupidly so. As if he were still my husband and I had to feel guilt.

How did I get on this tangent? What I really wanted to tell you was that, before evening fell, Toni and I were winding our way along narrow country roads flanked by moist green hills. Endangered sheep and darling little lambs watched our passage. Villages of clustered stone would pop out of a dip or turn. I don't imagine the wilds of the far grander Rockies have altogether wiped the Cotswolds from your mind, so I needn't go on.

Toni certainly didn't. His English really is minimal. Instead, he shot me an occasional knickers-wetting look as we listened to a bluesy tape. (I might, of course, have misinterpreted. He might just have wanted to get his hands on the steering wheel.

54

I couldn't let him go *that* far. A woman must keep her self-respect, as my mother might have said in the days when she still said things.)

Not that I held on to much of it once we got to Francesca's cottage. It's a glorious place, tucked into the end of a tiny village, so that when you look out the windows, there are gardens and fields everywhere. Night had fallen by the time we arrived. Toni lit the fire as if he had done little else all his life, and the sitting room, which takes up most of the ground floor, crackled and glowed. In the shadowy light it came to me that he looked a little like Gary Cooper . . . (Why are my tastes in men so antique? Black-and-white, really. Nell looks at Gary Cooper and her nose crinkles in disgust.)

He poured the wine we had brought. We had a sip or two while I chatted inanely, and then . . . well, despite my worries about my various sags and excesses and wrinkly bits and the silk nightie I'd brought to hide them, it all happened. It really all happened. Thanks perhaps to the happy murkiness of Francesca's lamps.

I had forgotten, you know. Quite forgotten what it's like to be with a young man. The energy of it. The beauty of him. The acrobatics. The sheer *boom boom boom*. What little of the night there was left for sleep found me so soundly at it that, for the first time in decades, I woke after ten. And then I have to say drizzle provided an excuse for the briefest of walks before — well, you can imagine the rest.

I have to be careful, Celia. I can feel it beginning already. That obsessiveness that sex engenders. And I can't allow it at my age. What's wrong with our generation of women? That dreadful romanticizing of lust, when we know better. That relentless way in which the emotions trample in and take over innocent pleasure. I'm already wondering what I might mean to him. I'm busy concocting ways in which we can have more time together. I've invented a background for him.

All I know, by the way, is that he came here from Bari to learn English and he's a dab hand at making lattes. He's pretty talented in that other department, too. I thought I might offer to help him with his English, but I don't think I will. The power relations are skewed enough as they are. In fact, yesterday I could feel myself playing the dumb blonde, so that I didn't overpower him. What did I just say? Hold on a minute. That can't be right. That has to be one of the many old habits that need to be shed. After all — the power is all in his court. Since I'm the one who wants him.

You see. I'm in a muddle and I should be singing.

I found an ancient picture of us, Celia. Sitting on the steps in back of my parents' house. We're wearing silly hats and you have one of those old fox furs draped around your neck, its snout clearly visible. We're pulling at something that sits between us that I can't identify. We look as if we might be blushing. The film is in black-and-white, so it's hard to tell. It feels as if the camera has caught us in some illicit act — probably some ten-year-old-dressing-up-in-parent's-clothes act. My father must have taken the picture without our knowing. It turned up in an old box of my mother's when we moved her effects. We look — I don't know quite how to put it — as if we've been gripped by something other, something bigger, zanier than ourselves, so that together we glow more fiercely than when alone.

Much love,
Jude

Dear Celia,

So troubling seeing Toni behind the bar today that I almost couldn't bear going upstairs. Almost. I've never had the experience of being someone's boss and . . . You don't think he's doing all this because he wants to earn some money out of a harassment charge, do you? No . . . no . . . That way lies lunacy. He smiled at me very sweetly and, apart from the fact that his eyes flickered over me, I couldn't see anything unusual about his behaviour. All the oddness was on my side.

I was taking some stock out from behind the sliding doors upstairs when he came up behind me and touched me on the shoulder and lifted the books for me. He gave me his dreaming look and asked in a whisper whether perhaps I'd like to go and see a film with him. Somehow I managed to trip over my feet and had to hang onto a chair, and before I knew what I was doing, I was shaking my head and saying, no, no, I was busy tonight. And then I realized that he didn't necessarily mean tonight, and so I rushed on, my voice rising like a whistling kettle, and said Friday, maybe Friday, 'cause I remembered something about Nell and a party, which meant she might be home late, which I had of course chastised her for earlier, bargaining away at the hours so that she'd promised to be back just after midnight. And now . . . Still, Friday was possible.

Toni nodded with that shy smile of his, which now seemed to me to be all admiration and approval, so that I went downstairs feeling I'd just won the lottery.

I had promised to go to a launch party with Francesca, something I rarely do, but she had insisted and I was glad now, because even by the time I hit Soho, I was flying. Ringing the bell to the private rooms at Groucho's fazed me not at all, nor did climbing the plush stairs or arriving in that first, smaller room, already crowded with journalists and liggers and publishers and writers — the literary world, in short. Francesca saw me before I saw her and came up to me with a slightly interrogating smile.

"You look fab, darling. Weekends in the country are evidently a must."

I nodded and grinned and helped myself to a drink, and Francesca introduced me to some faces whose names I didn't catch. (Isn't that one of the worst things about these mid-years of ours? You finally go to a party, and you can't hear a thing 'cause of all the surrounding noise. So everyone is reduced to a pair of those moving Beckett-like lips from one of his more minimal plays as you try and read what's being said.) Anyhow, I was trying to read the lip movements of a towering woman wearing a silvery sort of padded dress that looked like armour, and had just twigged that this was Germaine Greer as she was in person and not behind a table on the telly, when I felt a tap on my shoulder.

A tallish man with steel-grey hair and one of those trimmed, tanned faces that looks as if its owner goes jogging every day, works out the muscles of cheek and jowl and chin, and keeps tabs of his cholesterol intake on his notepad, was looming over me with uncomfortable familiarity. I sensed from his tone of voice and face that I should know him, but it took me a minute. When the penny dropped, so did my mouth.

"Robert?" I quashed the question mark as best I could. I don't think he noticed.

I know it sounds a little peculiar not to recognize your husband of fifteen years. I have no excuse, except that it has been well over three years since I've laid eyes on Robert — at my insistence. I thought it would make things easier. Turn down the gas on the resentments and recriminations. There were the phone calls about Nell and yes, he did pick her up to take her out at the beginning, but I usually made myself scarce. It took a supreme effort of the will, I can tell you. Why, I've seen his son more recently than I've seen him. (Ollie, in case you don't know, is Robert's "American" son, who lived with us for a year just before Nell arrived, and then again after you'd left for Canada. Robert had him when he was still a graduate student at Harvard with a first wife who predated me by twelve years!)

So yes, there stood this unfamiliar Robert behaving familiarly. Well, perhaps not altogether, since he was paying me a compliment and telling me I hadn't changed a smidgen except for the better. When I could hear him, I recognized him distinctly. Robert is the only person I know whose accent has grown more emphatically American with each passing year. It's a kind of perversity, since he never, as far as I know, had any intention of going back.

Well, there we were, Robert and I talking inane "How are things?" amidst the crowd at Groucho's (I finally twigged that the book party was his firm's), when this Sloany-looking woman in a cashmere rib-top and trousers so tight they might as well have been Heather's hot pants — except that they were more revealing — came up to him and whisked him away. But he was having none of it. He held her back and insisted on introducing her to me.

Lo and behold, I was meeting Emma.

She looked none too pleased to be meeting me, I have to confess, so I didn't have time to puke or shout before she took off, scowling in a way which made her brows knit and gave her face a particularly unpleasant expression, like one of Roald Dahl's incomparably nasty spinster aunts. Without the scowl, though, I have to admit she really was more of a dish than yours truly. Much more, if you like the type.

This Robert I didn't know and who made me rather uncomfortable had my glass refilled, and carried on talking to me in intimate terms about our daughter. From time to time he cast me a curious look from those cold blue eyes of his, which hadn't really changed. They still have a watchful edge. They still seem to see everything, but now I couldn't interpret what they were seeing.

When Francesca appeared, he finally excused himself with one of his little bows, though its courtliness had sat different-ly on the portliness of yesteryear. "See you sometime," he said with exaggerated casualness.

"I won't hold my breath," I muttered beneath it, but I watched him go. I have to tell you I was nonplussed, not to mention baffled and bewildered. He was himself and not him-self.

But it was me, too. How could I have managed to put his image so firmly out of mind so as not to recognize him, what-ever the trimming process he may have undergone? Here was an internal cover-up of truly heroic proportions, a veritable Everest of denial. Or maybe I hadn't really looked at him for years before our split, so one could say it was ten years since I'd in fact seen him. Or maybe my mother's Alzheimer's really was contagious and here was grisly proof of extra-early onset.

Oh well. I didn't really enjoy the party much after that, except in a kind of febrile way. I kept looking over people's shoulders to catch glimpses of Emma, to see how she deported herself, to see how Robert behaved with her. But also to see whether recognition would come from other points of view. I don't really like the notion that I've wiped out whole chunks of my life. It's short enough already.

Have I told you yet about the ghastly year that led up to Robert's and my parting? I don't think so.

In retrospect it all began with the summer hols. We'd decided we'd take Nell to Provence to give her French a little push in the right direction. We rented one of those wonderful houses near Gordes and then took little exploratory day trips through the region, even as far as Cassis and the Med. It was when we were at the seashore that I noticed it. Robert was huffing and puffing a lot after his swims and was distinctly out of condition. I mentioned it to him and suggested that maybe it was time to cut down on our evening smoking — which on hols persisted sybaritically throughout the day — not to mention the lunchtime lobster and the bottle of wine. Robert just grunted and pooh-poohed and we carried on as before. After all, we weren't wimps and we were certainly younger than our years. And in London we secretly liked standing outside with the young ones at those big do's where smoking is prohibited. After all, the most interesting people — if not the chief executives — were outside shivering, and not altogether with illicit pleasure.

The extra holiday exercise did nothing to stop Robert from huffing and coughing, so when we got home I nagged until he went to see a doctor, who promptly sent him off for a chest X-ray. When that was blissfully clear (oh, the relief), the cardiac unit followed. I was a little bemused by this, but Robert revealed that he'd confessed to the GP he'd also been having chest pains, very mild, but palpable. (Aren't these men something else? It's as if the only part of their body they can freely admit paying attention to is their cock — and that only if it's perpetually upright.)

I notice I used the word "promptly." This is, of course, a National Health Service euphemism. "Prompt" covers an expanse of time somewhere between emergency and death (though I guess the latter could also be the first). I mention this since you may have forgotten that we have the world's best medical system which never quite managed to work. Between each of the processes I describe, months passed, riddled with anxiety and slightly bizarre behaviour. Robert wanted me to know everything about his skirmishes with the medics and simultaneously didn't want me to know anything at all. Or maybe it was he who didn't want to know. Whatever.

The first visit to the cardiac unit at one of our major hospitals entailed a little tapping and prodding and being geared up to a machine that went *ping*, but mostly uphill running on a treadmill. The cardiologist — a woman who, according to Robert, turned the little white coat into a vehicle for Yves St. Laurent, while all the while holding on to diagnostic powers of Swiss precision — said there was something not quite right about his heart, not to mention his arteries, which had grown fur, like a kettle. She took it for granted that he now didn't smoke (this with a piercing look) and that he would cut fats out of his diet. She'd be writing to his GP, who would

prescribe the necessary blood-thinning aspirins and choles-
terol-reducing pills. Oh yes, and she was booking him in for
an angiogram.

An angiogram, in case you haven't yet heard, is one of the
wonders of modern medical technology. It's a "procedure."
Medicine now seems to have a lot of procedures. Maybe it's
hankering to assimilate itself into the legal profession which
has been giving it such a hard time. "Procedure" is the word
medics use for events which might once have been exploratory
ops but, thanks to above wonders, are now carried out by
computer and under local anesthetic. For the angiogram the
doctor punctures a hole in your groin, shoves a tube up your
veins all the way to your heart, whooshes some coloured liquid through it — and presto! — there's a video of your insides
which the medics (who are trained in film interpretation,
along with the best of the lot) can expertly read.

Robert, who's always preferred doing the interpreting to
being interpreted, didn't much take to the many chapters of
the book of his heart being more transparent to critics than
author. He put on a brave face, poor old thing, but he was distinctly grumpy, not to mention terrified. And without the
little boon of cigarettes, which calm and stimulate by turn,
time took on a distinctly funereal pace. We were easing ourselves slowly (and this only because of the rhythms of the
NHS) towards a verdict of instant death.

The dank odour of mortality came home with Robert at the
end of the day and wafted through a house which had taken on
a new solemnity. A house waiting for a very important event.
Nell and I were assiduously kind, which was so unnatural in
itself that she started to do badly at school, failing a test on

what else but the anatomy of the heart — an organ we had concentrated on rather more than even Mills and Boon might permit.

By the way, I gave up smoking then, too. Naturally. I didn't take any of the happy pills or stick on any patches or gulp at a plastic lump-filled holder, whose sheer ugliness served as a deterrent from it rather than cigarettes. (If it had been beautiful, like a Greta Garbo silver thirties number, and didn't advertise the fact that it was a prosthesis, I'm sure I would have felt differently.) No, I gave up solely with the aid of virtue, which was then in ample supply. It's a drug which in large doses can be almost as addictive as nicotine, though its astringent flavour is somewhat diluted when accompanied by innumerable snacks. Sadly, I can't seem to lay my hands on any virtue now.

After the angiogram came the angioplasty. This second "procedure" involves no mere reading of blood vessels and heart, but a thorough dyno-rodding of fur and scale and sludge and whatever other grisly blocking matter the passage of years has left behind in arteries. Then, to keep them plumped, little umbrella-like bits called stents are shot up through the vessels (from the groin again). When the umbrellas open — presto! — they hold up the artery walls.

Sounds great, if a little queasy-making, in theory and may indeed be great for most. Unfortunately, dyno-rodding couldn't blast through Robert's blocked pipes, which had evidently been blocked in the area of the heart for longer than anyone really cared to speculate. They speculated about the possibility that he had, unbeknownst to him or anyone else, suffered a heart attack. A slippery, shadowy attack actually known as a sleeper.

My own sense was that if he had, it really did take place in his sleep. Nothing wakes Robert, unless he chooses to be woken.

After the failed angioplasty, sleep became a little more difficult. The doctor had prescribed a triple bypass, sooner rather than later, but given the NHS, "sooner" was a vague notion, relative only to eternity. And unless Robert did actually suffer severe pains, which might be the beginning of a heart attack or, of course, a full-scale one, there was no way of making that "sooner" soon, let alone now. Meanwhile there were pills for this and that to take, beta blockers and cholesterol whackers and whatever else. Robert, who never took pills if he could possibly help it, suddenly became an assiduous popper, lining up bottles and times with military precision. There were, however, no sleeping pills, so that sleep, which might bring with it that sleeping heart attack from which nobody wakes, took on all the attractions of a night out on an out-of-control roller coaster.

Then, too, we had the new lodger in the house to contend with. True, he only hovered, and never showed his face at dinner, but he was there all the same. I could see him in Robert's newly slowed movements, in his theatrically forced attempts to show an interest in any lives beyond his, in any subject but that of hearts. This new, spectral lodger was certainly as present as my mother, who at that time was still living in her maisonette and rang us some six to ten times of an evening, and after the first conversation left mournful repetitive messages on the answering machine saying again all the things she thought she had forgotten to say. Anxiety churned at our innards together with the fruit and fibres of our new fat-and-nicotine-free regime. Death and aging mothers are hazards for digestion.

I'm ashamed to say that once or twice or maybe even thrice during this tensest of times, I sinned against the living and imagined Robert dead. Not his dying. Nothing gruesome. Just his absence. I imagined it all quite coldly and practically. I saw a tearful Nell attempting to blot out pain and collapsing in a heap. I saw myself getting out of bed bleary-eyed in the morning and looking around absent-mindedly, unsure as to what was missing. Mentally I adjusted the weekly shopping list. I found myself wondering whether Robert had looked at his will recently, whether I would be able to access his computer files, whether he had talked to his son in the United States.

Finally I confronted him, not so much out of courage as out of desperation. I asked him about all the above. But I also told him, in a tone rather more forceful than I would normally take, that he was behaving like some idealistic youth so blinded by a distant idea that he was about to fall into the abyss opening up before his feet. You see, Robert had always refused private medical insurance. He believed in the NHS with all the passion of a convert, and any chipping away at its edges through private medicine or queue-jumping was anathema.

I told him to bite the bullet of selfishness, since otherwise it didn't look as if he was going to be around to see the ultimate success of the NHS in any case, let alone Nell's flowering into womanhood. We had the money. He could easily go private. In fact, I ordered him to go private and get the whole grisly business of waiting over with.

He looked at me as if I were the whore of Babylon, a scarlet temptress who needed to be stamped out, and rapidly at that. He fumed. He pontificated. He succumbed.

Three weeks later he was on the operating table of the same NHS hospital and at the mercy of the same surgeon he would have had without the beneficial intervention of filthy lucre. The only difference was time — that inestimable commodity of which we have so little, and so little left as the years roll. It was also a Saturday — not, it seems, a day on the NHS operating calendar.

What I hadn't grasped until Robert made his decision was that it was not only the waiting game which tore at his being. He was scared of the op, too. Seriously scared. He didn't think he was going to come out of it alive. It was all fine and dandy for cardiologists and surgeons to talk of a routine operation they performed n times a week. They didn't perform it n times a week on Robert who had never had a total anesthetic, never lain on a hospital bed, never even had a nosebleed or an ingrown toenail removed, let alone had his chest and leg hair shaved, his body pierced and carved, his ribcage lifted, his lungs and heart bypassed, their functions taken over by a machine, while a surgeon pulled a vein from his leg, chopped it like spaghetti and clipped it at various strategic points to his heart, where it would have to serve as a detour for the unforeseeable future. So the trust and passivity and patience demanded of the patient were not characteristics Robert carried within himself at the ready. He was, simply put, bad at it.

I suspect most men are. Not only do we want them to be tough as old boots, but as a matter of course their bodies give them little with which to contend. No monthly bleeds; no pregnancy with its attendant prodding and poking and scanning; no piercing pains or ghastly throbs; no babe ripped from loins or cut from belly; nor a host of other little interventions.

Men are simply not accustomed to having their bodies tampered with.

So there was Robert waiting for imminent death and putting a brave-ish face on it, giving Nell and me long, tender hugs as we left him for the night. The anxiety got to me, too, I confess, though I tried to hide it and, of course, to keep it away from Nell. The morning of D-day, when I came into the hospital and they told me he was still in the operating theatre, I went out calmly enough for a cup of coffee, promptly stumbled off the pavement and all but fell under a bus. Whoops. No harm done. I was wearing a big coat which turned a little grey with passing bus grit. And the shock gave me the opportunity to cry, which I'd obviously been wanting to do. In private. Out on the street, away from my near ones.

Fortified by caffeine and a good cry, I made my way back to the intensive care ward.

Robert was out of the op. He lay in a high bed, eyes closed, tubes protruding from arms and legs and various orifices — some old, some distinctly new. Monitors went *ping* and *bleep* and showed wavy lines of varying shapes which were supposed to be the rhythms of pulse and blood pressure. His skin was a little waxy and his hand, which the nurse told me I could take, was ice-cold. "That's because they bring their temperature right down in the theatre," she explained. "Freeze them. To slow the processes."

Like cryogenics, I thought. When he wakes, he'll be in a different life. I held on to his hand to keep him in this one, while the nurse talked and explained. She was competent and beautiful and had a soft Irish burr to her voice and seemed to be there just for Robert. At one point I made her giggle irreverently and joined her. Our laughter counterpointed the *ping* of the monitor. It was then that I felt an answering pressure from Robert's hand.

He was all right. Well, he was in terrible pain and he had a bright puffy zipper which didn't zip down his chest and a sinuous snake of a scar along his leg. But by the day after the op he could walk along the ward and then along the corridor. It was a walk I didn't quite recognize, tentative, like the ground wasn't where he had left it. But it was a walk, nonetheless. Nell was thrilled when she saw it. She hadn't wanted to come to the hospital, was frightened, but I had urged her. And her relief at seeing him — seeing him move and address her — was palpable.

Robert spent another five days in hospital, then five weeks at home convalescing. I took the time off from the office. My assistant kept me in touch, fielded what she could and called in twice a day with whatever else. But mostly I tuned my clock to Robert's. We took a prescribed walk every morning, ten minutes to start with and building up to an hour or more. I made sure he did his exercises, cooked to his lighter diet, inspected his scars, lifted everything he couldn't lift, including his laptop, got lots of films out of the video shop, organized the rota of visitors and so on and so on. In some ways it was all really rather pleasant — a warm, cloistered time, like those first weeks after a child is born and you simply nest.

Given that I'm hardly a natural nurse, I don't think I did too badly. Robert was patently grateful. Or so I thought until he upped and left a mere six months later, bypassing nurse and wife and daughter on his way to a new life. It was strange. In some ways it felt as if a zombie had taken over his body and ordered or seduced him away. You see, we had never really been as close as we were in those months around the op and just before we plunged back into work. (Six weeks was back-to-work time and three months the notional moment, according to the doctors, when all systems were "go.") Maybe it wasn't the closeness of passion or of lovers, but it was a tender and loving intimacy. So his sudden bolt took me completely by surprise. I felt as shocked and traduced and betrayed as the greatest of innocents.

I suspect what happened to him wasn't as uncommon as I felt it to be at the time. You see, we had spent so many months in the shadow of his illness that it was almost impossible to find a language of relating which put it to one side. So inevitably I became the adjunct of his illness, its helpmate, the very image of the horror with which his condition had initially struck him. I was his dying. Life lay elsewhere. Certainly the life of his cock.

But I mustn't stoke that pain again, nor even rake over the ashes. His scars must be all but invisible now. Mine should be, too.

Sometimes when I'm in the old people's home, I think bodies remember longer than minds. An old lady will strike up a "how do you do" expression and stretch out her hand on seeing me — a set of gestures so engrained that the mere sight of a stranger elicits them. Five minutes later, if she sees me again, she'll perform the same ritual of politeness. And again, if chance occasions it, in another ten minutes. Her body remembers a smile, an outstretched hand, while her mind has already forgotten that she has seen me so very recently and already greeted me.

Tonight I failed to recognize Robert. I "forgot" him. I don't altogether know whether that's a good or a bad sign.
All my love
Jude

24 MARCH

Dear Celia,
In a little less than four months the Big 5-0 will be upon us, mine on the thirteenth, yours on the fifteenth of July. Do you remember how in Cambridge you took to saying that the true basis of our friendship was that we'd both missed the storming of the Bastille by one day? All my energies, you laughed, went into anticipation; whereas you were all afterthought and analysis. We both missed the present in the process, by looking either forwards or backwards. Don't know if any of that was quite true, but it was fun to consider. We had lots of time for considering in those days. Time had a wonderful elasticity, like my skin.

What I was working my way towards asking is shall we do something together? Something special to mark the occasion. A trip to Rome? To San Francisco? Or even a repeat excursion to Paris, where you can't have forgotten we celebrated our twenty-first on the all-important compromise date of the fourteenth. We splurged on a lavish dinner, got plastered, watched the crowds and the fireworks.

I'm finally going to post these letters to you so that we have time to plan. Yes, the more I think about it, the more it seems a delicious idea to mark the passage into this next stage (and I do feel it as such) with you.

What I don't want is a party. I would hate a party. I would have to spend weeks collecting together my music of the half-century, and I'd start weeping over the Rolling Stones or Gloria and Madame George or Judy Collins singing "My Father Promised Me." And Nell would insist on playing "When I'm Sixty-Four" for me, since she can't really see the difference between fifty and sixty-four. And the teenagers would watch us dance, their faces twisted in mockery and dis-belief, and we'd all feel like fools. I couldn't even invite my lover to a party.

Now that is a strange thought and should make me wake to reason.

I hadn't told anyone except you about Toni, not even Francesca, because much as I love her I know she's a formida-ble gossip and particularly good at secrets. She only ever tells one or just maybe two other people a secret, which I guess is marginally better than announcing it at a meeting of the J.P. Rutgers literary agency or taking out a whole-page ad in the *Sunday Times* — though the ultimate effect in terms of the circulation of knowledge isn't that different.

But I told Elizabeth yesterday. I didn't intend to. It just popped out. Elizabeth is like that. She makes things pop out. She's one of the few friends I have who've outlasted my mar-riage. That's probably because Elizabeth has been through everything, and if she hasn't been through it, then she knows somebody who has. And because she laughs. Never derisively. Wryly. Her laughter accepts all foibles. She sees the humour in life and makes me see it, too. She once told me that she could put up with the gradual erosion of all her senses, as long as she could be left with the most important one: her sense of humour. I've begun to see her point.

Elizabeth is about five years older then me. She's tall and plump and doesn't dye her hair and wears sensible shoes because she's a mass of energy always in motion. She's my guide to the pitfalls of the mid-life body. Elizabeth is all too aware that we've reached that age when the body is as much a desperate centre of interest as it was in adolescence, yet unlike those lucky teenagers, we don't want to be interested in it, 'cause it's only a signal of our decay. Elizabeth's energy, of course, is proof positive that decay can be overcome by a mere flick of the will.

For the last ten years or so, she's run an agony column for one of the grown-up women's mags. Before that, she worked in personnel, or what they've now renamed interpersonal relations — as if we have any other kind. And before that she was married to some British Council bod who kept moving them round Southeast Asia and Africa with dizzying speed. He died of some ghastly bug well before I met her. And she and the two children remade their lives here. Now she's married to a sweet man who's retired and seems to spend all his time creating improvements to their house in France, so is rarely here, which gives her lots of time for her friends, especially as the children have grown and flown.

So I found myself telling Elizabeth about Toni. I think I told her because I was wondering how on earth I could carry on this relationship, which had suddenly blossomed into ridiculous importance, fuelled no doubt by the fact that I see Toni daily, but privately only in snatched moments.

I haven't told you yet, but I didn't have the nerve to bring him back with me on Friday. What if Nell were to get home early? She'd collapse on the floor in a paroxysm of disgust.

She'd run off and make love to her boyfriend and never come home again. She'd . . .

So Toni and I really did just go to a movie. (A movie for him seems to mean a picture palace, and therefore Leicester Square, which I haven't been to in years 'cause of the hordes of young who gather there.) Not that I remember much of what we saw — some ridiculous Hollywood garble of his choice, with lots of chases and exploding guns. Some explosions in my head, too, I can tell you, over what he was doing to my legs.

I think he was a little taken aback after that when I said I'd drop him off at his place. He looked as if he might argue, but the words didn't come. He just gave me one of those kisses which leave me gasping and went off into the night. I don't think he wants me to see how he lives. I know it's off the Caledonian Road — probably one of those ghastly shared accommodation places which are little better than tips with crumbling walls round them. We didn't notice dirt so much when we were students, did we? Funny, that. Layers of grime on floor and sink. Mugs ringed with whorls of tea and coffee. Dust balls flying across the floor. Windows which let very little daylight through. Heaps of forgotten clothes in odd corners. Hardly a place to take that strange creature called an older woman. She might start tidying up — like mother.

Anyhow, I was saying some of this to Elizabeth on Saturday evening, probably in the hope that she'd talk me out of this mad pass in my life, when her eyes started to twinkle and she said, "Stop feeling so guilty. There's nothing to feel guilty about. No . . ." She put out a plump, staying hand. "I don't want to hear anymore. You'll talk yourself out of it. Have a little secret, darling. It'll do you good."

Will it do me good? I'm not sure. I'm no dab hand at secrets — as you know. If only I could talk to Toni about more than latte and cappuccino and working hours . . . Maybe I should take some Italian lessons. Or maybe I should remind myself that when I was young, relations with men were not all about talk. Quite the opposite, in fact. Talk is probably inimical to passion.

It certainly is in Hollywood, in any case. Have you noticed that dialogue in films has all but vanished? Elizabeth said something interesting about all that. What was it? Oh yes, that she suspected there was far more sex happening in the culture — in movies and mags and soaps and advertising — than there is in the home. Sex has become so banal we've wiped out its basis in desire. She also suspects that, when asked direct questions, people lie in all those questionnaires that have to do with sex. Because now it's shameful to be celibate or not to keep doing it well past the age of Viagra — whether you want to or not. (Which is all very well, except that since last week I seem to want to.)

Nell surprised me by coming home before Elizabeth had left. The pre-midnight return was unusual, and the first thing that leapt into my mind was that it was a good thing I hadn't brought Toni home and that I would have to keep on being wary, since my daughter's hours, which had always seemed far too late, were in fact erratic. Simultaneously, it occurred to me that Nell might be in some kind of trouble. I stared at her eyes to check for those telltale glistening pupils, but they seemed all right within the ghoulish circles that the kohl outlined. She even pulled out a chair to join us when Elizabeth asked her to.

Nell's always liked Elizabeth, who teases her.

"Don't tell me." Elizabeth reaches into her capacious bag

and brings out a wonderfully wrapped parcel. "You've come back specially for me. And to collect your birthday present."

Nell ogles it. "Do you want the truth or will a lie do?"

"A lie, please."

"I came just for you, then." Nell grins and adds sheepishly. "And 'cause I didn't fancy the club. Shall I keep it till Sunday or open it now?"

"Now. Is that where the fifty others went?"

"Only twenty tonight."

"The pack's dwindling."

"Competing venues. Some like hip hop, some want garage."

Nell tears open the parcel to reveal an assortment of choice toiletries and creams and makeup. She gasps and kisses Elizabeth, who basks in her pleasure.

"So what are you doing over Easter? Is your mum taking you somewhere wonderful?"

"Dad this time. We're going skiing. Well, actually he's taking me away from London so that he can watch me revise. Otherwise he doesn't believe I do. Half-days with the notes, half-days on the slopes." She gives Elizabeth her wicked grin.

"That reminds me," I interrupt their banter. "I bumped into your dad the other night. Forgot to mention it."

"Oh yeah?"

"Yeah. And Emma."

Nell suddenly looks up at me. There is distinct surprise on her face, but she quickly masks it. "That's good. Now you can finally stop badgering me with those endless questions about her."

"I've never badgered you," I splutter.

"Haven't you? That's sure what it felt like to me. It's not so bad now, but at the beginning . . ."

"That's not true, Nell." I look towards Elizabeth to be the judge of the unfairness of this attack, but Nell has already put on her adamant voice.

"It is. You went on and on about her. Endlessly. And I had nothing to say 'cause Emma only went into a sulk whenever I turned up. Still does. Not when Dad asks her to take me out shopping, of course. That's okay. She doesn't sulk then, just drags me along to all those designer shops."

This was the first I had heard of any of this.

"You never showed me anything she bought you."

"That 'cause she doesn't. Like, what am I gonna do with designer clothes, Mum?" Nell's expression is all stormy contempt. Then she giggles at Elizabeth. "I much prefer it when Dad just hands me the cash and tells me to go off and treat myself."

"I never asked you many questions about Emma," I persist in my self-justification.

"It's okay, Mum." Nell gives me a crooked little smile.

"It would be altogether unnatural if you hadn't," Elizabeth intervenes, and I don't know whether I'm miffed more at her interruption or its content. The two of them are ganging up on me to tarnish my self-image.

"So what did you think of her?" Nell asks.

"What?"

"What did you think of her? Of Emma?"

I grit my teeth. "She's very pretty."

"Not half as pretty as you were at her age, I bet, Mum." Nell throws her arms around me and gives me a peck on the cheek. The gesture is so surprising that tears leap into my eyes. I adore my daughter. I shall never allow any man to come between us.

Yours,

Jude

PART TWO

When Celia first turned up in the little school and we became fast friends, I used to fantasize that she was my sister. My sister come back to me.

There had been a sister. Nothing explicit was ever said about her. Only that she had existed too briefly and died. A grave in the churchyard marked her place. Lottie, they had called her, and she had died two years before I was born. My mother didn't make a big thing about it. But sometimes I would catch her wearing a peculiar expression and staring out the window into the fields beyond. There would be a dishtowel in her hand, say, and a plate half dried, and she would have stopped right in the midst of whatever it was she was doing. Just stopped to stare out the window as if she was looking for something. If I said anything then, she would jump. That's how I knew. Knew she'd been thinking about Lottie. I'd caught her in the act and she'd jumped because she didn't want me to know. My mother prided herself on no-nonsense practicality.

I used to tell myself that she didn't want to talk about Lottie because my sister was really only a half-sister. She hadn't come from my dad. He never talked about Lottie at all. And probably he didn't want my mother even thinking about her.

Anyhow, when Celia turned up and began to spend almost as much time with us as she did at her grandmother's, my mother really took to her. "Such a confident, well-brought up little girl," my mother would say to me, half intimating that I would do well to follow Celia's example. Celia had the gift of talking to adults. She was utterly unfazed by them, indeed even seemed to find them genuinely interesting at the dinner table. In front of Celia, my usually quiet father happily discoursed about the differences between Roman law and common law and why a jury was made up of twelve people rather than four. Or whatever. It came to me at these family occasions that what had been missing all along was a sister. And Celia took her place admirably.

Once when we were playing near the churchyard, I took Celia to visit Lottie's grave. "That's my sister," I told her. "But now you're my sister."

Celia gave me a troubled look. I could tell that beneath her fringe her forehead was all scrunched up, 'cause her eyes had grown narrow. "You want me dead," she blurted, and ran off in the midst of my denial, so that I had to look for her everywhere.

I've done it now. I've sent her the letters. That makes me jittery. I have no idea who the present Celia is and how she might receive them. Receive me. I'll wait for her response before writing any more. Though the temptation is great.

Dear Celia,

I haven't written for a bit — in part because there's been no sign from you, and I've been wondering whether you so thoroughly disapprove of your old mate that you've given her up. You should have had my first batch of letters by now. It can't be that far to Vancouver, even if the plane does have to get over the Rockies. You know, I always think of you as living in some dramatic meadow in the foothills of the mountains from which you can watch the rush and tumble of distant waves — or have I got my geography all wrong? Then it occurred to me that the letters probably had to be sent on from an old address to a new one, and we all know that can take forever . . .

To tell the truth, I haven't written for another reason. I don't know quite what sense to make of myself.

What a strange old time it's proving to be. There's been Nell's absence on top of everything else. And with it, my sudden freedom, which feels weird — as if I've been unleashed, but the master is just around the corner and will start to bellow the moment I head off too fast or too far. So I'm a little tentative about my freedom, but I'm taking liberties with it nonetheless.

Yes, I did it. I brought Toni home. I invited him to my bed, which used to be Robert's bed too, since I never thought to get rid of it, only of him. I have to admit Toni's presence taxed the mattress as it had rarely been before.

Toni seems to be blossoming under his boss lady's tender love and care. Really. Yesterday he came into work in a creamy linen suit. He looked altogether devastating, and I kept a beady eye on him and the customers who lolled too long in the café. I've been up and down the stairs so often I seriously think those sagging thighs are firming up just a little. Or maybe it's the night-time acrobatics. But back to Toni. He's showing more initiative, too. He suggested that we introduce one of those newspaper racks — the kind they have in Viennese cafés. I agreed, though my thought was that we should stock it with the weekly review pages and maybe add the TLS and the other literary rags to that.

Toni is less interested in what we put there than in the feature itself, but it did seem to me he used several more words of English in the process of explaining it all. He also wondered whether we could put some café tables or a bench or two out in the garden under the tree, only to be used in good weather, of course. But it has been crowded of late and we could do more business. As he said this, Toni beamed a beatific smile at me which had something a little conspiratorial in it. My heart — or do I really mean some nether region? — went pitter-patter. I watched him from the top window as he went out to explore the garden and measure up, and I had this unrecognizable feeling. It struck me that it might be happiness.

On Tuesday evening we had a reading by a travel writer who's written a book on unknown Europe. His adventures in Bulgaria, Albania and Ukraine really do rival exploits in more exotic lands. It wasn't meant to be one of Toni's nights, but he stayed anyway, perching at the coffee bar and listening with seeming intentness while Hamish McCrae read. And whom did I suddenly see on a stool just in front of him, when I turned around from my place near the front? Heather. Heather Glover. And her eyes were not on Hamish McCrae.

Afterwards I had several uncomfortable moments. We were all milling around nursing a glass of wine and I thought I should introduce Toni to McCrae and his accompanying publicist. I hesitated because McCrae was telling us some silly story about always being able to identify aging romantic writers by their startling leopard or tiger tops which fail to match the papery crinkle around their dull eyes. When I looked around for Toni, he had vanished as if he'd read my embarrassment. Or was it because Heather, too, had vanished? It came to me that I had never trusted her or her hot pants.

But Toni reappeared alone when everyone else had gone and it was time to close up. I decided to interpret his ability to make himself scarce as a sign of his innate tact. I'm impressed. I'm very impressed. (And I shall never again wear a leopard top.)

The next day, I was reminded that happiness always comes with an expensive price tag.

I was putting together a list for a promotion I thought might work well in my shop, a promotion of anthologies — you know the kind: humorous quotations, politics, invective, death — when the phone rings. I pick it up and it's the head of staff at my mother's residential home. Her voice has a forced calm which fills me with foreboding. Could I come to the home, please. No, no, it's not an emergency. Well, not quite an emergency, but she's sure I'll want to come and see my mother.

I rush out, driving so recklessly I all but disappear into the pothole at the top of the road. Potholes in London have grown gigantic. Like New York in its heyday, even if we haven't got the weather for it. It's because the government is so interested in e-stuff, in the immaterial, in puff, they've forgotten there's a world outside the virtual. These potholes are not virtual. Nor are they merely the appearance of a pothole. They may signal an absence, but an absence of road is a material event, like an absence in a train track. Life can disappear down it.

When I get to the home, I find that it's my mother's life that's disappearing. She's had a stroke. Sometime in the night, they think. The carer who comes to dress her in the morning found her quivering and unable to move. The doctor has been. She's resting now. Angela, who is in charge today, tells me all this. Angela is built to Amazonian proportions. She's big and black and very, very brusque. When I first met her, she terrified the pants off me.

A major Caribbean bully, I thought, but whereas I might have just about been able to tell a white woman to be gentler with my mum, I couldn't possibly say anything to Angela. I'd wake up in the night worrying about how she was treating my mother. I'd have ghastly scenarios running through my guilty mind, sadistic scenes of retributive horror in which Angela took out all the accumulated rage of her people on my help- less mum in order to get her to give up the key to her room, have her baths, eat her morning gruel. Twice I said to Nell that I would either have to lodge a complaint or get Granny out of there. "And bring her home to us?" Nell asked with simulated innocence, knowing full well I'd back down.

It took some six months for me to realize that Angela's brusque bullying was only half in earnest. The other half was masquerade which could crack into hearty laughter. Beneath both there was a soft enough heart which beat to the rhythm of sympathy, as long as everything was running according to the rules. I don't really know whether my mother would have bent to these sooner if the initial approach had been more visibly persuasive. Maybe. But even the staff members whose manners were overtly gentle had steely sides. Institutions demand a certain discipline, and discipline has an inevitable edge.

But I'm running away with myself. Running away from the image of my mother. My mother on her narrow bed. My mother lying on her side. Her face and hair the colour of her pillow, her eyes closed. My mother, who looks as if all her life has drained away into the girlish pink of her coverlet. I hadn't noticed until now how tiny she had grown. Her bare arms are shrivelled, the skin crinkled parchment. I stare at her and my pulse grows erratic, my mouth bone dry. She could be dead and no one has noticed. I want to scream. Instead I whimper. Inanely.

"Hello, Mum. How are you feeling? I would have brought you some flowers. I . . ."

Her eyelids flutter like wounded birds. A blue gaze floods me for an instant and disappears as quickly. A spasm goes through her hand and arm and, as I watch, becomes rhythmic. A master puppeteer has taken charge of her limbs. I rush out to find Angela, who reassures me.

"That's norrrmal," she sings in response to my cries. "Norrmal."

Normality has become a moveable feast. I guess if you live one step away from an emergency ward for the demented, "normal" is an elastic term.

Angela comes back to my mother's room with me. She takes my mother's hand and pats it. "That's a good girl," she

87

says, and strokes my mother's blind face, her hair. "Good girl."

I watch her with something like awe. I couldn't do that. I haven't been able to do that. Take my mother's hand, stroke her, offer physical reassurance. Comfort. And here is this stranger, whom in my thoughts I often characterize as brutal, doing just that.

My mother and I rarely touch each other. We never have. I don't know if it's her doing or mine. My only memory, but perhaps that already dates from early adolescence, is of wriggling out of her grasp. I hated her smell. It wafted from her clothes, from her drawers and wardrobe to clutch at me — a mixture of lavender and thyme and perspiration, or more womanly things that I thought would infect me.

That smell has gone now to be replaced by an odour of institutional mustiness, a mixture of thrice-used cooking oil and bleach and something indescribable. But I still have to overcome disgust to take my mother's hand. Does Nell feel like that about me? Probably. Or maybe only in part. Her hugs are far rarer than they were, but they still take place from time to time, warmly enough, though it's hard to know who makes the first gesture. Sometimes I catch her nostrils twitching and there's a second's recoil. If she's in a good mood, she doesn't say anything. If she's feeling a little resentful, her lip will curl and she'll mutter something like "What have you been eating, Mum?"

The mother's body is a tricky place. After all, we came out of it. No wonder men can be squiffy about women. We are, too.

I sit by my mother's side and babble. Even if I can't quite bring myself to hold her, the sound of the voice, they say, offers comfort. At one point her eyes open and she starts to speak. At least that's what the movement of lips and emerging sound seem to imply. She is making words; the words fall into rhythms. They have the rise and fall of sentences. But none of it makes sense. None of it.

I want to scream again and run for Angela, but I force myself to sit there and I say things in response to my mother's incomprehensible speech. She appears to be utterly unaware that I do not understand her. At last she closes her eyes and seems to fall asleep again. I wait for a little while, then sneak away.

Angela is in her tiny office. "How do you find her?" she asks me.

The question seems as incomprehensible as anything my mother has uttered.

"Terrible," I say. "Is she going to . . . ?"

Angela cuts me off. "The doctor says she's doing all right . . ."

I stare at Angela. Has she gone off the deep end?

"But if you want her to go into hospital, he can arrange it."

"Go into hospital?" I repeat, my mind blank.

"Yes. Though she's fine here."

It takes me a little while to make sense of Angela's non-sense. Only then do I realise that she's been hedging. She won't make use of the D word. It's not part of the vocabulary of the home.

A scene I witnessed some months ago drops into my mind. I am sitting in a corner of the lounge with my mother. Across the room there is suddenly a whispered exchange between two staff members. With practised calm, they whisk everyone into the next room, one by one. In the far chair I see a woman whose head is lowered. She has dropped off. From the way the care worker is patting her hand and whispering, it seems she has dropped off into death. None of us is meant to see. To recognize the fact. Even here in this waiting room for death, the D word can't be mentioned. "Mrs. R is no longer with us" is the euphemism, as if she'd packed her bags and Zimmer and gone off to some smart resort on the Riviera.

What Angela is trying to tell me now is that I have a choice to make. My mother can stay here to die or go off to the hospital, where intrusive techniques may be used to keep her alive or accidentally speed her way to death. My choice.

"She'll be very confused if she wakes up in hospital."

"Verrry," Angela nods sagely, her face a drama of my mother's confusion.

"And the doctor said she was doing well?"

"You can ring him yourself. He'll be checking in sometime tonight. You can wait for him, if you like. But she's doing just fine."

Angela wants my mother to stay put. She doesn't think the hospital will be good for her. But she doesn't want to be seen to be influencing me. That would never do. It might indeed land her in a complaints procedure.

"I think she should just rest for the time being. To put her into an ambulance would only make her worse," I say tentatively.

"That's right. That's right," Angela rushes in. "Then they stick tubes in her. No good." She crinkles her nose with even more disapproval than Nell can muster.

I find myself sniffling on the way back to the shop. I tell myself I am just going to check in and make sure everything is in order and then I'll go back to my mum and wait for the doctor and have an early night. But no. Toni is there waiting for me. I'd forgotten we had said we'd have dinner out together. One thing leads to another, and before I can put a halt to it, he's back at my place. The proximity of death has a strange way of heightening passion. Carpe diem and all that. I finally understand what it means. I'm seizing the day, or the night in my case, 'cause tomorrow may not come.

But it does. And in the morning I urge Toni away. I'm frantic with guilt. I ring the home expecting an announcement which contains one of the many euphemisms for the D word. My fault. It's all my fault.

I don't believe whoever it is who answers the phone and after a little hesitation tells me my mother is better. I rush for the home as soon as my assistant, Kate, has arrived in the shop. Kate tells me everything will be fine. She won't take her lunch break. She'll stay late. Whatever. And it's raining, so it will be quiet until at least noon, when Toni and Sandra come in.

Fifteen minutes later I turn the handle on my mother's door. She's there. She's really there and not in a coffin. She's lying with her back to me, so I move round to the foot of the bed where I can see her better before whispering a hello.

Her eyes flutter open and then she does something which makes me reach for a chair to sink into. Her right hand lifts shakily and careers towards her left. And misses. Again and again, it lifts and misses. She is trying to clap. But her hands refuse to meet. One of them lies dormant. The other can't quite reach it. Yet the gesture is undeniably a clap. And she looks like a joyous toddler. A child trying to clap her pleasure. Her eager pleasure at seeing me.

The tears stream down my face. With them comes a mad recollection of one of those Zen parables that made the rounds in our youth, all about the sound of one hand clapping. I'm sure it wasn't what the Zen master meant, but I think I have now heard the sound of one hand clapping.

I think it won't surprise you to learn that I sat by my mother's side for the rest of the day.

Yours, a little in awe,

Jude

15 APRIL

Dear Celia,

Events have been running away with me, not to mention the paperwork in the shop. If I have to fill in one more form this month, I'll have myself committed. No, I know, there aren't many places left to commit oneself to. Committing to "care in the community" doesn't have the same ring to it. The aura of those old institutions, however vile, was of a solidity which blocked the world out. The streets are another matter. It'll have to be those cloisters we used to dream about.

Nell is back from her ski and study trip. She came home a day earlier than I expected. I must have miscalculated. I expected her on the Sunday, not the Saturday. As fate would have it, Toni was here. We were just sitting down to a light supper when I heard the key turning in the lock and almost jumped out of my skin. Thank heavens I was dressed. Another hour and I might not have been.

On top of it all, Robert insisted on helping Nell in with her cases and up the stairs to our first floor, which contains our sitting and dining space. He seemed in no hurry to leave, either. He stopped to chat and had a good look around. Maybe he wanted to see what I had done to the family furniture. I think he expected me to offer him a drink as well. No way.

He hasn't really crossed the threshold of this place in years. Usually he rings the bell and waits for Nell outside or drops her at the bottom of the stairs. I certainly didn't want him doing any more than that now, but Nell was busy urging him in and on. She wanted to show him the guitar I'd bought her. Apparently he'd been telling her about his misspent youth and his early career as a Dylan sing-alike. So I cut my losses and sent them both up to her room, not, however, before Toni had made himself wonderfully visible leaning against the column by the dining table. Robert glanced at him, threw me a quick, assessing look, and patted Nell's bottom to speed her up the stairs.

He must have forgotten how to strum the desired chords, or maybe he never knew how, because they were downstairs with perverse quickness and before I could gently show Toni the door. It always takes a little time to explain things to Toni. It's the lack of language. Mostly his intuition makes up for it, but that evening he seemed to have gone particularly thick, and he was just refilling our wine glasses when Robert and Nell came into the kitchen. A few distinctly uncomfortable moments followed. Robert decided to prolong them by reporting on Nell's skiing technique and pontificating about the condition of the snow in the Swiss Alps. Finally he gave Nell a hug goodbye — a giant hug which left me in no quandary whatsoever about the relative nature of cuddles for Dad and Mum — and left. After which Nell flounced into a chair and asked "What's for dinner?"

And you know what? She took over. She was exuberant, funny and more flirtatious than I've ever seen her. So much so that I began to wonder whether she had learned all these new mannerisms in just one week from Emma or whether they'd been there all along and I had just never seen them in action. She sipped wine and crossed and uncrossed long legs and made eyes at Toni and told tall tales about zooming down black runs and was really so bewitching that I found myself retiring to my principal role of cook and maidservant.

But no sooner have we finished eating and I've managed to get Toni out of the door, than she turns on me.

"What was HE doing here?" Her finger points with all the assault power of a nuclear warhead.

"Having dinner."

Her eyes narrow into melodramatic slits. Her whole face scrunches. "Mum, you're not. I don't believe it." Her voice rises into a shriek. "I really don't believe it. And I've got my GCSEs coming up!"

She races towards her room and I'm right behind her.

"It's not what you think."

"What is it, then?"

I stop the door of her room from slamming.

"You're disgusting." Her face has turned red and puffy and breathes venom. "You're altogether disgusting. No wonder Dad left you."

She has a way of going straight for the jugular, my Nell. The tears fill my eyes, willy-nilly.

"Your father hardly left me because of a younger man. It was more the other way round."

"*Both* of you are disgusting."

This time she manages to slam her door in my face.

I leave her. There is very little I can say.

She, however, says it all. In actions, not words. Two days later when I come home from the bookshop, without Toni, of course, she's sitting on the sofa with a man I've never seen. And he is a man. Not a boy, though he could look like one to me. In fact, he's probably about Toni's age, and he's not her usual boyfriend. But it's clear that they've been up to something. Both of them have these very pink cheeks and bright eyes, and Nell is straightening her skirt (a skirt?!) with a deliberately provocative gesture. The provocation is aimed at both of us. I see this and stop myself from shouting and kicking the man out of the house. Anyhow, he's up and murmuring something made incomprehensible by twin lip rings and out the door before I can collect myself. And Nell has already bolted upstairs.

"You're meant to be studying," I shout after her. But I shout half-heartedly. Nell is trying to tell me something. I know she is, which is why I don't follow her upstairs and start to rail. She's telling me that it's her turn for all this, not mine. Sex, passion are for the young.

I want to struggle and argue, but in my heart of hearts, I know she's right. I suddenly feel depressed — not only because I already miss Toni. But because somehow I've failed her: all my gentle nudges about waiting for sex until she's older, when she's sure she feels something that will last for more than a month, all my interminable attempts to insert sexual and relational good sense into haphazard snatched conversations, have come to naught. Because of my own actions. Will she ever forgive me? Will I?

I still haven't been able to confront Nell about this new, older man. The furthest I've got is to ask her softly about what happened to her nice Simon, the seventeen-year-old boyfriend. Whereupon she told me to mind my own business, in no uncertain terms. I did.

I'm sure my cowardice is bad for her, but I don't know how to tackle it all without her running off in a huff. Well, I do really. I could drop Toni. And fire him.

I could, but somehow I don't think I will. Not yet.

My love,
Jude

Dear Celia,
Life grows stranger and stranger.

I've been going to visit my mother daily. There is no one else to whom my presence brings such open joy. Not Toni (who would be ardent, but whom I'm training to circumspection). Certainly not Nell.

But yesterday when I went to my mother's room, she wasn't there. My stomach performed a somersault.

I rushed to the staff office trying to keep euphemisms and the D word from ransacking my mind. I couldn't have been successful, because Angela, who was again on duty, gave me one of her distinctly bullying looks as I blurted out, "Where is she? What have you done with her?"

"Calm yourself now, Judy." (She always calls me Judy and I've given up protesting.) "Mrs. Brautigan is right next door. Yes, yes, she's sitting up today. A major improvement."

Indeed, when I go into the lounge, there is my mother. Her head lists to one side, she is distinctly overbalanced on one hip, but she's sitting up, and she blurts out a cascade of incomprehensible language when she sees me. The oddest thing is that, some twenty minutes later, this mimic language which only she can understand gradually slides and merges into English. I am so thrilled that I sit by her side for far longer than I had intended. What I don't understand is why I am so thrilled. It's not as if my mother makes much sense when she is speaking English. But there we are. Small comforts are important in such distressing times.

They are distressing.

When I get back to the bookshop, guess who is standing behind the till? You can't guess, I guarantee it. Nell. Yes, my daughter. What is she doing here? You may well ask.

Just a few days after I caught her more or less at it with her new boyfriend and she sullenly refused all my (half hearted) attempts to talk about this unacceptable state of affairs, Nell suddenly announced that she wanted some work experience. Never mind GCSEs. She will come into the bookshop to work for a few hours every day until the end of the Easter break. She imagines I can use the extra hand. And the change from tedious revision can only do her good, she claims. Being stuck in the house for too many hours will send her raving . . . literally and metaphorically.

I can hardly say no, since a stint in the bookshop is something I have been trying to persuade her into for months. But Nell isn't at work to work, though she makes a stab at finding out where all the stock is and helping the occasional customer. She's there to use her mobile from a new site and to embellish the life of the bookshop with little beeps which need instant messaging responses from her nimble fingers. I swear she has written more into the tiny window of her mobile than she has in all her years at school.

Apart from that, Nell is in the bookshop to police my activities. She follows me everywhere, more assiduously than a private dick waiting to jump in for the kill, which I imagine is the sight of Toni and me doing something unspeakable together, like talking. I suspect she has visions of interposing her body to save me from this terrible brute.

On top of all this, Heather has taken to dropping in for coffee around closing time. I can't complain, 'cause she's bought a book or two as well. But she looks wonderful, all fawn and maroon, as if she's decided to live up to her name and stride across highlands with Rob Roy or some such. And she spends much of her time ogling Toni and trying to engage him in conversation. Perhaps she succeeds. I can hardly stalk her the way Nell stalks me. But I'd like to claw her eyes out.

Yesterday I sent Nell out on an errand and caught a few moments alone with Toni. I don't think he understands my sudden coldness, and I wanted to explain. It was a beautiful day, at last, and we stepped out into the garden. I confess I had a cigarette or three. I never do when Nell's around, but these last weeks have been nothing if not enervating, so I took the opportunity.

Anyhow, I say something like "I'm really sorry, Toni, but until my daughter is back in school, life is a little complicated."

"Complicated?"

"Yes."

"Why complicated?"

He seems genuinely not to understand. How can he? He's never had children.

"It's just difficult. She doesn't approve."

He stares at me dumbly. Then suddenly a light comes on in his eyes. "I see. You marry me, then no problem," he blurts out.

"Marry?" I squeak.

"Yes, why not? Would be good. Good for Nell." His voice has taken on a sonority.

I don't know whether to hug him or burst out laughing. It's so sweet being proposed to. Perhaps he's a Catholic and he thinks what troubles Nell is the immorality of our relations. Perhaps he's completely age-blind and really doesn't see that my daughter might find our coupling curious.

"I'm sorry, Toni. I can't," I say.

"You can't?" His face falls. He stubs out his cigarette in one of the ashtrays he's bought for the two new outdoor tables and looks at me with the ardour of a romantic swain. "Why not? I would like marriage. You divorced, yes?"

I see Nell at the top of the stairs and I draw away. "Let's talk about it another time," I say as lightly as I can.

Celia, how to describe how flattered I feel and how, for one mad moment, I think yes, why not. He's so lovely. He's so kind to me, so sweetly passionate. In a few years' time, Nell will be away at university and I will be left alone to brood into my lonely old woman's teacup with the crack running down the middle. So, why not? Why not be daring? The way we were when we were young. Shed this old fuddy-duddy's skin I acquired with maternity, which makes me anxious at every turn unless I douse myself in alcohol.

Give me reasons why not, Celia. Reasons which aren't merely to do with decorum and propriety and those things we never thought we cared about.

Yours, but not as ever,

Jude

P.S. One reason I haven't heard from you yet has just presented itself. I omitted to give you a return address. Silly, silly me. I've simply grown out of the habit of writing letters by hand. I shall rectify this omission immediately.

20 APRIL

Dear, dear Celia,

At noon today Elizabeth appeared in the shop. She looked ghastly. Her hair was a frizzled mass. She had put on her lipstick at a drunken angle and her jacket had the chic of an old rag used to wipe down oil stains. She dragged me upstairs and all but fell into a chair at a corner table. Toni had asked to have his day switched and wasn't there, so I gestured to Manou, my new French bar girl, to make us two espressos and bring them over. There was nothing stronger I could offer Elizabeth, though she looked as if she needed it.

"What is it?" I asked gently.

"Stuart."

Stuart is her husband.

"Has he been taken ill?"

"Worse."

"He's dead. Oh, Elizabeth, I'm so sorry. What can I do?"

"He's not dead. It's worse than that."

I'm trying to work out what can be worse than death, when I realize the worse applies to her and not to Stuart. Simultaneously Elizabeth says, "He wants a divorce."

"Why?" I blurt out this inane question, then clamp my hand over my mouth. Stuart must be almost a hundred. Well, certainly almost as old as my mother. Or so it seemed the few times I've actually met him. Can it be worth getting divorced even that late in life?

"All those weeks he's spent, months, maybe years, working on the French house, on the garden . . . or that's what he told me . . . In fact he's been down there because some woman . . ." her voice cracks and chokes.

I give her a big hug and murmur solace and let her shed tears. As I hold her, I'm suddenly back in that moment of being left, abandoned for no reason one can think of, and the nausea comes, that feeling that abandonment is tantamount to a wiping out, an extinction. If you have no value, you don't exist.

"He'll come to his senses," I murmur. "No one could be better than you."

"He says that, too." Elizabeth suddenly yelps out a shrill laugh. "No one better. But he doesn't want the better, does he? No, he wants the worse. Why can't we ever learn that? Remember Woody Allen. If it's done right, sex is dirty. Wives never seem to be dirty enough, not after all those years."

"But if you're not around and she takes over, she won't stay dirty for very long," I say reasonably enough. Elizabeth gives me a look which is the other kind of dirty. We are not in the realms of reason, as I should remember only too well.

"I think you should just go down there and sort him out. She's only got her clutches into him 'cause you're always here and not paying attention to him."

Elizabeth stares at me as if I were uttering statements of profound novelty. Why is it always the first time when it happens to us — and a cliché when it's anyone else? Now I've become Elizabeth's agony aunt.

"I've decided they need attention. Men, I mean — like children. Not only the food on the table at a regular time, but constant stroking — looking into their eyes and telling them they've done the garden or the barbecue just right."

"Stuart isn't like that."

"Isn't he?"

"No . . . But I guess I have left him to his own devices rather a lot."

"Who's the other woman?"

"She's a widow."

"So she can't be twelve."

"She's French," Elizabeth says, as if that were the same thing — or at least designated an irresistible siren with layers of invisible makeup which created flawless skin and body, plus an assortment of envy-me-till-you-die designer clothes.

"Oh. What does she do?"

"How should I know?" Elizabeth bleats. Tears streak her cheeks. She takes a soiled hankie from her pocket and stabs at them. "She has a farm. Lives on one, in any case."

"I take it you don't want a divorce."

She looks at me as if I had suddenly taken leave of all my senses.

"Of course not. Why should I?"

"I just thought . . . Because you seem to spend so little time together."

"That's ridiculous," Elizabeth cries, then grabs hold of my arm. "I'm going to fly down there."

"Of course. You must. Immediately. Fly down there and spoil him. Cuddle him, cook, clean, garden, whatever it takes. Tell him it's all a mistake. A misunderstanding. You do want to spend more time in the French home, I take it . . ."

Elizabeth doesn't answer. She's crinkling her hankie and crying again. I see Nell hovering by the stairs. She signals to me and I murmur to Elizabeth that I'll be straight back.

"I just wanted to know, Mum, is it okay if I take the rest of the day off? It's just that I'm meant to go to the British Museum. To do some sketching for art, and I've only got a few days left."

"Of course. You should have told me sooner." I look at my beautiful daughter and an imp of the perverse takes hold of me. "And you don't need to worry. Toni isn't in at all today."

Nell has the grace to blush and develop an inordinate interest in her toes. But she still stands there.

"What's wrong with Elizabeth?" she asks after a moment.

"She'll be all right. It's just husband problems."

"Just. She looks as if she's met Beast 666." Nell looks scared in turn. "Like, I tell you, Mum, you lot are going to turn me into a lesbian."

I want to hold her back and shout, "No, no," but she's already dashed away and, as I watch her, I wonder why I think I should protest — except that at her age, I didn't even know what lesbian meant, and it certainly didn't cover anything we felt for our lacrosse mistress.

Elizabeth is staring into a space which doesn't include my bookshop when I sit down again. Only the scrape of my chair wakes her.

"You come with me," she says.

"Come where?"

"To Carcassonne, of course. To see Stuart."

"Whatever for?"

"You can tell him how preposterous it all is."

"Why would he listen to me? I hardly know him. You're the one who needs to convince him." I hesitate. "But I wouldn't make him feel bad, if I were you. I'm sure the other woman doesn't. Probably makes him feel like the Prince of Wales — not the current one, of course."

"Yes, come with me. It will give me courage. And two of us will make him see sense."

"What sense is that, Elizabeth?" I don't know why I'm saying this, except that, looking at her at the moment, I can see that maybe she isn't much of an advertisement for herself. And when she's the Elizabeth we all know and love, she's so self-sufficient that I don't really think she notices Stuart's absence. "Elizabeth, tell me the truth. Do you really mind Stuart having an affair with this woman?"

"Of course I mind."

"Did you notice, before he told you?"

She looks as if I've bludgeoned her with a large stick. "What are you suggesting, Jude?"

I shrug.

"Okay, okay. So it's not the affair per se that gets to me. It's . . . Come with me, Jude. Tonight. Just for a day or two."

"I can't just leave, Nell. Or this place."

"Take Nell along. I'll pay. Yes. The evening flights cost next to nothing. And she's still on holiday. And get that bloke of yours to do a little extra work here. The place won't fall apart. It gets too much of you already."

Elizabeth is sounding a little more like herself, though the way she says "bloke" makes me think that she suddenly bears poor Toni a grudge. Maybe I shouldn't have cancelled my last night out with her in his favour.

As I think of Toni, I have a traitorous moment. Wouldn't it be nice to bring Toni with me instead of Nell? Of course not, that would be impossible.

"Where is Nell?" Elizabeth is on her feet, her stupor partly gone. "Let's go find her. And then I'll dash home and book our tickets." She runs not altogether clean fingers through her tangled hair.

"I'll have to get Nell on her mobile. Elizabeth, you know what? Why don't you go across the road to my hairdresser? Have him give you a new cut. Something to surprise Stuart with."

"You think I look awful."

"Not at your very best."

She considers me, then grins. "Do you want to take over my column, Jude?"

It did flit through my mind for a moment as an interesting proposition, Celia. But only for a moment. If I were doing a column I'd have to be honest and say that Stuart probably wouldn't notice Elizabeth's hair unless she cut it in spikes and dyed it in pink and purple stripes. And then he wouldn't approve. But one mustn't give up all hope. And a new hairdo does something for the seratonin re-uptake whatevers, not to mention one's pride.

It's ten at night now and we're all on a late flight to Carcassonne. Elizabeth, Nell and I. Elizabeth is looking good, with a smart new haircut which swoops smoothly and cheekily down over one eye. I think she must have popped into the beauty salon, too, because she's got makeup in areas where it's never reached before. And her trouser suit is becoming. Nell and she are sitting together. I thought Elizabeth's company at the moment might make her think twice about her earlier threat, though she's probably plugged in to her Discman and only alert to the manias of the Manic Street Preachers.

I've been ushered towards a seat right at the back and have a neighbour who makes letter-writing a positive godsend.

Nell didn't want to come at first because she was meant to be seeing her friends and, of course, revising. So I did ring Toni. He wasn't at his flat and the person who answered sounded a bit confused. But I remembered he had a mobile number, too, which Kate gave me, and I managed to get hold of him. It was a little strange, I confess. I'd never rung him before and I really didn't know what to say, so I simply told him I was going off for the weekend and had made arrangements for extra help in the shop.

I wonder what he's up to tonight. I sincerely hope Hotpants Heather has nothing to do with it.
Love,
Jude

SATURDAY, 21 APRIL

Dear Celia,
When we arrived at the Carcassonne airport, it was so dark there was little to see. But a definite balm perfumed the air, a

106

delicious southern fragrance which instantly soothed some nervous corner of the bowel and made me sit back and relax, despite Elizabeth's jerky ways with the gears of the car she had hired.

The house is only about twenty minutes from the airport along wonderfully empty country roads. It's a big, slightly squat stone structure which sits behind two flowering Judas trees at the end of a pebble drive. I loved it instantly, loved the jasmine clambering up the walls and the window frames painted bright blue and the sweep of the roof and the lantern illuminating a stretch of distinctly cottage garden.

The front door was locked, which surprised Elizabeth, and she had to search through her bag for so long I began to think it was a lost cause. When at last she let us in, there were tears in her eyes again.

"Stuart," she called out.

"Maybe he's gone to sleep. It isn't early."

She left us in a large tiled kitchen which seemed to have been carved out of one of those *Sud* magazines and sped away, only to come back minutes later to say, "He's not here."

"Did you tell him we were coming?"

She shook her head.

"Elizabeth wanted to surprise him," Nell said with authority. Ways of surprising Stuart had evidently been one of their subjects of conversation on the plane.

"I guess we'll have to surprise him in the morning."

"That's where you're altogether wrong, my darlings." Elizabeth's voice had taken on an edge which could cut glass. "Quite wrong. Just leave your cases here and get back in the car."

I looked at Elizabeth and witnessed the sudden birth of a Valkyrie. I could feel her mind screeching.

"If you're thinking what I think you're thinking, Elizabeth, dear, I'm not sure you're thinking clearly."

"I've never been so clear." She gave Nell a little prod and moments later we were all back in the car and the screeching wasn't just in my imagination.

It only stopped when we had veered past several fields, turned down a dirt road and pulled to a halt in front of what looked in the headlight beams like a slightly ramshackle farmhouse, smaller than Elizabeth's, but perhaps only because the neighbouring barn was still a barn. She was already letting a large brass knocker fall against the door with a bang loud enough to wake the dead.

"Are you sure that he's here?" I came up beside her.

She pointed to a beat-up Renault in the drive and let the knocker fall again.

From inside a woman's voice shouted "*Qui est-ce?*" in a frantic pitch.

"She probably thinks it's her priest of a brother coming to smoke her out."

"So you know her?"

"In a manner of speaking. We've exchanged the occasional greeting."

The door finally opened, but this time Elizabeth offered no greeting. "Where is he?" she asked in French.

A sleekly black-haired woman in a white chenille robe stood at the door. Her face was sultry, her built statuesque. In the dim light her olive complexion gave away no age. She could have been anywhere between forty and sixty.

"Ah, it's you," she said, without stepping aside.

Elizabeth heaved past her like the prow of a Viking ship.

Nell and I followed nervously in her wake.

"He's hiding, is he?"

"I don't know what you mean."

The woman stood her ground, her arms crossed in front of her really rather superior bosom. It displayed one of those cleavages that demanded serious consideration — as one of my favourite writers once noted of a distinctly mature woman. Her feet were firmly planted on the tile floor. A scent of perspiration and what was probably sex came from her. I began to feel that Nell and I were about to catch a round of marital gladiators and I wondered whether this was suitable material for her eyes, then reminded myself that she had probably already seen every possible variation on the theme in *EastEnders*.

Nonetheless, I murmured something about waiting outside. Nell didn't budge. Her gaze was glued to the staircase as if she were willing Stuart into view. He appeared soon enough. He had obviously pulled his trousers on in a hurry. One side of his shirt hadn't quite managed to get tucked in and his thin white hair stood up in odd matted spikes.

"That's what I mean."

"Hello, Elizabeth," Stuart said evenly enough. His tone was far less ruffled than his hair. "You didn't say you were flying over."

"Yes. I thought we needed to talk. Immediately. And I've brought some friends along who wanted a break. You remember . . ."

"Of course, Jude . . ." He came towards me to shake my hand. "And this is . . ."

"My daughter, Nell."

"How she's grown. Good evening, Nell."

Stuart's insistence on polite normality seemed to bring the temperature down some fifty degrees. What was it Elizabeth had told me about him — something about a prior life in the navy managing stores for some fleet or other? I could see it now. Despite the sparse hair and untucked shirt, there were still the remains of something military in his bearing.

"I thought you'd like to come home and fix us all a drink. I can never find anything in the place." Elizabeth had suddenly grown embarrassingly feminine. "And we'll need to sort out the spare rooms."

"Of course." Stuart was avoiding our current hostess' eyes, which crackled like burning coals as they moved from him to Elizabeth and back. It was clear that she had no idea what they were on about.

"Why don't you drive Jude and Nell in your car, dear? I'd like to have a word with Madame Varigues."

I have to say I admired Elizabeth's understated composure, so different from her manner when she arrived in the bookshop not all that many hours ago.

"I'm not sure that would be a good idea." Stuart suddenly moved towards his lady love, who had put out her hand towards him. A look passed between them and I could feel Stuart's backbone beginning to disintegrate. The woman obviously had him by the short and curlies.

"Oh yes, I promise you that would be an extremely good idea." Elizabeth interposed herself as I had sometimes imagined Nell might between Toni and myself. She literally placed herself between them, and since she was a good head taller than Madame Varigues and her eyes on a level with Stuart's, the electric charge of the fatal goddess was momentarily obliterated. "Off you go now. You haven't left anything upstairs, have you? A jacket, perhaps?"

"No, it's right here. *A bientôt*," Stuart managed to murmur to Madame Varigues as we preceded him out the door.

Nell and I clambered into Stuart's car. He drove us back to the house at a pace which bore no trace of nerves. He managed to chat to us about the region as we went.

By the time Nell had been tucked into a small four-poster and I was sitting opposite Stuart in an exceedingly comfortable living room, I began to think I might be hallucinating. There were oversize plush sofas. There were vegetable prints on the walls. I was nursing a glass of excellent claret. The reasons for my being winged here bore no relation at all to the ordinariness of Stuart's and my chitchat. I decided I should say something. What came through my lips had an overwhelming banality.

"Elizabeth is very upset. That's why she asked us to accompany her."

"Yes." He looked vague. As if all that — the divorce, the woman, maybe even the ties of passion which had made him contact Elizabeth — belonged to some different region which he didn't really want to tap into. He examined his glass, swished the wine around it so that it caught the light with a ruby glow. "Yes. Sorry. How's your bookshop doing?"

Stuart would have been a dead loss on the Jerry Springer show. I have to say, I rather admired him for being so buttoned up and out of touch with his feelings. I couldn't really press him, so we ended up talking about the book trade until I heard Elizabeth's car in the drive, whereupon I thought they really ought to be alone together, and I snuck off upstairs.

The next morning, Elizabeth was already in the kitchen when I made my way down. Bacon sizzled, mingling its aromas with a rich dark coffee roast. Toast popped. Eggs were being poached. Elizabeth stacked a plate for me while I poured myself some coffee. She was looking good in a man's silk burgundy robe.

I told her so and she smiled.

"So . . ." I prodded, wanting a hint about the lay of the land before Stuart came downstairs.

"So I sorted her."

"You sorted her?" I asked puzzled. "What about Stuart?"

She lowered her voice. "Stuart's not very good at all this. I suddenly remembered from when we got together. I had to do most of the running. So I imagine that's what she's been doing. So I sorted her. First."

"How did you sort her?"

Elizabeth calmly buttered a piece of toast.

"I told Madame Varigues that the house was mine and would certainly never be hers. I told her if it came to divorce, I would claim special wife status and Stuart would be left with the shirt she had just seen him in. I advised her to think carefully about whether she really wanted a penniless Englishman — one her pious brother would consider anathema, since he certainly wouldn't and couldn't be married in church, being twice divorced. Twice? she asked. Well yes, I told her, I was hardly the first, and if he didn't die in advance of himself, she would probably not be the last."

I giggled. "And you said nothing to Stuart?"

"I took your advice. I was kind to him. I only talked a little about the relative longevity of passion and claret. Stuart likes his claret."

"So, no divorce?"

"Well, now it's up to fate." Elizabeth sighed. "I've done what I can."

"I'm sure you could do a little more."

"You'll help me, darling. I need you as ballast. To remind Stuart that there is an England. What on earth will he find to say to this woman once passion is spent? His French is execrable!"

Treacherously I think of Toni and how his conversation isn't what I miss about him.

Love is such a complicated and messy business. Sometimes I wonder why we want it at all. Oh, I don't mean love for our children, though they do put a serious strain on the word from time to time. Luckily we have the adjective "unconditional" to help us through that one: we're meant to be programmed from birth to put up with their lapses and see them through — even through adolescence, when unconditionality takes on heroic dimensions.

No, I mean the kind of passionate love that binds us to the various men in our lives, makes us abject and triumphant in fits and starts. Yet the passion always goes — either because the object of our love leaves or because he stays and time intervenes to transform everything, so that what was once there is gone anyway. Loss seems to be the name of the game, yet we go on and throw ourselves into it all again and again.

Elizabeth interrupts my thoughts. "The best thing would be for us to find a ploy to get him home, for a little while at least. Until he comes to his senses."

"What ploy?" Nell's silent arrival startles us and I hope she won't repeat her question, since I can hear Stuart's footsteps on the stairs. So I give her a big smile and show her the array of cereal while Elizabeth moves into a not altogether convincing rendition of the surrendered wife. It's hard to tell whether Stuart is convinced either, but he makes a good job of being pleasant and evidently enjoys his bacon and eggs.

Meanwhile Nell is spooning cereal into her mouth with the rhythmic concentration of someone under hypnosis. We're all rapt by this ravenous, trance-like eating. My daughter has become appetite incarnate. Only gradually does she grow aware of her assembled spectators. She looks up suspiciously, grins with prima donna aplomb, then astonishes me by announcing that since we're here, we really should have a walk and take in the sights and get some sun.

For some years now, you understand, Nell has been oblivious to sights. The seven wonders of the world, let alone country roads or visits to Florentine museums, cannot penetrate the swoon her Discman produces. It's a kind of generalized catatonia and only disperses when other catatonics of the same sneaker-wearing ilk appear. I don't think we've joined their number, yet today she's sitting up and paying attention. In fact she's engaged in mapping out our day with a more-than-willing Stuart.

Watching her, I realize what's different. There is nothing attached to her ear. Neither a music-producing bit of encasing technology nor a telephone. Nor is there a screen in front of her on which messages can be sent and received. Nell has suddenly been released from all apparatuses which make the far near. And she hasn't begun to suffer from withdrawal symptoms yet. She is actually and fully present. For this brief hiatus, my daughter is an alert and recognizably human being. It feels like a miracle.

As for Stuart, I have a passing sense that the poor soul may indeed have been suffering from neglect, or just sheer loneliness, which is what got him past shyness and into the capacious arms of the siren down the road. I'm going to have a serious word with Elizabeth about this. She's so busy with everyone else's problems, she's forgotten that one can also grow them close to home.

Yours in French,
Jude

LONDON, SUNDAY NIGHT, LATE

Dear Celia,
A quick one, just to catch you up on the French journey before I drown in London life. We had, I have to confess, a glorious two days traipsing through countryside, visiting castles and tombs and such like. Nell, who was constantly at Stuart's side and seemed to be drawing him out effortlessly, imbibed more history than I imagine she's done so far in all her courses. She's become a passing expert on the Albigensian heresy (it was the word "heresy" that did it) and the Cathars' hatred of the material world (they were against consumerism, she announced to me, when I stopped to look at a rather fetching dress in a shop window).

Anyhow, Nell kept Stuart so busy that he certainly had no time to visit his lady love — unless he did it in the small hours of the night. And when we left, he said quite forcefully that he'd be seeing us soon and that he hoped Nell wouldn't forget the promised expedition to Medieval London — wherever that is.

On the plane I asked her what she and Stuart had talked about when Elizabeth and I had fallen behind, which was often enough.

"We talked about Elizabeth," Nell declared, with a look of such blatant triumph it made me wince.

"Oh?"

"Yeah, I told Stuart what a star Elizabeth was and how she had been such a good friend to me when I was having problems with my stepmother." As she says this she gives me a look of wide-eyed innocence, then rushes on, "And how I wished I'd gotten to know him better, too."

"Really?" I am three-quarters skepticism.

"Really. I like him. I also told him how great it was for my mother to have one happily married friend."

"What did he say to that?"

"He coughed once or twice." Nell has the courtesy to giggle. "But he didn't contradict me." She reflects for a moment, then looks solemn. "I hope we were of some help."

I give Nell's shoulders a reassuring squeeze, and I think to myself that maybe men, come a certain age, don't really want sex most of all. What they need is a regular dose of adoration to bask in — preferably offered from unwrinkled, daughterly skin. What else is old Lear really about?

I doubt that we've saved Elizabeth's marriage, but perhaps my newly wise daughter has eased the difficulty of those first steps. Now it's up to them — and probably fate.

I forgot to tell you that Elizabeth recounted the most horrendous divorce story while we were trailing behind Stuart and Nell. About this woman who had not only won her claim for five million — a clear special-wife status, half of all his business interests — but had then told all and sundry that he was bisexual, so that his current lady love started to suspect him and dropped him. Anyhow, the man eventually topped himself.

Do you think hatred is a stronger emotion than love? I suspect it must be. If you raise it to the level of society, it's clear that at best we tolerate or make do with each other, while at worst we massacre each other. The first is hardly equal to the second.

When Robert and I split up the depth of my passion against him was far greater than any love I remembered feeling for him. (This could be a trick of memory. Even now I can feel the hot coils of my hatred, whereas the other kind of heat doesn't seem to burn retrospectively.) Strangely enough, the hatred didn't manifest itself in financial claims, maybe because Robert likes being generous and I find money matters more demeaning than I could then face in myself. We had always had separate bank accounts in any case, and he paid for all household stuff while I handled extras. No, my loathing took on another shape, the shape that I obviously suspected would most hurt him, give him the kind of pain that doesn't go away.

I almost came to the point of telling him that Nell wasn't his. That his fatherhood was what the American geneticists like to call a "non-paternity event." After all, fatherhood is largely presumptive. Every time he came to collect her, I wanted to throw it in his face, like a bucket of acid that would burn and blister its way beneath his skin and fester forever. I wanted to see his pain, to taste it.

Of course I didn't say anything. Not because Nell really is his, as the shape of her frown makes manifest. Nor because I imagined the eventual disproof through DNA testing. That would at least have given him a few months of mental torture. Nor even because I suspected it would all rebound on Nell. I wasn't being that reasonable. It was simply not something I could do. I'd stand there at the door, having fantasized the exact words, and remain completely mute. So I was left without that robust stew of vengeance to feed on and had to make do with the thin, pallid broth of good behaviour. I told myself that as soon as his bimbette was pregnant, I'd do it. She never was. And I didn't.

Oh well, all long in the past now.

Much love,

Jude

SATURDAY, 28 APRIL

Dear Celia,

What a week it's been.

Toni was over an hour late coming in on Monday (a new extra day for him) and I had to send Kate upstairs to take over the café service. It's not what she likes doing best, so it made her grumpy, and by the time Toni came in, so was I.

He didn't look his best. Rather weary and dishevelled in fact, without his sleek animal glow. He wouldn't meet my eyes. He only offered some lame excuse about the tube being delayed. I couldn't very well probe, there in the midst of everything, though Nell is thankfully back at school, so I made light of it and urged him upstairs to work.

I only managed to catch up with him after the lunch-hour flurry. When I asked him if anything was wrong, he grabbed my hand and squeezed it between both of his and looked into my eyes, and said he was "sorry, so sorry," so that I had two simultaneous thoughts. One was to be a daredevil and lock the doors of the shop and do it right there against the counter. The second was to wonder what on earth this desperate "sorry" was for. What had he done that necessitated such gravity? Naturally I thought of Heather. But then he added, "I see you tonight, yes?" and of course I melted and thought of nothing else for the rest of the day except how and where. My place was utterly impossible. As it was, I would have to go home first and make sure everything was okay for Nell. It would have to be, for once, his place. What did the place matter, after all?

Well, to cut a very long story short, I rushed home for Nell, made her dinner, picked up the car and then picked up Toni from the bookshop, whereupon we fell into each other's arms. But cars, I have to tell you, Celia, are definitely no longer my preferred sites of passion. Not only has the physical agility gone, I'm mentally incapable as well. That particular forbidden — the threat of a constable or an elder tapping at the window — is more likely to rouse anxiety than passionate fantasy. So, after a moment, I suggested we go to his place. Toni looked like someone who had seen a vision of massed cockroaches battling ravening rats. "Not possible," he said softly. And I believed him. It was then that I suddenly remembered I had Elizabeth's keys with me. She'd asked me to tend to her many plants, just in case she and Stuart ended up tarrying a little.

Elizabeth's London house is a wonderfully comfortable double-fronted affair, just off West End Lane, which is a mere hop and skip away. Toni and I ended up on her floor, which luckily has a rather soft rug. It was on that surface that he asked me again, "Why not we marry?" I can tell you, but for the lack of a handy registry office, I was just about ready. But there was no registrar to hand, so we ended up ordering in a pizza instead. When he suggested with those wonderful cat's eyes of his that we just stay the night there, it was as convenient for the bookshop as my place, I almost succumbed. Almost.

What I didn't have the heart to do was to send him back to the inferno of King's Cross. Elizabeth's house was evidently a billion times more comfortable than his place. So, in a fit of transferred generosity worthy of some adolescent who had mistaken Elizabeth for her mother, I told him he could spend the night on her sofa. I left him the keys and, already consumed with guilt, added that he had to remember to double-lock carefully and of course to leave everything supremely tidy. I could hear myself beginning to sound exactly like his mother, so I fed the cats and sped off — though not before he had repeated his proposal.

The next day he was late for work again, which upset me. I began to think that perhaps he was beginning to take advantage of me, on the principle that the hungry lover would forgive any sins against the shop owner. She did. But I took note. I also noticed that Toni made no attempt to fix a date with me for that evening, though he did dutifully return Elizabeth's keys as soon as he came in.

Sometime the next afternoon, I saw him pacing in the garden. He had his mobile to his ear and his lips moved with great speed. There was an intensity I had never seen before in his face. It shadowed his animal vigour with something I couldn't quite put my finger on, something troubling. I wanted to ask him whom he was talking to, yet I couldn't muster that kind of brash courage. But for the scent and touch of his body, I realized that I knew him so very little. It's presumptuous surely to assume that the young are bland, uncomplicated. Ageist, really.

I did find a moment to ask him if he was all right. He nodded, smiled and I think pretended not to know what I was talking about, though the worry was still there on his forehead, in his unfocussed gaze. He also pulled away because someone had just arrived to sit at the counter. When I turned I saw Heather. Heather looking stylish in crumpled linen with a little wisp of a crumpled shirt beneath. The very crumpledness gave off an expensive odour.

She threw me a look of brazen complicity. It made me bristle. I barely managed a "How are things?" before escaping downstairs. By the time I reached the front of the shop, I was furious and ready to go back up. How dare she assume we both had designs on him, even if we did. It's so rude.

I was saved from myself by the sound of the telephone. For once I picked it up before Kate got there. It was Elizabeth at the other end. She sounded a little strained, but not despondent. But maybe it was just me, 'cause I was burning with guilt about using her floor. Anyhow, she asked me to pick up some stuff from her desk. Someone from the paper would arrange for it to be collected from the bookshop at eleven tomorrow morning, if that was convenient. I asked her how she was, but she was obviously not alone, and then I had to see to some customers.

I haven't yet managed to acquire that extraordinary contemporary habit of always giving priority to telephone conversations over live ones. I imagine this has happened to you, too — but I've stood in front of hotel and hospital staff, not to mention shop assistants, for what's felt like hours, while they carry on vapid conversations on the phone. And remain utterly oblivious of the breathing being in front of them. They're wholly tuned in to the invisible party. I suspect if God had used telephones as his means of communication, we'd still be living in a deeply religious country. Certainly my daughter and her friends would qualify for sainthood.

Now that I think of it, it's probably Nell's constant use of the phone which has made me take up letter-writing again . . .

Anyhow, by the time I got back to the café upstairs, I was quite calm. Or so I thought until I did something completely barmy. I invited Heather to dinner that very night — and Toni, too, since he was standing there, and of course keeping him at my side and her away, or at worst, within my view, was the point of it all.

Heather surprised me by accepting with alacrity. Toni hemmed for a moment, said he would have to see to something after work, but would eventually join us. Where?

At home, of course. There was Nell to consider.

I was already rueing the rash invitation and mentally going through the contents of the fridge, which didn't take long, since apart from a bottle of milk and some dry cheese, it was empty. So I had to leave the shop early and them together — though thankfully not alone — and dash off to the local Italian deli to stock up on ravioli, a little artichoke sauce, a stack of Nell's favourite little canapé pizzas for starters and ice cream for desert. And while I was at it, I stopped at the green-grocers and bought a host of salad things, not to mention grapes and nuts and sundries, so that by the time I got home dragging my ton of shopping, I was readier for bed than for dinner.

When I called out for Nell to help, I heard the inevitable click of the receiver. My daughter appeared wearing not much more than her guilty look above her robe. Guilt in Nell's adolescent gestural vocabulary comes with downcast eyes and a grim uncommunicativeness which leaps into hostility at the first comment that a reckless fantasist might deem critical. Guilt to me signals sex or drugs, so I didn't know whether to empty bags first or scoot upstairs to check bedroom and sheets and ashtray. I decided on the bags.

"God, these are heavy."

"Like no one asked you to shop for a month. I've been working." Nell opens the greengrocer bag clumsily and apples spill out on the kitchen floor.

"Working on the phone?"

"Yeah, Cassie's been helping me with maths."

"Really. Cassie?"

"Yeah, Cassie. And I had a bath, 'cause I was feeling grim."

"Hmm. We've got guests for dinner."

"Oh no, Mum. I've gotta work. Can't I eat something quickly now?" She pops a baby tomato into her mouth and gives me a challenging look.

Nell knows that we have a time-honoured rule about meals which dates back to our days with Robert. If we're home together, we eat together, even if it means a pizza in front of the telly. Or, if it's on the cards and not too late, a dinner with friends.

I think you're indirectly responsible for that rule, Celia. Do you remember when I came to visit you in Paris, just before you got together with Jim and were still living with that French academic woman, the sociologist Monique, and working at the French equivalent of the World Service? Well, Monique went on and on about the horrors of English children, how badly behaved they were, how they had nothing but contempt for their parents. She had been an au pair in England and I think it must have marked her forever. Anyhow, she said that she had gone over and over the reasons for this marked difference in the French and English families and decided the really telling bit was that the French family ate together regularly and the English didn't. And somehow that stayed with me. So, when Nell came along, I tried to make sure we all ate together at least once a day. I don't know if it's made any difference. (Nor do I think it's what made Robert leave the marriage.)

"Who's coming to dinner in any case?" Nell asks.

"Heather Glover. An old friend I went to university with."

"Oh yeah?"

"And Toni."

"Oh, Mum. Not Toni. What are you trying to do? Get me used to him or something? He's not about to move in on us, is he?" Nell is wailing.

"Don't be silly. He's just coming over for a bite. He doesn't know all that many people. He's foreign, remember."

She studies me carefully and I know that she's going to be there at dinner, even if it's the last thing she wants to do.

Heather arrives first and talks to Nell, who has now donned a skirt. A skirt again. This one is so short I even begin to rue her street-sweeping trousers, but I stop myself from sounding like my mother — well, my mother as she used to sound when we wore skirts that weren't quite. Heather addresses Nell as if she were an intelligent being, which has its desired effect, since Nell gradually emerges from her silent trance and begins to speak an English which has more syllables in it than grunts and is really altogether comprehensible, even without a dictionary to indicate that "random" and "jacked" have acquired new meanings.

Having told Nell about her work at the museum, Heather even offers to take her and a friend around one day for a special tour. She also tells Nell about her son, who is studying biochemistry up in Edinburgh, and as she talks about him I realize I really like Heather, and that all this business with Toni has robbed me of reason. At which point, of course, Toni comes in looking lush and dreamy and a good part of it flies out the window again.

It's not only my reason that goes. Heather's no better — there's a subtle shift in her laugh, which grows richer, more frequent. And her posture, her gestures become more pronounced, somehow artificial, like a bird that has suddenly entered the mating season. Nell, of course, resists any charm Toni can propel in her direction — and he tries. But her resistance, too, is unreasonable, since it's only verbal. Her voice may be charged with unnecessary malice, but her hand caresses her bare crossed leg, and Toni can't help his eyes straying, so I know I'm going to have to get him out of here very, very soon, before he notices that my daughter really is irresistibly attractive, if he hasn't already.

What is it with us women? You'd think that no sooner did we see the potent male than instinct went to work and display began. But it can hardly be instinct at work here. According to evolutionary biology, there's no reason at all that Toni should be in the least interested in Heather or me, or we in him. His sperm will produce zilch in us, according to neither selfish nor co-operative genetic models. It's too late. Too bad. So if he's here with us, that instinctive part of him is either dead or has suffered a perversion.

Oh well, I never put much faith in evolutionary biology. Though I have to confess that the moment I've managed to persuade Nell upstairs, where the rest of her homework awaits, I clap my hand over my mouth in a semblance of sudden recall. "I forgot. I've got to get over to Elizabeth's. You'll have to help me, Toni. There's stuff to be moved. For tomorrow morning, when her office are coming to pick it up. I'll never make it in the rush-hour traffic."

I'm not sure Toni altogether understands me, but Heather does. She gives me a little knowing look, not devoid of admiration, as if I'd won and she's a good loser.

"I'll be off, then. Thanks. It's been great." At the door she looks back at me and says cryptically, "If you want to talk sometime, give me a ring."

Believe me, Celia, I really hadn't intended doing anything more with Toni that night than keeping him away from Heather. I told Nell where we were going and that we'd be straight back. But Toni evidently hadn't understood that and when we got to Elizabeth's, well . . .

Still, I wasn't very late. Not late enough really for Nell to have turned off all the lights and insist on punishing me with her sulky silence. I could tell she was awake by her breathing, so I whispered a soft "night-night, darling" and crept guiltily back to my room.

It's funny. I usually know when Nell is pretending or indeed lying about something. But mostly I don't pause to catch her out on it. It's terrible not being able to have secrets — or thinking your mother can see through you like some persecuting jailer.

We talked about that once, you and I. Do you remember? It was when you came to stay at my parents' house during some reading week or break. It must have been spring, because the sky was clear and we walked a lot, tramped over fields, revisited old haunts, giggled about childhood exploits. One of the walks led past the convent of Poor Clares. They had always worried me, the Clares. They were a silent order. The sign in front of the convent announced it. Through all the years of my childhood, I had never seen a single one of them, and I used to wonder whether their silence also made them invisible.

You knew all about the Clares. Your mother was French and Catholic. That much I had already known, but what you added during that spring visit as we stood in front of the convent was that you had gone through a phase of great devotion, then stopped believing when you were about fourteen. You stopped because you realized that God really couldn't always see you being naughty, nor did your mother always know when you were lying. Those two disruptions of omniscience had shattered your faith and brought you an incredible sense of freedom.

I remembered the lying and the freedom. But as I look back now on that scene of the two of us standing at the gate of the convent, something else comes back to me. You were gazing at those convent walls with a kind of mingled longing and distress. When I asked you if something was wrong, you said no. Yet you didn't move, and a little later you murmured that you missed your faith, the intensity of it, the ritual, the glorious abnegation. You confessed that during your childhood year in Arundel you had gone into the convent one day. You had waited until a van pulled in and then covertly loped in behind it. There was a single Clare in the gardens next to the ivy-covered building, and she saw you. She stared at you from an ancient yet innocent face — that's how you described it — and with eyes made huge by her bare forehead, her wimple. You waited for her to shout out. You wanted to provoke a verbal prohibition — or that's how you explained it to me with hindsight. But nothing happened. The nun didn't speak. She came toward you, smiling a little, as if she were curious as to what kind of species you were and didn't want to frighten you. But she didn't communicate verbally, and eventually she continued on her way. So did you, though you had to wait for the van to go before you, too, could leave the walled grounds.

Your silence suddenly begins to worry me, Celia. Are you all right? You haven't decided to give it all up, have you? Become a poor Clare?

I can see the temptation now. The temptation of structure and silence. The contemplative life. Ageing French courtesans of the best calibre used to go in for it in the nineteenth century.

It comes to me that it was probably only a few weeks after this confession of lost faith that I found out about you and Patrick.

Ah well. All in the past now. The distant past. Even a change of century to underline that. Hardly feels possible.

Sometimes I think this twenty-first doesn't really have space for us. All these new technologies we have to master. Messaging, Mini Disks, banking on line — and the digits are always so tiny you can't possibly count the zeros in your balance, let alone tell the numbers from the wavering lines. I may have to succumb and get specs. I've been avoiding it. Their presence would somehow constitute a symbolic moment — a rite of passage.

Besides, I don't really want to see my face all that well.
My love,
Jude

15 MAY, 2001

Dear Celia,
Time has been scarce and I haven't written for a few weeks. Though I've missed the letters. Addressing you has become something of a habit, even when I don't write. In fact, it's become altogether like that unsung addiction of adolescence — keeping a diary. I had one. Nell has one, which she guards with all the stealth of an aspiring MI5 recruit. Guess it's a way of taking stock of racing emotions, not to mention making sense of the jumble of the everyday.

But just to underscore the difference and prove I'm not sixteen, I had been hoping for a response. And now it's come, even if it isn't the one I'd wished for.

You've moved. Of course, you've moved — though the people in your former house took their own sweet time telling me about it. Maybe the post doesn't work very well in Western

Canada. I received a curt note giving your new address and telling me to send no more letters or parcels (I guess they mean those fat envelopes which contained several of my letters all bundled together). It occurs to me that the new address might already be an old address and the reason it took so long for them to write to me to pass it on is that they'd lost it or some such. It was mad of me to think that you'd stay put. I haven't, though I've hardly moved as far as you have. Minneapolis. I can't guess whether that means you've followed Jim and are still with him — or with someone else. Or, indeed, footloose . . .

Nor do I have any inkling whether the people in your old house did indeed send on my stack of letters or simply dumped them. I hope they sent them, since none of this may make sense otherwise. Never mind, it hardly makes sense to me, and I've been here in the midst of it all. Everything has been happening so fast.

First of all, my friend Francesca, aged thirty-eight and one-quarter, is pregnant. Only just — but, she asserts, definitively. It all began a few nights after we went to the launch party where I didn't recognize Robert. She hadn't mentioned it to me, but that evening she bumped into an old gay friend, Hugh, who was in a bit of a state 'cause he'd recently split up with his long-term partner. Francesca and Hugh met up a couple of times for dinner and chats and such like, and it turned out that they both hanker after children. So, quick as a flash, Francesca (having checked on his HIV status) suggests a syringe job. Hugh, it seems, is very handsome, very intelligent and pretty rich. In fact, he's perfect, says Francesca, the small matter of his sexual orientation apart.

Well, Hugh thinks it over for a few days. They discuss ways and means and parenting strategies, and by the next weekend they're up at her place in the Cotswolds bearing the necessary and intently dreaming babies and nurseries and schools. Then Hugh suggests that the real thing might be easier than syringes, so off they go.

When Francesca tells me all this, I can't hide my astonishment nor, to be frank, a shiver of disapproval, which is really concern for her and this tricky adventure she's embarking on. And you know what? She bites my head off. She tells me (me who's kept the lunacy of Toni from her) that I'm turning into an old fogey. She attacks me — though the attack feels a little like one of Nell's when she's busy convincing me I'm utterly wrong about something she herself has secret doubts about. But it reminds me that one really shouldn't comment on one's friend's lovers — not ever, not even when you know they're about to be done for fraud or bigamy. So I apologize to Francesca.

A couple of days later Francesca rings me up and suggests we meet on a neutral patch — a brasserie fashionable, I think, for the quality of its din. If a five-foot-nothing woman can give off a glow radiant enough to light up a warehouse, then Francesca does it when she walks in. She's luminous. Like Napoleon doing his history-on-horseback number.

What she explains to me, once we've downed our first glass of wine, is that the possibility of raising a child with Hugh feels wonderful to her. In any case, if one thinks about their potential "union" in an unblinkered way, it bears far more resemblance to a really existing old-fashioned marriage (particularly among the upper classes) than any of my silly and girly illusions about Mr. Right. Why, I had to wait for my Mr. Right for years, only so he could cheat on me and up and leave me for a version half my age. At least if Hugh cheats on her, she'll still know she's the only woman in his life.

I couldn't really argue with that. So I said nothing.

She told me that once I met Hugh I'd understand. She also stressed that it wasn't about passion and forever. It was about fatherhood and partnership.

I suspect Francesca thinks she can convert him. I wanted to tell her to be prudent, but it was a little late for that. And in any case, every time I think of the word "prudent" I can hear our esteemed chancellor rolling the word, with its eternal Scottish Rs, over his lips so that it begins to sound like some enthralling perversion which includes a miserly rubbing of the hands and whips.

I did point out, however, sometime after the first course, that if she was really in for an old-fashioned marriage, as she put it, then any emotions should be kept firmly in the closet, and property and paternity given unsentimental pride of place. Francesca's emotions were definitely on display.

She didn't make a comeback until we were counteracting too much claret by sipping double espressos (I didn't sleep that night, but I hate ordering ersatz — it's like going on Oprah for the single purpose of confessing your age). Then Francesca smiled at me with sweet innocence and told me that it wasn't my fault; I was subject to the very prejudice that the hoary gay movement had made an item of political correctness. I could think of homosexuals only as, well, gay and all that that entailed — a lifestyle which put sex at the top of the agenda. That might have been instrumental at a particular political moment, but now . . . Well, now it was bollocks. Or at least old hat. No one was their sex all the time. We women didn't think of sex all the time. Especially as we grew older. *We* didn't have to be trapped in an identity. Okay, so Hugh was gay, but he was also bisexual and a lawyer and a Brit and loved opera and was even a little bit Jewish.

I giggled and gave Francesca a kiss. I half agreed with her in any case. She's obviously head over heels about the man, and who am I to advise anyone on what's right or best in life. I can't even have a ten-minute conversation with my daughter without one of us snapping. Nor have I managed to give up Toni, despite Nell's disapproval and my own. I've just turned even more secretive. As for my mother, now that she seems to have got over the last crisis and is on an even vegetative keel, my visits have dwindled in number.

Then, too, you can never predict what the future holds, so Francesca might as well have her season of happiness without any interference from me. And now that she thinks she's pregnant . . .

Whoops, work call. Gotta go. More later.

J.

P. S. The only matter of any substance in my possibly dumped last letters is: would you like to travel somewhere wonderful for a mutual fiftieth? I promise not to bring any cigarettes along if they bother you. In fact I'm going to give up on my fiftieth. That's a promise I intend to keep. Really. I'm even going to eradicate all those quotations that have imprinted themselves on my mind and somehow survived senior moments, viz.: "Smoking is, as far as I am concerned, the entire point of being an adult," or "A cigarette is the perfect type of a perfect pleasure. It is exquisite and it leaves one unsatisfied."

Neither of the above wits, needless to say, belong to the twenty-first century.

16 MAY

Sorry, Celia,
I got interrupted the other day 'cause my wholesaler rang up and asked if I'd like to do a promotion on gardening books. It's spring at last. The sun has finally shown its face again.

I succumbed, though I don't really like the idea. We now have thousands of gardening books and as many television programmes, and they're all so successful you wonder how anyone has time to do any gardening for the watching of it. I suspect it's really those new professionals — with little printed cards they drop through the door of the house — who have taken the actual activity over. It's the same with cookery: thousands of books and programmes where these sexy guys and gals run their fingers through dough or squid with the sensual rapture prohibited from the faces of lovers — except in French films. Yet everyone's always on some sort of diet or goes out to eat or pops a packet into the micro.

Part of the newly triumphant virtual world, I guess. More important to watch than to do. Forget about the material plants and living bodies. They decay and die, after all. Don't want to be reminded of that.

Whoops. I've let the tangent take me away. It's because I'm

unsettled. And my back started to ache this morning. Just like that. Out of the blue. Elizabeth's floor is taking its revenge.

Elizabeth is still away, tending to her Stuart. I do wish she'd come back. I feel I've been abusing her hospitality with these surreptitious visits to her house. But I miss her, too. Life feels distinctly odd when your closest friends are in a tizz. I almost rang Heather the other day to invite her over. She's stopped dropping in on the shop. Maybe I'll do that tonight. But I wish you were here, Celia.

What I really wanted to tell you about was what happened on Tuesday. There was something strange about it all, but I can't quite put my finger on it.

It was just after the lunch-hour rush and I was upstairs. I was going to have a quick word with Toni — about work this time. Some of the regulars had been asking why we didn't stock more than biscuits and cake. They want sandwiches. But I've been loathe to move into another supply chain and have been quite happy for them to bring their own, if it comes to that.

Anyhow, I heard the roar of a motorbike and I looked out the window and saw this biker parking to the side of the shop. I assumed it was a delivery and Kate would sign for it. A few minutes later, the biker is coming up the stairs. He's got his helmet under his arm and his face isn't a messenger's at all. It's topped by steel-grey hair and the features are those of the new slimline Robert. He's looking at me with a lopsided grin on his face while his eyes also take in the café, Toni, the smattering of clients and my sudden and inexplicable embarrassment, as if I'd been caught out in a compromising position with a camel.

"What are you doing here?" I manage to say by way of

greeting. I'm edging away from Toni and the coffee counter towards a remote corner of the room.

Robert is untroubled by my grumble. "I was passing by and I thought I'd have a look." He looks at the tables, the chairs, the bright walls, and his gaze settles on Toni, who's busy polishing the counter to a sheen.

"It's hardly a shop that opened its doors yesterday."

"That's true. Let's call it a slightly delayed visit."

"They haven't demoted you to being a rep, have they? Can't imagine what else you'd be doing in a bookshop."

"Not yet." He chuckles. He's dressed so incongruously that I chuckle, too. Robert has never been known for his sartorial splendour. He errs on the side of functionality. And now, beneath the biker's jacket that he's removed and above the leather trousers, he reveals a white shirt, an outrageous tie and a grey waistcoat which is evidently waiting to be covered by the suit jacket he's left in his office. Personally I wouldn't trust him to remember which jacket he's left behind, so there are probably days when he's very oddly attired. Maybe Emma takes care of that.

I've never seen him on his bike before, though Nell has told me about it. Apparently he took it up not long after he left me. Guess the excitement made his heart beat with reassuring loudness and proved he wasn't dead. But it can't be safe for our streets having these seniors racing along. Does he have to wear glasses?

"There was something I wanted to talk to you about. Two things, in fact."

"Oh?"

I'm standing there awkwardly with what I imagine is an inane expression on my face. I haven't had a live conversation

— a real conversation — with Robert for so long, I've forgotten how one goes about it.

"Why don't we sit down? And let me get you a coffee. Nice place. You're clever to have made a go of it. Not easy, I know. It looks great. And so do you. Espresso?"

"Latte," I mumble. I'm wondering what Robert wants. More precisely, I'm wondering what Nell has told him. But I'm also remembering something. Something from a long time ago.

There are two kinds of seducers, Celia, as we know. Those who tell you how wonderful you are. And those who tell you how wonderful they are. The latter are usually poets and writers and, of course, our erstwhile Patrick. The first, in my experience, have usually been those courteous old central Europeans. Both are usually pretty successful, since what more does a woman want than that undivided attention . . .

Robert confuses the issue. He manages to be both kinds of seducer at once. But then I only knew him as a seducer for a relatively short time. Too soon, he became a husband. I wish he'd stop behaving seductively now. It makes me suspicious.

So does the inordinately long conversation with Toni, which I can't quite hear, since I've put myself in the far corner of the room. Nell couldn't really have said anything, could she? I guess I can always put it down to frenzied adolescent fantasy. But why should I care? Shouldn't I be flaunting Toni?

By the time Robert comes back with the coffee, I'm in a complete tizz. He's brought a giant piece of carrot cake, too. Can that be good for him? Is it my business?

You can see that I'm not at my most settled, Celia. The cues with past partners are so askew. There's a terrible familiarity mixed in with the strangeness, like a wood one happens upon in an unaccustomed season. The ground is now shaded by a canopy of leaf or bare or newly covered in bramble. The paths have disappeared and you can't quite get your bearings, but you know, know with an uncanny certainty, that you've been there before.

Anyhow Robert doesn't keep me in suspense too long about why he's here.

"I wanted to have a word about Nell." He examines his carrot cake for a moment without digging into it, then gives me the full force of his icy eyes.

"Go on."

"Do you know she's been seeing someone much older than her? Far too old." His lip curls, just a little, and in that sudden gesture which signals contempt and controlled anger, I see Nell as clearly as if she were in the room.

"Far, far too old," he repeats and jabs at the cake.

I look at him in amazement. The amazement comes in part from the fact that I'm struggling against the guilt his comments induce in me. It's my fault. I'm a bad mother. Simultaneously I'm wondering why I should feel this and in a rage because he makes me feel it.

"What do you mean too old? A man of forty? Fifty?"

"Don't be daft. Oh, I see." His expression shifts swiftly from recrimination to surprise to uneasy humour. Robert is nothing if not quick.

"You're not seriously suggesting that our darling Nell is setting out to follow in Emma's footsteps in order to please her dad?"

"I hadn't got quite that far in my thinking."

He glances at Toni and I avert my eyes. No way am I going

to admit that I might be partially responsible for Nell's sudden leap from a seventeen-year-old to a twenty-something-year-old.

"No. He's in his twenties. Quite old enough. And Emma, unlike Nell, may I remind you, was hardly in her first youth when I met her."

"Her dad might not have been of the same opinion on that."

I mutter this beneath my breath, but he hears me and his voice rises. "I didn't come here to talk about Emma and me."

"Sorry. Sorry."

Toni is suddenly hovering beside us. Robert's little outburst has evidently alerted him to possible trouble. His fists are clenched. I reassure my defender with a smile and he moves slowly back to his post at the counter.

"Me too. Let's start again. So you didn't know and you haven't been worried?"

"I'm constantly worried."

He nods, then swallows hard. "Do you think she's sleeping with him?"

"She won't talk to me about it. And she's been at your place for as many weekends as I can remember. So you'd be the first to know . . ."

"That's the problem. She's out so late that I inevitably fall asleep before she's back, no matter how hard I try. So I can't see her face . . . I've only caught glimpses of the boyfriend as he sneaks out in what is my morning."

He looks so sad that, despite myself, I'm suddenly filled with compassion. He loves his daughter.

"Does she know you're here?"

"I told her I was going to have a word with you about her. I reminded her exams were coming up. I told her I wasn't pleased. Is she doing any drugs?"

"Cannabis." I shrug. "Not a lot, I don't think. They all do."

"Ecstasy?"

"Not as far as I know. We've talked about that . . . And she tells me all her girlfriends remind each other not to leave their glasses unguarded at the clubs."

He nods with the expression of a condemned man.

"What did she say when you told her you weren't pleased about the age difference between them?"

Robert looks down at his coffee and fidgets slightly, then suddenly chuckles. "She must have been talking to her mother. She turned to me with supreme innocence and said, 'You *were* pleased when Em liked you.'"

I'm definitely in love with my daughter, Celia. She's a star.

But Robert has another reason for coming to see me, which he only divulges after we've talked at length about Nell's state of being. There's a second child in the equation. No, not the one I imagine he'll have any day now with nubile Emma, but a much older one. His son.

It turns out that Robert's son, Ollie, has been in London for some three weeks now and staying with them. I don't know why Nell hasn't mentioned it, but maybe it's because Ollie hasn't really seen her properly yet, since he's been away on the weekends. And he hasn't rung me, according to Robert, because he's depressed. Seriously depressed, Robert thinks. His dot-com company folded. He had to sell the house he had bought north of San Francisco. His girlfriend had left him in any case about two years back. Anyhow, poor Ollie has apparently decided to spend some time in England with his dad and maybe see if he can make a go of things here for a bit.

Robert took another round of coffee and a good while to come out with it, but the gist is that he doesn't really want Ollie staying with him. I had the impression from his general discomfort and the flicker in his eyes that the reason he doesn't want Ollie staying on lies somewhere in the area of how Emma treats him and he treats Emma. Ollie, if I haven't told you already, is wonderfully attractive, a kind of mixture of Harrison Ford and Johnny Depp, if you can imagine it (though I'm not sure I mean Johnny Depp — I get that entire generation of actors mixed up with one another). And he's more or less Emma's age.

So the long and the short of it is that Robert asked me if I'd be willing to take Ollie in — for a while, in any case. It's not the moment, apparently, for him to be too much on his own. On the other hand, nor does it seem to be the moment for him to be with his dad. Which seems to leave only the haven of his ex-stepmother, if that relational function bears a name.

Did I say yes? Of course I said yes. What is an ex-step-mother for, particularly one who hasn't seen her ex-stepson in some three years nor her ex-husband for about as long (in non-virtual terms)?

Oh well, I like Ollie. And Nell used to when he was around more in her childhood. Though I suspect having him to stay will see my relations with Toni out the window. I barely seem to have time to catch up with myself as it is. And Toni has asked me again to marry him. I don't think he's joking. He tells me I'm the best thing that ever happened to him. Maybe he's one of those textbook Italian men who really do love their mamas . . .

Well, I said there was something strange about my meeting with Robert, but now that I've written it all down, I can't quite see what it is — except that it was something of a marathon talk — as if we'd reached some significant juncture and managed to get to the other side.

I got Kate to close up for me and went home early to have it out with Nell. I told her that I'd had a long talk with her father and he was worried about her, as was I, and I wanted to know then and there about her relations with this character she'd been keeping from me.

"He really came to see you, did he?" Nell manages neither to snap at me nor look sullen. In fact, her expression has a distinct gleam of triumph.

"He did."

"And you talked?"

"We did. So what's his name?"

"Who?"

"The new boyfriend."

"He's not my boyfriend."

"The new friend who hangs round with you on sofas and things."

Nell giggles.

"Damian. Damian Fry."

"Good name. What does he do?"

"He does lighting. For gigs. At the Kentish Town club. The Forum. I know, I know." Her voice rises. "It wouldn't be your preferred occupation. But he's fit and he's cool."

"I had no doubt he could be anything but 'fit' and 'cool.'" ("Fit," in case you haven't heard the word used in this sense, Celia, means handsome. I think it's come to Nell and her lot via the new Darwinians and the evolutionary biologists. Fitness, after all, is Darwin-speak for the capacity to reproduce, in which race only the fittest survive . . . none of which reproduction talk is calculated to make this mother sanguine.)

"So you met him at the club?"

"Yeah."

"What drugs does he do?"

"What kind of question is that, Ma? Do I ask you whether your friends drink whisky or beer? What has it got to do with anything anyway? Why don't you ask me what music he likes? Or whether he votes Tory or Green? Or whether he's good for me? Or what he read at university?"

My insufferably middle-class ears perk up, as if graduates didn't make out with underage girls or do heavy stuff. "You're right, you're right. I'm being stupid. Why haven't you introduced me to him?"

"Because you're embarrassing."

This is one of Nell's standard accusations. Apparently I am the most embarrassing mum in the annals of embarrassment. No other mums wear the clothes I do. No other mums ever mention books or know about the existence of museums or certainly ever hint of their secret presence to teenagers. No other mums try to stop children fighting in the street. No other mums ask teachers questions about the syllabus. No other mums ever attempt to talk to their children's friends.

"How on earth could I be embarrassing?"

Nell gives me her basilisk stare. "You'd flirt with him."

I feel myself growing hot and stifle my response. "Have you slept with this Damian?" I ask, with as much equanimity as I can muster.

Nell turns on her heel and races upstairs. "Like, I'm not you, Mum!" she shouts before I hear the door slam and the music come on with deafening decibels.

Part of me wants to shout back. But I find that I'm smiling. The inevitable has been put off for just a little longer.

Well, Celia, an hour later Nell comes downstairs to see what I'm making for supper and, miracle of miracles, to help! I tell her about Robert's suggestion that Ollie come and stay with us.

"That would be just great," she says, her eyes wide, her expression suddenly eight years old again. "He hasn't been around when I've been at Dad's and it made me think he didn't want to play with me anymore." She catches herself and giggles.

I giggle too and hug her, and I promise myself (though I can't believe that it's me thinking these things) that I'm going to give Toni some kind of promotion or rise and then give him up.

Love,
Jude

17 MAY

Dear Celia,
I feel so virtuous, I think I'm growing a halo. Or maybe that slight heaviness on top is just the beginning of a headache.

No, I haven't given up smoking. But I will, I will. As soon as that birthday comes. The virtue comes from something else.

This morning, not too far after dawn, which I see with increasing regularity as the Big 5-0 approaches, I went for a swim. I've been intending to start the exercise regime for months, but the incentive is hard to find. I'll never even look like Bridget Jones again, let alone a *Harper's* model. On the other hand, when I catch a glimpse of my thigh next to Toni's, my narcissism plummets. You'd think that I'd have made a sensible accommodation to all that by now. After all, I've been old long enough. You'd think, too, that at least in my mind Toni and I could have a sensible division of labour. He can do the youth-and-beauty number, while I'm left with the comforts of wisdom appropriate to my years. Don't know why it doesn't quite work out like that. Maybe it's because I just know that, any day now, he'll abandon me for that delicious little underage brunette who's been flirting with him on a regular basis for weeks. Or maybe it's just the sight of that bit of chicken skin that's beginning to flap from my upper arms.

Anyhow, I went to the local pool, where you can do lengths-swimming indoors before nine.

The best thing about our local pool is that few of its users are regulars of the Croisette in Cannes. Delicately bronzed flesh is not *de rigueur.* Nor does one even need to qualify as an advertisement for the benefits of swimming. Muscles are rarely on view and sizes range from the obese to the merely overweight to the purely functional. Greying skin and sagging bits you haven't even begun to dream of are regularly on display in the changing rooms. As for the swimming, I started off in the slow lane and graduated to the middle and then the fast lane within ten minutes — and I've always assumed I swim with the speed of a tortoise. In short, it's a great place unless you have a magazine spread in mind.

I did once go for a free trial to one of those bright new exercise spas which have replaced hospitals and factories in our city landscape. The pool had no chlorine in it and was a beguiling ozone turquoise. There were palm trees in terracotta pots artfully poised here and there, plus a few loungers in which the beautiful people lounged. Far too beautiful for me. Not only did they all swim capped and goggled and with various prostheses which turned the activity into hard exercise work aimed by personal trainers at specific areas of muscle lack, but by the time I left the changing room and had peeked at the glossy machines and glossier bodies in the gym, I was ready for a course of psychotherapy, so low was my self-love, so acute my mourning for lost time. Incidentally, at about a thousand pounds a year, each of my infrequent swims would have ended up costing about the same as a session with a therapist. So I've resigned myself to the local pool, where a swim costs less than a packet of cigarettes and is at least twice as good for you.

My second virtuous act is that I didn't go to the cinema with Toni tonight — or indeed any other night this week — despite his fervent wish to do so. Instead I came home and helped Nell with some English homework. The GCSE course is dire and about as challenging for her as crossing the street, only to find that you have to cross it again and again and again. Can you imagine — if you've already conquered literacy — taking an entire four months to read *To Kill a Mockingbird*? To Kill a Novel, more like. Any novel would die on you over that stretch of reading.

Don't get me wrong. I understand the need for standardized exams — but spending one's entire school life preparing for them has got to be something far short of an education.

Anyhow, I helped Nell moan and then do a synopsis of some pretend visit to Stonehenge, and after that, before writing to you, I decided I might as well get rid of some tasks I'd been putting off. So I bombarded local councillors, our MP and our newish London mayor with letters about our latest urban blight: The Dumped Car. Has this one reached you yet?

Local streets here have taken to spawning unlicensed heaps of once-motorized steel at an alarming rate. The council does little to remove these wrecks, even the ones that could still be driven to a recycling plant. It simply isn't cost-effective, now that steel prices have slumped. Even the vandals and car thieves can't be bothered with these heaps. I suggested that the council might consider doing a secret deal with those kids who are obviously adept at making cars go without the need of keys and are particularly brilliant at setting them on fire, too, once they've had a little joyride. I'm sure something could be worked out where we could save ourselves one of the costs of policing by signalling to these kids which cars are dying to be vandalized, joyridden, turned into pyres . . .

Seriously though, these wrecks are even more unsightly than I am. And soon there won't be any space left to park cars that move anymore. Our streets look like graveyards for the unburied dead, forcing the fast and the quick underground.

As a once-dumped old model myself, I have a certain sympathy for these cars and I've tried to think up some positive uses, even some form of recycling (short of compression into a steel block of which a ton is needed to yield £20 at today's prices). But all I can come up with is the notion that these abandoned cars could be transformed into shelters for the homeless. Quite a few I've looked into already contain old syringes and dirty blankets. Trouble is, we don't want the homeless littering our streets either, nor our up-and-coming saved-from-sinking estates. So what is to be done? I've promised my vote to any councillors who come up with a solution. In fact, I even wrote to our Euro MP and suggested a Europe-wide competition for the best scheme. My own favourite is that the old and the dumped have to be driven back to their individual dealers — who by some Europe-wide edict are permitted to sell cars only with the guarantee that they'll take them back again at the end of their days.

All this letter-writing in one evening has got me seriously tired, particularly on top of this morning's swim. So I'll sign off, Celia. Though I did want to ask you whether you had heard at your distance that Marie Cardinal had died. I read it in today's obits. Do you remember how you used to love her books? Didn't you also go and interview her once for French radio? I have a vague memory of you finding her wonderfully frank, somehow joyous. Douglas Adams died, too. Suddenly. And too young. Our age. But that news must have reached you, since he was in California — a place where I thought no one except ghetto youths ever failed to make it past the age of reason and into the age of plastic surgery. Oh dear.

Do you think my worrying about these dumped cars is just a way of worrying about what will happen when Toni dumps me? I know it can't and shouldn't last — particularly because of Nell. But things have been so good between us that I can't bear the thought of it all being over — which is probably why things have been so good between us. Knots is what we used to call these kinds of tangles in our youth. I suspect the young today are better at simply cutting through them.

Heather just rang and I was strangely glad to hear from her. I told her I was writing to you and she said the only reason you

could possibly be in Minneapolis is that you must be working at the university. Are you? I'm going to check it out on the Net. Because I really do want to see you, Celia.
Goodnight and love,
Jude

26 MAY

Oh, Celia, what a week it's been.
On Friday, because he so wanted to and he's mentioned it several times before, I took Toni along to the home to see my mother. He really did want to. Really. I think it's that Mediterranean thing about family and respect for the old. I forewarned him about what the place was like. I'm not sure whether he understood. He bought a big bunch of tulips to take to her, and when we walked in, I can tell you, all eyes were on us. Well, on Toni, in any case. And it wasn't only because of the flowers.

I've already mentioned to you how the residents adore the young — in particular, the old ladies adore young men. Well, if Toni had been a Beatle on tour in '65, he couldn't have gotten a warmer reception, given, of course, the restricted capacity for movement of the local population. But there were lifted arms and pointings and calls of "Come here, you" and "Hallo, hallo" as we walked through the hall, not to mention a sudden stirring from a hunched woman I've never before seen awake, despite her open eyes.

To his credit, Toni took it in his stride. He didn't stop and stare or quake and quiver. Or indeed retreat back into the car — something I might well have done in more youthful and

149

less courageous days. He only nodded and grinned and saluted like a practised star, and when we reached my mother, who for some reason was sitting in the smoking area near the gardens, he bowed with graceful formality and proffered the bouquet.

To my surprise, she took it and even said a comprehensible thank you. She was having a good day, though she didn't have her teeth in. On the other hand, her cardy was spotless and her stockings hadn't gathered into a coil around her ankles. So once I had settled Toni in front of her and introduced them, I felt I could go off to find a vase for the flowers.

When I came back, my mother was telling Toni something at great length in that new language of hers which is babble interpolated by common words. Toni wasn't in the least fazed. Maybe he thought it was yet another English accent. In any case, he nodded and smiled at appropriate junctures. We sat there for a while making all the semblance of polite conversation. I explained to my mother that Toni worked in the book-shop café. Toni mimed the art of making espresso and added sound effects, which had all the old dears listening in. At the point where he steamed the milk, my mother made a sound I haven't heard in a long time. She laughed. Yes, it really was laughter — loud, uncontrolled — the kind of laugh toddlers have. All uninhibited joy. I stared at her in disbelief, then laughed with her. It felt heavenly, like a cascade of sunlight after winter's long gloom.

Toni took her hand. No Englishman would have managed that gesture with quite his degree of naturalness. He took her hand as if he really intended to take it. As if he wanted to. He wasn't afraid of her touch. And his gesture carried both respect and affection. I watched with something akin to incredulity and, yes, love, damn it.

But it was when he started to speak that my mouth fell open. Do you know what he was saying to her? He was asking her permission to marry her daughter. He was saying he wished his mother was here to speak on his behalf. She would say that I was a good woman and that he would try to be good to me. And on he went, in that broken English which was probably as incomprehensible to my mother as hers was to us. But you know, the scene made me think for the first time that he was serious. I stared at him, those dark, glowing good looks in this grey shabbiness, his kind focus on my batty mum. I grew all tearful and I covered his and my mother's hands with my own and thought how lucky I was, and my mind raced into a sentimental dreamland where an extension to the café and a managerial Toni figured large, not to mention a vast and comfortable queen-size bed, a double wedding ceremony for odd couples, with a pregnant Francesca and her beau standing beside us . . .

Which was when I heard it. A gasp, a stifled sob, something like a squeak. I turned. And there stood Nell, white-faced, gazing at the scene our little threesome made. Nell. She hadn't told me she was coming to visit her gran. She hadn't told me or I wouldn't be here holding hands with Toni and my mother.

I swallowed hard. How much had Nell heard? I extricated my fingers, but before I could utter a word, she had already turned and was racing along the hall. By the time I was up and after her, I heard the unmistakable slam of the front door.

Behind me, my mother, ever alert to changes in animal mood if not much else, was calling in a distinctly troubled fashion. Her neighbour took up the call, like a plaintive echo. I turned back. I would sort it out with Nell later. We'd been getting on well these last days, after all, so it shouldn't be that difficult. Nor could I just abandon Toni now. We'd been looking forward to this evening together.

I didn't get home until quite late. It was dark downstairs. Ollie hasn't moved in yet. He has decided to spend a little more time in Oxford. And Nell's light was out, too. In the morning she was, of course, asleep when I left for the shop. It wasn't until that evening that a faint tremor of anxiety went through me. When I checked for her up in her room, I had a sense that she might not have been in all day — nor, perhaps, the evening before. Of course, reading clues from the community dump which is Nell's room is not an altogether simple matter. You have to wade through a jumble sale of trousers and sweats and T-shirts, mingled with underwear, sheets of school work, magazines, old photographs, chocolate bar wrappers, an assortment of CDs and Mini Discs, chicken wire — and that's only to get the door properly open.

Still, looking around, it came to me that maybe after she had witnessed the scene at my mother's home, she had rushed straight off to her dad's, despite her prior decision not to visit him last weekend.

I tried Nell's mobile to no avail, then rang Robert's number. The answering machine came on with Emma's voice telling me that no one was in, but if we had the alternative number we could try that. I have the alternative number, by which Emma means the country number, which they don't give out much so that they can pretend at seclusion. (The second thing Robert did when he left me was to buy a country cottage in Gloucestershire. The first thing was to buy a vast loft in soon-to-be trendiest Clerkenwell, where he could more easily masquerade as young and with it.)

I rang the country number. There was no answer. I knew there wouldn't be. One of the things Nell has told me about her dad's new life is that Emma doesn't cook and he usually prefers going out to donning the chef's hat. If I had my life to live again, Celia, I wouldn't bother with cooking either. Or cleaning or washing or ironing, for that matter. I've noticed a lot of younger women get on quite happily without it all and it doesn't seem to make them any less deserving in male eyes. Perhaps the opposite. Helplessness in chosen domains can be a real plus. We were all far too competent.

Though I don't feel at all competent by Sunday evening — competent as a mother. In fact I'm in a state of minor panic which is soon to become major panic. It's six o'clock and Nell isn't home and her mobile isn't responding. Then it's seven and eight and eight-thirty and she still isn't home. By which time I'm on the phone to Robert again. His answering machine is still on. I leave a message to ring me the minute he comes in. The minute is 10:02.

"What's wrong?" he asks by way of greeting. I don't know whether I should be chuffed or resentful that he can still tell by my voice that something is wrong.

"Has Nell been with you?"

"With us? No, we've been in Norfolk with friends. What do you mean with us?" His voice rises and cracks like a boy's. "She told me she was staying home with you this weekend."

"That's what she told me, too. But when she wasn't here, I assumed she'd changed her mind. We had a little — well, a little misunderstanding."

To his credit, Robert doesn't ask about what or chastise me. He tells me to ring all her friends and then to ring the police. He'll be straight over.

I've already rung a couple of Nell's girlfriends, and it was when one of them told me Nell had rejected a clubbing night because she was off to the country to get some revision done, that I had felt confident enough to get through the day without going mad. But now . . .

Now the panic produced wave after wave of unwanted images. Nell hit by a car and lying unidentified on a hospital bed. Nell mugged, her mobile stolen. Nell kidnapped by some lunatic rapist. Nell in a drug coma, pipes protruding from her mouth. Nell in . . . The last image came just as I dialled the second nine. I put the receiver down with a clatter. It wasn't a violent image. But nor was it desirable. We were talking about another kind of pipe.

I raced for the directory. I couldn't see the entries by the light of the living-room lamp. I needed a magnifying glass, torrid sunlight, a host of brightest spots. (I'm going to have to get those specs, Celia.) Finally, the kitchen glare saved me. I looked up Damian Fry.

There were too many Frys, though only three Ds. I tried each of them in turn and they were all home. But none of them was a Damian. I was just ringing directory enquiries to get the number of the club where Nell had told me Damian worked (I could visualize it and its location perfectly, but I was having a senior moment and for the life of me couldn't remember its name, which is why I thought the operator could help) when the doorbell announced Robert.

"Have you reached the police?" he asked as he put his helmet down on the hall table.

I shook my head and explained my hunch to him.

He looked a little grey around the gills. Queasy. "Well, what are we waiting for? Let's go over there and check it out. I'll wring his neck. She's a minor. Just a child. Damn, I didn't bring a second helmet. Have you got one here?"

"No." I repressed a surge of gratitude. "Easy enough to go in my car."

It took no time at all to get there. It took substantially longer to convince the guard at the door to let us through. We were obviously the wrong sort of folk or had come at the wrong time. Maybe we should have arrived on Robert's bike. A Harley-Davidson might have impressed him rather more than Robert's grey-haired orders and my tearful pleading. Judging from his threatening, dictatorial manner, the man was a paid-up member of the National Front, except that he was black.

At last, when my repeated insistence on the fact that Damian Fry worked there had no effect, Robert resorted to that time-honoured method, a bribe. Twenty pounds saw us through to a lobby which doubled as a bar. It was dark and noisy and smoky and I couldn't make out any faces. Nor, when we finally located a kind of box office, did the chalk-faced Goth behind it admit to knowing anything about Damian Fry. In fact, she stared at us as if we might be rather more deranged than all the lunatics inside who were gyrating to sounds far more deafening than The Who had ever dreamed of. Maybe they have an unspoken age limit — no one over 28 allowed.

The strobe lights didn't help any processes of identification either. Everything moved even when it didn't. Robert gripped my arm like a vise: either he was afraid to lose me in the heaving crowd or he thought he might pass out and be trampled. This couldn't be a good place for the weak-hearted and thick-arteried.

We bumped round the room and peered into unknown faces. The young, as you realize when you reach our age, all look alike. By the time we managed to get to the front, Robert had turned a colour which matched our box-office Goth and which had been achieved with no help from makeup. It was then I decided we needed to come up with a better strategy. I urged him towards the bar.

"Thought you'd never ask," he grimaced when we found a spot we could shout and be heard in.

"Shall we see if there's a way into the lighting box? That's where this Damian would be, if he's here."

"I'm going to make him see some new lights when we find him."

Sometimes I think Robert read too many comic books as a child. They peep out when he's upset or excited.

Well, to cut a far-too-long story short, we never managed to get into the lighting box, which had to be reached from a separate entrance. Once we were outside we didn't have the strength to go back into the club, so we decided to sit in the car and watch people coming out. Finally, around one, when my eyes were clouded with tears and I was thinking of going to the police after all, we saw her. She emerged from the shadowy alley where the side door of the club stood locked. She slinked along the lane, hair waving, elephantine trousers sweeping rubble aside, fashionably bare belly gleaming with the jewelled piercing I had agreed to after months of argument. (I still harbour the suspicion that all these body piercings are trial runs for cyborg implants: lip rings are tomorrow's phones and messaging systems; navel rings, the National Health's internal monitoring equipment; and so on ad miserandum).

Robert raced towards Nell, shouting her name. I was right behind him. I wanted to hug her, drape a jacket over her, but her tone stopped me in my tracks.

"What are you doing here?" Her eyes pierced us with a horror that might attend the appearance of purple-spotted aliens emerging from a spaceship on Highgate Road. Then they flickered and went dead as she tried to walk around us. Evidently being seen with aliens is deeply uncool, and a gaggle of her own kind were upon us.

"Hold on a minute, young lady," Robert gripped her shoulder. "We're the ones who are asking the questions here. Get into the car. Where do you think you're off to, anyhow?"

"Home," Nell says. "If it's still that." She flings me a hostile look and adjusts the rucksack which is slung over her shoulder.

As soon as we're in the car, I scold and rant. "Where were you all weekend? You had me worried half to death. I've told you that you have to check in."

How is it that with teenage children relief can turn to anger in the snap of a finger — or a voice?

"I'm surprised you noticed I was out."

"Nell. Really!" The tears leap back into my eyes.

"Has she announced her forthcoming marriage to you, Dad? Has she told you who she's having an affair with?"

Robert stares at me for a moment, then back at her. "What I want to know is who you've been with. Your mother is an adult. You're still in our care."

"Not much care if it took you three days to notice I was out," she challenges beneath her breath.

I can feel that Robert is about to lose his temper and bark, but I've already succumbed to my guilt. I'm so happy to see her in one piece that I'll forgive her anything.

"You're right there, Nell. If anything had happened to you, I could never have lived with myself. I rang and rang. I assumed — or let's say I hoped — you were in the country with your father. Another hour and the police would have been on the case."

"Oh well. I'm here now," Nell says, undeniably pleased with herself and the impact she's had on us.

"I can see that, but where were you?" Robert growls.

"With friends."

"With Damian?" I ask.

"Him too." It's in the emphatically careless way she says it, in the way that she flings back her hair with just that extra jot of confidence, that I know. Her assertion of equality with me gives away the game. Or at least I think so.

"Where is he? Why isn't he seeing you home?" Robert asks, as if it were a given that Nell's boyfriends had to be gentlemen trained in an old school.

"Oh, he's still working. And I've got school tomorrow, haven't I?"

"You most certainly do, young lady. And let me tell you right now, we're not standing for this kind of behaviour again. We need to know where you are at all times. All times. If you switch off your mobile again, I'll stop paying the bills. You forget that it's principal use is for contact with us. You hear?"

Despite the sound of it, this is a serious threat, and one Nell seems to have respect for. It displaces the more serious discussion we should be having, but it sees us home, by which time Nell has decided to burst into tears.

A few minutes later, it's hugs all round. She does recognize that we've been out of our minds with worry. And she has made her point with resounding emphasis. Any weddings around here will be hers.

When we tuck her in and kiss her goodnight together for the first time in years, she looks up at us with the innocence of an eight-year-old. "Both of you came to fetch me. That's nice. Night-night."

Like the exhausted parents we are, Robert and I sit down together and nurse a quiet drink. After a moment he squeezes my shoulder and says in a low, companionable voice, "You want to tell me about this forthcoming marriage?"

I shake my head. "Nell witnessed something and misunderstood. If she'd talked to me rather than run off, I would have put her straight."

He stares at me and I feel myself starting to flush. For a moment I wonder whether I'm lying and then think that probably I'm not. The trouble is I'm already feeling deeply nostalgic about Toni.

There's more, but I have to sign off now.
Much love
Jude

PART THREE

I'm still writing to Celia — even though there's been no response yet. Maybe Celia really doesn't want to be found this time.

Part of me thinks, never mind. I'm not altogether sure I want a response. After all, Celia and I have had our bad moments. When I confronted her about two-timing me with Patrick, all she said was, "Well, you talked so much about him and his perfections, you made me want him." And that was that. I raged. Of course I raged. And fumed. And considered taking eternal umbrage. But by the following term, we were friends again. Celia and I went further back than Patrick. And outlasted him.

Maybe that's the thing about friendships which are formed before we have professions or functions — formed when we're still children or footloose. They feel deeper than those which come later and as a result of shared interests. They feel as if they've been imprinted on us, have become part of our self-definition. We've taken the other in and she has a share in our inner landscape forever. Celia certainly has a place in mine. And I know it means something that I've felt the need for her now, have dusted her off and brought her into the light again.

Celia belongs to two key moments in my life. Two moments of transformation, really. She is the keeper of my rites of passage. She belongs to the moment when the pastoral of my childhood metamorphosed into something more dangerous, something bigger. In Celia's presence, for the first time I became intensely aware that there was a world beyond home and school and fields and town. She also belongs to the later turbulence of my young womanhood, with its rampant desires and first profound betrayals. Celia betrayed me. In the process she showed me that I, too, could be a betrayer. Showed me that virtue was only a trick of perspective, that clinging to rightness was often only a synonym for clinging to hypocrisy.

It was a good lesson. I'm not altogether sure she learned it herself. I'd like to find out. I'd really like to see her. Meanwhile, I write. Celia helps me with Toni, helps me be hospitable to this new Robert, too. Without her hovering, I might simply stifle him in old resentments.

27 MAY

Dear Celia,
What I didn't get a chance to tell you in my last letter is that Ollie, Robert's son, has now arrived and is occupying the spare

room and, indeed, the house. He's not as bad as Robert led me to believe. I thought I'd have a basket case on my hands, a born-again adolescent who never got out of bed except to grunt or groan and empty the fridge. But it's not like that. Ollie moans a lot about the wasteland that his life has become. He complains about how he's got no future and only a virtual past, since he spent most of it in front of a screen. But he's funny with it and utterly charming, and he's become a definite plus on the household scene. Which is probably what Emma thought, too, so Robert decided to pass him along. Ollie's grown, if anything, even more attractive. I don't remember Robert looking that good when I first met him, but perhaps the years cast a backwards pall.

Ollie's presence has meant that I haven't been able to confront Nell about her activities with Damian. I must do so, but I don't quite know how and I can't very well just blurt it out as a direct question, or she'll stomp away. Terrible that I'm afraid of eliciting her bad moods. Motherhood is a ridiculous function with children of her age these days. Here I am, an enlightened woman of some intelligence and more experience, and I can't even ask my daughter what she did on the weekend for fear of igniting her wrath, which may lead to . . . well, lead to exactly what?

Adolescence has grown fraught with so many bogey men, half of them of our own conjuring, with a little help from Hollywood and the media, that we end up by imagining our own children are halfwits or monsters, victims or agents of a chain of horrors. If I'm sensible, I think I know that Nell won't quit school. She has distinct ideas about her future. And she is now seriously studying for her exams, which begin next week. She eats regularly and I've detected no signs of anorexia.

There's probably far more chance of her crashing a car than ODing, yet I've promised her driving lessons as soon as she turns the right age, and I patrol her eyes and her room like a Gestapo officer. I offer her wine, yet regularly ask her what she's drunk on her evenings out. I have nothing against sex, yet I seem to have a lot against it for her. (Can it be that this is simply the mirror image of what she feels about me?)

Maybe part of the problem, hormones and moodiness at both ends apart, is that we see teenagers as giant, uncontrollable toddlers who need protecting and from whom in turn the world needs protection. And we tremble because we can still recall the terrible things we got up to at their age, while earlier years are cloaked in amnesia. We couldn't bear our children replicating that remembered adolescent omnipotence. Nothing then was too risky. Nothing was going to hurt. Time, that great mortifier, has taught us vulnerability. So we fear for them and fear them.

Sorry about all that, Celia. It must be the Sunday afternoon blues. Not only haven't I confronted my darling daughter, I haven't confronted Toni either. I'm a coward. I don't want to hurt him. To tell you the truth, I don't want to lose him either. There'll probably never be anyone else. I'll just have to curl up at nights with a hot water bottle. And how does one fire someone as a lover and still keep him on as an employee? Funny, whenever I read those office harassment stories, I never thought of myself as the employer.

So I'm steeling myself for the moment when Toni reverts to being what he started as — simply a reliable part-timer. I'll just have to think of Nell when I go up the bookshop stairs. I'll cut down my coffee intake, too — which can't be bad for me.

My racing heart may have as much to do with caffeine as with Toni's presence.

Have I mentioned, Celia, that I visited the Web site of the University of Minnesota in Minneapolis to look for you? You weren't on any of the staff pages. So Heather's hunch must have been wrong. I imagine Jim has dragged you there because of his work. Perhaps I'll try directory enquiries to see if I can dig up a phone number for you, though I'd really like to know first if you've received my letters. Otherwise we'll just sit there with nothing to say, listening to silence travel up to the satellite and bouncing back.

While I wait to hear, I think I'll just bundle some of these letters, like the last lot. Do you still remember that wonderful series of letters you sent me from France — even up to the first stages of your love affair with Jim?

Oh, there's Heather at the door now. I've invited her around for dinner. She invited me, but I thought it best if she came here — so that I can keep a steadying eye on my charges, She reminded me that Patrick's book is coming out next month and was surprised I hadn't asked for an advance copy. I'm surprised, too. Life has just been too busy.

More soon.

Love,
Jude

Conversation with Toni as we walk towards the local pub for a quick drink after work:

"So when we make the wedding? Two weeks, three? A month latest, yes?" He tucks his arm round my waist.

I wait until we're sitting down and can search out his eyes. They're round with hope and innocence. And he looks so shiny and new with his glossy hair and azure shirt. I glug the wine and cough.

"I can't, Toni."

"You can't?" His face falls. "Why not?"

"I just can't. It's not . . ."

"It's not what?"

"It's not . . . appropriate."

"Appropriate? What means?"

"Means it's not right."

"Why? Because I have no money? No house?" His face has grown grim. There's suddenly something brutal in it. Maybe it's just the bruise of his fingers on my arm. I edge it away.

"No, no. It's not that. We . . . it's difficult for us to speak. Your English . . ."

"What matter English? I good to you."

"And my daughter . . ."

"I like Nell."

Everything is so simple for him that tears leap into my eyes. "I just can't, Toni. Seeing each other is one thing. Marriage is . . . well, it's something else."

I say it and I feel like a cheat and a coward. And maybe like an old rake telling a blameless young woman, "That's not what I meant. Not what I meant at all." The registers are at odds.

"We really have to stop seeing each other, as well . . ."

I'm about to add "after tonight and except at work, of course," when the sound of his chair interrupts me. It's an

168

angry scraping sound, and his face is even angrier. His eyes, too, scrape, though I'm the floor this time. I have the feeling that if we were alone, he wouldn't be using only his eyes. He scares me.

He mutters something which I take for an expletive and then, before I can do anything, he's gone.

I feel ghastly, Celia. Not even a shopping spree on Bond Street could alter that. I don't think I can face going in to work tomorrow.

Sleepless,
Jude

30 MAY

Dear Celia,

I'm sure the last thing you want from me is another letter about T — so I won't go on, except to say that he didn't turn up today. At first Kate and I thought he was merely late; and then she swore when she had to take over the coffee. She says she hates the vibrations of the espresso machine. They make the baby leap in terror. Maybe she's right. Anyhow, I took over, but not before getting hold of Sandra, who was luckily able to come straight over.

I have a hunch that Toni has enough pride not to come in for a few days. I tried putting myself in his shoes and the only analogy I could come up with from my own experience was the split with Patrick — way back then in our Cambridge days. I was devastated when he told me in no uncertain terms that it was over. After all, he was my first. He had taken that precious virginity I didn't quite know how to get rid of. (Or I had given it to him . . . a present. Wonderful how archaic that language now sounds. I can't hear myself asking Nell, "Have you given him your virginity?" But then I haven't yet managed to ask her using any language whatsoever.) And I was head over heels in love with him. He was simply the handsomest, most intelligent, cleverest man I had ever met, and I harboured all these secret fantasies. That we would secretly elope together to some hideaway in Spain, whereupon his wife would grant him a divorce and I would become his wife and amanuensis. Or we would live together in blissful sin in Rome, just a few steps from the Vatican, and join some exciting revolutionary grouplet.

So, when he told me it was all becoming a little too serious and we mustn't see each other again, not like that, I couldn't believe it. I cried and cried. I didn't go to his supervisions for three weeks. I sulked. I was certain he'd send for me. I had my pride. (To be fair, he did write a note asking for an essay I owed, but there wasn't the hint of an amorous addendum.)

Then one day, sentimentally, I cycled over to Madingley, stopping at a place by the river where . . . but I won't go into that . . . Then I went on to the pub we used to go to because it was at a little distance from the usual student haunts. I was full of that bittersweet melancholy which, in my youth, became the mood emblematic of those periods at the end of affairs. An almost delicious sorrow and world-weariness that made us reach for poetry and wonder about the suicide we knew we would never commit — though the melancholy was a real enough emotion. I think I was crying when I opened the door to the pub.

That's when I saw you with him. I knew instantly, of course. What I didn't yet know was that it had started while I was still under the illusion that Patrick was all mine — bar his wife. It was when I found you together that the anger came. At you as much as at him. But you know that. It seemed to me a double treachery. You were my closest friend. I had talked to you about him, and now — well, now I'd been not only robbed of Patrick, but could no longer cry on the shoulder I'd grown used to. (It comes to me that this was the second time you'd taken someone that was mine. There had been Jessie, as well, at school. Jessie, who had been my Best Friend until you came along; but then you gave her up and the two of us became Best Friends.)

I didn't intend to go into all that now. I was really thinking of Toni. I suspect the brush-off, however kind, may be a little different for men. The anger will follow the hurt more quickly. But maybe it'll blow over more quickly, too, and he'll be back to work by next week . . . I'll give it a few days and then I'll ring — as his employer, of course. I do miss him. Miss him so much that I'm back on the ciggies with a vengeance and find myself in the garden café every time I can manage a break. Unlike Patrick, I haven't got another string.

I'm probably going on about Patrick because the proofs of his book arrived today. You can imagine I had my nose in there at every opportunity.

What a rogue he was. A rogue and a scholar. He came back to me with all his youthful splendour, before the slight seediness set in. Those slanted green eyes. The devilish eyebrows. The thick blond-red hair. Like a Silenus. Or maybe that's just the portrait the second chapter of the book conjures up, which is as far as I've got. We're in there. In those groves of academe the satyr roves through. At least I'm pretty sure we are. Not named, of course. I'll have to check the descriptions with Heather. He has the effrontery to pay homage to us as a group — the young women in flower, he calls us. Cheek. Proust he isn't — even if the first chapter is all about the smells and sounds of childhood. Not that I'm a judge. Anyhow, I think Heather comes in as the irresistible bluestocking in hot pants. There couldn't have been another.

I suspect I'm the long-legged blonde. Though apparently he loved me for my riotous and infectious laughter. (Was my laugh riotous, Celia? I can tell you, it isn't anymore.)

You, however, are unmistakable. He describes you as having the sweet patience of a nun, a "purity of visage" which made him dream of doing naughty things, just to see if he could ever rupture that aura of serenity. He says he succeeded, but only once. It's a tease, though, because he doesn't tell us how.

I'll send you the book as soon as I'm certain of your address, and maybe you'll tell me. It all took my mind off Toni for a while.

I think Nell has sensed that something's changed. She was incredibly sweet to me this evening. As was Ollie. He cooked, with Nell as his kitchen maid. They made a ton of pasta with some kind of complicated Californian sauce, replete with asparagus and lemon. Quite delicious. I must have put on three pounds at the sitting. (I don't like to smoke in front of Nell.) There was salad, too, and chocolate brownies.

Nell is good for Ollie. Either that or he's eating his way out of depression. It could also be that Robert simply exaggerated in order to elicit my sympathy and get him established here. Not that I mind. Ollie is even helping Nell with her revision — a true blessing, since I'm hopeless at maths and all her sciences, which is what he's good at. This is her study week, too. So the timing couldn't be better.

I'll go back to Patrick now.

My love,

Jude

8 JUNE

Dear Celia,

Another mad week.

Toni hasn't turned up and he doesn't answer on phone or mobile, which has gone dead. I almost thought of setting out to find him at his flat, but that seemed excessive for the employer-only that I'm now meant to be. Though I might still succumb and go and look out for him on Sunday. When we talked at the pub, I had no sense of finality. I was sure that I'd see him the very next day. It didn't occur to me that I might never lay eyes on him again.

Strange that I haven't a clue about any of his friends, so I can't even ask after his welfare. For all I know, he might have decided to go back to Italy. That makes me feel quite desolate.

Nell's mood, on the other hand, undoubtedly related to my mentioning Toni's absence, continues so angelic that I haven't dared to rupture it with any prying questions. But then, she needs her equilibrium more than I do at the moment, what with exams begun. We haven't managed to talk about her

Damian and, with a gigantic effort of the will, I've kept away from her diaries. In the past she's always told me about things when she's ready. I don't know if it'll hold true for Damian. The readiness is taking a long time . . .

Never mind. I don't think he's been to the house in the last little while. And she's been having such a good time with her tutor, Ollie, she hasn't even asked to go out on the weekend. The phone calls still take about an hour out of the evening and lord knows how many out of the day. But that's only to be expected. About the rest, I'm crossing my fingers . . .

What I didn't get around to mentioning to you was Robert's telephone call last Wednesday. I was still at the shop. He wasn't ringing only about Nell, it turned out. He wanted to know why I hadn't replied to his firm's invitation to their sales conference. It was imperative that I be there.

Why was it imperative? I asked him. I don't respond well to any kind of orders from Robert, even ones veiled in silk. It's an old habit.

He hesitated. "I want you there. The reps want you there. I'll send a car for you, if it's difficult."

To tell you the truth, Celia, I had simply bunged the invitation somewhere and forgotten all about it. I've had rather a lot on my plate this last while, as you know better than anyone.

"When is it?" I asked him.

"Tomorrow, of course."

I protested and said it was impossible. I was short-staffed. He offered Ollie. Robert is wonderfully high-handed when he sets his mind on something. It didn't occur to him that Ollie was not his to offer. But I did succumb. I was more than a little curious as to why Robert wanted me there. And Ollie had already offered his services to me with a degree of eagerness that meant he was serious. I hadn't accepted for a variety of reasons, including the fact that I was extra pleased to have him at home with Nell during her study week. But a few hours in the shop would do him no harm.

So, at three o'clock on Thursday, a car came to fetch me and take me to this swank hotel in Hampshire. The car was pretty swish, too. I couldn't work out what Robert was up to. Maybe he thought if I drove up in my old Peugeot it would reflect badly on him. After all, really powerful men keep not only their present but also their past wives in style. Yesterday's slightly worn trophies they may be, but trophies nonetheless. In Hollywood you might even say that the size of a man's alimony payments is a good indication of the size of his fortune . . .

I don't know why my bitchiness is slipping. Robert might just have been trying to be helpful. And nice. He used to be capable of it, after all. A few bits of steel — or was it staples? — in the area of the soul, plus a new woman, can't transform a man totally, can it?

I hadn't before been to a sales conference given by Robert's firm. Invites had come, but I'd stayed away for evident reasons. This one was a tasteful affair in comparison to some. The hotel was charming, not one of those custom-made-for-conferencing resorts attached to golf courses and swimming pools. I was half sorry I hadn't signed up to stay the night, as so many do for these things. Drinks and tea were at the ready when I arrived, and a room set aside for the euphemistic nose-powdering or change of clothes. I did the first, then went through into the meeting room.

Most people had already gathered, including a fine gaggle of the firm's star writers, all being passed around to meet the booksellers, those most important of people in the trade, as the publishers like to tell us without quite believing it. I had managed only a first sip of wine and a first introduction when Robert appeared at my side. This time, needless to say, I recognized him, even in the crowd. The aura of that other Robert, that genial larger man who had a marked resemblance to the late Hemingway, still hovered around this trimmer model, but the two images had almost become reconciled. I wasn't constantly seeing double.

Robert behaved like a host who had set himself the task of making certain that some total unknown (myself) was treated with the respect due to royalty, the Victorian variety, of course. I allowed myself to be charmed, but I was inevitably just a little suspicious. Was this his way of saying thank you for Ollie. Or something else?

I found out only after some hours. First there was the sales presentation — a series of snappy videos about lead titles, with banter scripted by resident wits singing praises of authors, detailing promotion and such like. Then there was dinner — yes, the inevitable fluffy hotel chicken, but it had a rather good caper sauce and the veg were firm. Editors and writers circulated with the changing courses, gracing us with their company.

I had the good luck to be at a window-side table. Invisible all day, the sun was now setting in pink splendour over pleasantly humped hills. A youngish editor from the firm came to sit beside me. He had sleeked-back hair and an air of mid-Atlantic chic, signalled by half reclining in a chair as if it were floating at 35,000 feet. He turned out to be Patrick's editor.

I had forgotten Robert's firm was Patrick's publisher. Two courses went by in gossip about you-know-whom. I learned that, from the publishing house's point of view, it would have been far better if Patrick had postponed death and hung around until at least four weeks after publication. This would have meant that reviews could have been followed by obituaries and provided twice as much free copy — whereas P's untimely disappearance had meant that copy had been unattended by books. Not, of course, that Rupert J. Rivers (name on card) was callous enough to say quite that, but that's what it amounted to.

When I mentioned that I knew Patrick from way back when, he gave me a wide-eyed and slightly disbelieving look and promptly asked me what bits of the book I thought were invented and what true. I said I supposed that all of it was probably true, bar a few of the necessary decorations memory provides to give a book and a life pace. His disbelief grew more prominent. Then he sighed, "I assumed most of it was spin. There was something about the way he talked to me about it all."

"As if he couldn't believe it himself?" I asked.

"Yes. That's it exactly."

"Happens to one as time passes. You'll see."

"Really?"

"Really," I confirmed, just as Robert propped himself against the back of Rupert's chair.

"What's really?"

"Ms. Brautigan here knew Patrick Mahoney. Quite well, from the sound of it."

"Did she, now?" Robert throws me a curious look, then edges young Rupert away. "You never told me."

"Guess you never asked." I favour him with my best smile and am tempted to laugh in the manner that Patrick described as riotous, but I don't think it becomes a woman who's kicking fifty.

In any event, Robert has pulled his chair a little closer to mine. He looks disapprovingly at the glass of creamy parfait that's suddenly been placed in front of him and confides, "I hope you're ready for the speeches."

"What speeches?"

Robert pushes the parfait glass away, just in case it jumps up to pour itself into his mouth and strangle a few arteries. Then he gives me a truly glowing smile, the kind that must have set young Emma's heart ablaze. "You'll see. But pay attention. Don't have too much more wine. And hold off on those fags."

Which comment, of course, is guaranteed to make me do the exact opposite. I empty my glass, but I stop myself lighting up out of respect for Robert's ticker. At which point I hear a tinkling of fork on crystal and the room grows silent.

A pear-shaped man with extravagant eyebrows and ruddy whisky-drinker's cheeks has stood up. I know him to be the chairman of the group, Robert's immediate superior. He's a locker-room sort, loves broad humour and slightly salacious jokes of the kind that make the under-thirties cringe and raise their napkins to their lips in disapproval, but go down well with the older crowd. They love to be jollied along like star footballers in the team effort to sell books.

I stop listening. I'm hoping someone will refill my glass or perhaps, better still, offer me coffee. I'm fascinated by the shape Robert's hand has taken on the table, like a nervy frog kicking out its hind legs to some inner rhythm. But not a green frog. His hand, it comes to me, is much paler than Toni's. And then I hear my name and everyone's clapping and Robert is urging me up and kissing me on either cheek and whispering that I have to go and make a little thank-you speech, and I'm looking at him as if he's turned into some obscene gargoyle on a Viennese church and is about to tumble down and crash on my head.

He leads me towards the front of the room, where the chairman has his arms open for an embrace. I stumble into them and wish I could just hide my hot face against the cool smoothness of his shirt for the rest of the evening, but he's already urging me upright and towards the mike and simultaneously placing a mahogany-and-bronze plaque into my hands. I manage not to drop it. Letters twist and dance before my eyes and coalesce into the words "Independent Bookseller," and some murky light goes on in my foggy brain. I've been given an award.

"Thank you," I say into the mike, which screeches back at me so that I jump. "Not you." I prod it away and focus on the chairman. "Thank you. I'm overwhelmed." I must look overwhelmed, because everyone laughs. "It's not easy being an independent." I think I get "bookseller" and "woman" mixed up, because I suddenly hear myself thanking not only my backers, but my daughter, Nell, who unfortunately isn't here and my assistants, Kate and Sandra, and yes, Toni, over whose name I can feel myself flushing, but no one can tell because I'm already far too hot with wine and confusion and Robert grinning into my eyes as he leads me away amidst a chorus of clapping.

After that, I remember nothing, though I must have been taken to the car and driven home, because this morning I certainly woke in my bed. Ollie, who had made breakfast, insisted on whistling through it rather than offering speech. He force-fed me on orange juice, however, which can only mean he was probably party to my indecent arrival.

I hope this isn't an indication that the age of my being taken care of by the children has already arrived.

Yours, headachy, but as ever,
Jude

9 JUNE

Dear Celia,
Still no word or sign from Toni. His pride is obviously greater than his need to collect the wages I owe him. It makes me miss him all the more. If it weren't for Nell's continuing good behaviour, I'd be slitting my wrists. But she's making every effort to show me that the sacrifice of what is probably the last man ever to make love to me is well worth the while. Imagine, not only did she not go out on Friday night, but she even stayed in on Saturday night! To top it all off, my daily imprecations about the state of her room have suddenly resulted in action. Her floor is visible. So is her bed. A quick look around revealed no hidden mountain of socks and knickers. I just about managed to keep myself upright until a chair was in sight. A shock like that can topple the middling-aged, you know.

Then, on the way to the shop, Ollie revealed something that made me stop hyperventilating with maternal anxiety.

(Ollie's been coming to work almost daily since my Hampshire jaunt. He says he really enjoys it. He's fine with books and his cappuccinos are almost as good as Toni's. My young women customers, who had developed a distinctly disgruntled air last week, are looking happy again.)

I had been saying to Ollie that I was a little worried about the company Nell had been keeping. The men in particular seemed just a tad old for her, too experienced. And he said straight off, "Oh, you mean Damian."

"How do you know?"

"She told me about him."

"Really."

"Yeah. She's decided he's more of a friend."

"But she spent two nights at his place!" My voice was a squeal, and Ollie shot me a concerned look, then shrugged.

"Hey, Jude, I spend quite a lot of nights at your place."

"What are you telling me, Ollie?"

"A lot of people apparently bunk down at Damian's. He's got a cool pad."

"A cool pad."

"Yup. Just that."

He gave me his candid grin, then changed the subject. Did I want him to upgrade my PC, which was camping out somewhere with the dinosaurs, and really needed to enter a more recent epoch?

I did. But I wasn't thinking about PCs. I was wondering whether Ollie knew what he was talking about, wondering indeed whether Nell was being the secretive girl she is or open with her big brother. After all, she hardly knows him.

Aren't the families we breed these days extraordinary? Governments don't have a clue. They still talk about this mythical unit with a mum, a dad and 2.5 children separated by up to three years (and perhaps some grandparents in the background waiting to sell up the family home to pay for nursing care). While in fact, families come in wondrous permutations which are hardly nuclear (more like brain cells with lots of synapses). I think they always have. Statisticians just don't know how to cope with it. Take Elizabeth, for example. She has two children by her first marriage. Her son married a woman who already had a daughter by a previous marriage, and they have a child together. The woman's former husband married someone who already had a son, who became good friends with his all-but-half-sister. He comes to stay with Elizabeth's son, who is a quasi-stepdad and kind of family, but no blood relation, and they all sometimes come and stay with Elizabeth, who is grandma to everyone, regardless of origin. Undoubtedly Nell will bring back to me any sibling Robert and Emma produce for her, even though she's now almost old enough to produce her own. Perish the thought. But you get my point. And now that people live longer and divorce more, rather than dying off to produce "step" children, the "steps" in the family ladder are going to increase dramatically.

But none of this is what I meant to tell you about. What I really meant to tell you was that Robert called. I instantly thought he had called to draw attention to my less than composed behaviour as winner of the great Hoffinger's Independent Bookshop Award and I had a slew of excuses ready, but all he said was that I had forgotten my award in the car and his assistant would bike it over to me. I did want it, didn't I?

Yes, yes, I effused. Of course I wanted it. I would hang it in some strategic location in the shop. In fact I had been worried about where I had managed to mislay it in my state of, well, exhaustion.

Robert was kind about that. Yes, he said. He imagined running a bookshop couldn't be easy. Then he asked after Nell and Ollie and rang off.

The bronze plaque arrived an hour later. Thanks to Ollie it now hangs in a prominent location right next to the coffee counter, rivalling it for shine. Win some, lose some, I guess.
My love
Jude

15 JUNE

My dear, dear Celia,
I've been too depressed to write. I've spent my evenings in floods of tears instead. Floods of tears mixed with the smoke of countless cigarettes. The puffiness around my eyes has now reached astronomical proportions. I think, in fact, the eyes have disappeared altogether, lost amidst puff and wrinkle. Probably been like that for ages, but I've been too loopy-in-love to notice. That's the only way I can account for my blindness.

I don't know where to begin to tell you all the things that have gone wrong. Is it really possible to reach this ripe age of mine and remain as idiotic as a Victorian parlour maid fed on penny romances? No, what am I saying? I insult the parlour maid. I insult the young. My stupidity is vastly superior. I should go and bury my head in sand, and maybe the rest of me with it.

In fact, I should have done it on Sunday morning, when this run of bad luck and worse revelations first announced itself.

I'd been dreaming about Patrick, a Patrick who looked as fresh as Toni. Or rather a Toni whose tongue was as fluent as Patrick's. It's the book. The voice is so very much Patrick's that he's been with me a lot. That sharp, clear-sighted intelligence, that wit which occasionally has a whiff of the fatuous — it's so vividly there it's hard to tell yourself that in fact he's dead.

Ashes to ashes, dust to dust . . .

Toni, on the other hand, is only dead to me.

Anyhow, those are the kinds of half-thoughts that were flitting through my mind while I stood at the back window of the living room. I was also gazing at the rampant flowers and thinking that I really wanted a garden of my own again. Somewhere to muck about in. That's when I noticed an unusual item on the path. A brown rucksack, it looked like, though I couldn't be sure. What was certain was that the object wasn't usually there. It didn't belong. It disturbed the view, like some eerie deposit from an escaped X-filer.

I knocked at our downstairs neighbours' door and pointed it out to them. They rushed outside and rushed back with an ungainly and rather smelly cloth bag. It contained an unknown woman's necessaries, including a wallet emptied of money but complete with credit cards. It also contained a turd. My neighbours grimaced, said they were in a rush, dashing off to a country picnic, and could I please phone the police and alert them. The bag had evidently been tossed over the wall by hoodlums.

So I take this yucky bag, leave it by the front door, having removed the wallet, and ring the police. I wait for ages and ages, get passed from pillar to post and back again, until some-one at last listens to what I say, then tells me that I should bring the bag to the station. I clear my throat and am about to rage and say that I've already wasted enough time trying to fulfill my civic duty. But I'm a coward. I end up whimpering a pathetic "couldn't they perhaps come to me?" It's hard work being citizenly these days.

Anyhow, I'm waiting for the young ones to show for a late breakfast and worrying about this poor woman who's worry-ing about her stolen bag and some lunatic using her credit cards, and I decide that I might as well pop around to the police station. So I'm just getting into my car when I see a police car pull up. The officer runs off to ring my bell.

Having determined that I'm the person who phoned, he asks about the bag, which I've wrapped in plastic. I place in his hands, at which point he upbraids me for having touched it. How was I supposed to bring it to the station without touch-ing it? I ask him. He has no answer, of course. In any case he's wrinkling his nose at the smell and I can see he'd like to tell me off for not removing the turd. Then he tells me there's been a burglary three doors down, which is why they've come so swiftly. Amongst other things, a woman's handbag was stolen. He interrogates me as if I had stolen it.

Meanwhile Nell has come in, all agog. Watching me being turned into a criminal by the police's demeanour seems to please her. She takes her time to say she thinks she heard the bag being chucked into the garden. It was about 12:30 last night. She was just switching her light off.

By the time the policeman has finished grilling her and has left us and I've aired the room, which still carries a ripe fecal whiff, I'm feeling depleted. But the whole story has to be repeated to Ollie, who's just arrived downstairs and fancies a fry-up. He and Nell are off for a big walk on Hampstead Heath, he tells me. He's decided to deploy the Socratic method to help her with her revision, since it keeps one going in body as well as mind.

Do you know what this means, Celia? Nell is actually WALKING. If we're lucky, she may even purchase a pair of trousers that don't clean the pavements.

Ollie asks if I'd like to come along. He doesn't think I get enough exercise.

I'm about to say I'll come if we stop off first to visit my mother, but then realize that's hardly fair. There have been so few sunny days this year that all the chatter about global warming has gotta be about a planet that doesn't contain England. And Nell really should get out in the light as soon as poss. I agree to meet them later on in front of Kenwood.

My mother, when I arrive, is in a state. It's as if she'd read my mind and decided to incarnate it. She's picking up wave-lengths, or signals, like the mad used to do in the fiction of the sixties and early seventies. They don't seem to do that any-more. Break down, I mean. Or be susceptible in the same way. Or at least the stories we're told about them have changed dra-matically. Funny, that. "Voices" seem to have gone the way of tics and muteness and strange paralyses. Maybe madness comes in fashions, like everything else. Or maybe it's the drugs they pump into you. They create different illnesses. Now that we've got antidepressants, we get lots of depression.

Sorry, sideline. What I was really saying is that my mother hasn't noticed that change, anymore than she has in the clothes domain. She still picks up signals. Today it was the

Toni signal. She kept seeing him or looking for him over my shoulder.

"Has he gone out to buy flowers?" she asked three times. I knew very well who the "he" was. Then she said, apropos of nothing, "He's lost." And a few minutes later, when a youngish man walked in, she literally shouted, "Over here, young man. Here. Here."

I smiled at him in the way that one does in that place, a big, vacant smile covering imminent tears. On top of it all, this was one of the days when my mother's speech was altogether decipherable.

When I left her after only a half-hour, 'cause I simply couldn't take it, she squeezed my hand and said, "Bring him. Come soon."

Then off I went to meet Nell and Ollie on the Heath. I told myself it was a glorious day. I walked past the flower beds in Kenwood and stared at the greenest of greens against the bluest of English blues. A pastoral idyll complete with glittering pond and white *trompe l'oeil* bridge and racing dogs unfolded before me. I pulled myself together; it was ludicrous that I should miss a man I could barely have a conversation with. When I saw Nell and Ollie, I hugged them both as if they'd been away for months.

Nell was on her mobile, but she hung up quickly, her face slightly flushed. The walk was doing her good.

We strolled past Kenwood House and downhill towards the massive Henry Moore sculpture, its bronze glinting in the light, its holes somehow more prominent in the brightness.

"That reminds me, Elizabeth rang the other day. They're coming home . . . Oh. I guess it was last night."

"Nell," I wail. "How could you forget to tell me?"

I'm thinking about all those plants I haven't watered this week. Haven't watered since I had it out with Toni. I've been avoiding the cascade of memories that wait for me at Elizabeth's. I had been planning to force myself to go there today.

"Elizabeth didn't specifically ask me to tell you." Nell shrugs. "Otherwise I would have written it down."

"She'll be upset. I . . . Her plants will be wilting."

"You should have asked me to tend to them, if you're so busy." She charges off in front of us.

"Don't be silly, darling. I'm not blaming you." Though I am, of course.

I catch up to her and we all walk in silence for a few minutes until Ollie says, "Nell's been telling me how bad things are for teenagers these days."

"Bad for *teenagers*?" I look from him to her in disbelief and just manage to change my "bad for their parents, more like" into a nondescript "humpff."

"No, it's true. Everyone complains about them hanging around streets, causing problems . . . But there's nowhere for them to go. Even nice middle-class girls like Nell and her friends."

"What do you mean?"

"You know what he means, Mum. I've told you often enough." Nell has her grunt voice on again.

"Nell told me that she and a group of friends were chucked out of some coffee shop . . . Coffee Costa?"

Nell nods.

"With no forewarning, they'd introduced this new rule of no one under twenty-one allowed in."

I remember Nell mentioning this and thinking that I'd write to the management to complain. But I hadn't. I'd simply been too busy.

"And they don't even serve alcohol, like the bars and clubs which won't have us," Nell grumbles.

Ollie continues, "And she says when they go to places like Pizza Express or whatever, if they try and share a pizza or a main course, like all adults are allowed to do, they're told off or told to leave."

"No one wants us," Nell moans. "Just wait until they have their own kids."

"It's because there are always too many of you. Gangs frighten people."

"It happens even when there's only a few of us. They just don't want us. Our money isn't the colour of yours, right? Or our faces." She kicks a stone and sends a bit of turf flying. "Everyone's so nasty. Only the Chinese welcome us. I think I'm going to study Chinese."

"That would be great."

Nell doesn't seem to have heard me. "It's like you'd created all these aliens. Or we turned into them at the age of twelve or something." She pauses and studies my face carefully. "And then when we behave like these monsters you think we are, you're surprised."

"You're right," I say after a moment. "It's appalling. But to give us old ones our due, you can behave pretty wildly. Not to mention rudely."

"In some tribal societies," Ollie cuts me off, "they send adolescents away to live in their own houses until they're ready for the rites of passage."

"Great," Nell says, shrugging the opposite. "They're probably the same guys who send menstruating women off to live in their own houses, too."

She's running her hand along the hole which is the middle of the Moore woman, and I study her carefully. I'm more surprised by her comment than I am by her behaviour. It's true. I've fallen into this common abyss of parenthood. Teenagers have been terrors for so long in the media and, I guess, in everyday life, that when varieties of the worst take place, we're hardly astonished. But when my daughter, who's spent a good three-quarters of her waking life away from me at school or camp or wherever, utters a statement based on material I haven't communicated to her, I'm genuinely surprised.

I smile at her. "You could always bring your friends home to our house more often, Nell. I'd love it."

"No, you wouldn't," she comes back at me, quick as a flash. "You'd be hovering over us all the time checking to see no one had dropped ash on the floor or spilt their drink. Or you'd be making naff conversation. Or you'd be worrying and we would feel you through the floorboards."

"That's not quite fair, Nell," Ollie intervenes.

She looks up at him and grins. "Okay, it's not *quite* fair." Then suddenly she waves.

I turn and think I'm going to fall over. Instead I manage to step into a pile of dog mess.

Robert is making his way towards us. "Hope I haven't kept you waiting," he says, kissing Nell, then hesitating before he does the same to me, so I have time to pull away and groan as I point at my shoe and start wiping it on a patch of moist grass, like some twitchy old bat. Decidedly there's been too much shit in my life for one day. There's also been rather too much of Robert of late. I look around to see if Emma is about to trot up behind him, but he's evidently left her at home, far from Ollie, whom he's pounding on the shoulder in true American dad style.

So we all walk together, as if nothing had ever rent us asunder, and by the time we're having a very late lunch back in Kenwood, even I'm feeling relatively lighthearted, despite Robert's rendition of my acceptance speech at the booksellers' event.

"He's exaggerating," I insist to Nell.

"I know," she giggles. "He always exaggerates. But it's funny." She leans towards him. He embraces her and she cuddles into him. And you know, I'm jealous. Jealous of the affection she so naturally gives him and he her. This isn't altogether the effect of divorce, is it? I have a vague recollection of feeling something similar when Nell was little, feeling a little jealous of that extraordinary father–daughter bond. Like bondage. Like that bittersweet Judy Collins song I would have as one of my choices if I were to have the fiftieth I won't have.

Robert comes back to the house and stays far too long, testing Nell on her history. You'd think he had nothing else to do. Emma must be away, but I haven't the heart to ask him. It's as if we're playing at cosy families and putting more into the play that we probably ever did into the reality. It's then that I see this expression on Nell's face — a mixture of longing and triumph, if you can imagine that. There's something familiar about it. It reminds me of a girl in a video of an old movie she used to watch over and over. What was it called? It had Hayley Mills in it playing manipulative twins.

My daughter is up to something, and I'm not sure I like its nature.

It must be about half an hour after Robert leaves that the telephone rings. I manage to reach it before Nell. It's Elizabeth. She's in a state of hyper-excitement through which the hostility shows. Her beloved plants must be dead or on the very verge of extinction.

After the initial greetings and my queries about her and Stuart's welfare, over which she rushes as if there had never been adultery and divorce on the horizon, she asks curtly, "When were you last here?"

"About a week ago." I lie just a little. "I was going to come and do the plants today; then Nell told me you were already back." I say the latter a little coolly, as if she really ought to make such announcements to the responsible party.

She cuts me off. "We just got back. And it's not the plants I'm worrying about. I think there's been a squatter in the house. Either that or we surprised a burglar in the act."

An unbidden balloon pops into my mind, as if I were a cartoon character. "OUCH" is clearly written in it before a pin splatters it and I'm drenched in wet goo.

"What did he look like?" I ask, then quickly cover my faux pas. "Did you catch him?"

"We saw him running off. But I wouldn't let Stuart go after him. You never know what ghastly substances people are on these days. Or whether they're carrying guns. Stuart's talking to the police now."

"Shall I come over?" I ask lamely, hoping she'll say no. I can't bear it.

"Yes, yes. Straight away. They may want to ask you some questions. And bring the keys."

So forty minutes later I'm with Elizabeth and Stuart and two police, which makes three in one day. Too many for anyone. I'm grateful to see that neither of these two is the man whom I saw this morning. Otherwise he might think I was involved in some heinous plot. Nor would he be altogether wrong, though its nature might not be quite what he'd suspect.

Elizabeth, despite her fluster, is looking wonderful. A healthy ruddy flush has settled over her face and throat and all visible limbs. She's lost weight, too, and her pale trousers and ivory top flow around her with sophisticated chic. I wonder whether the weight loss bodes well or ill, but it's hardly the time to ask. Stuart is unchanged and does little more than wave, so intent is he on his conversation with the police.

"Was anything taken?" I ask as I hug her.

"That's the odd thing. I can't tell. Some silver, perhaps."

"Maybe . . . maybe you've imagined it all?"

She gives me a sour look. "I'm not that far gone yet. Despite the ordeals of the last months. No, no. There was definitely someone. I could tell as soon as we came in. I wanted to put the kettle on and it was hot. HOT. There were dishes in the sink. For a moment I thought maybe you'd dropped around to give the place a lick and a polish before our arrival. And had a cup of tea, and we'd just missed you."

"I would have done just that," I interrupt. "But Nell forgot to tell me you were coming until a few hours ago. You have to give that girl specific instructions or she . . ."

"I won't have a word of criticism about our Nell. She's been a boon to me over these last weeks. I've really enjoyed our conversations."

"Oh?" Nell hasn't told me about anything that could be called "conversations."

"Yes. Don't look so surprised." Elizabeth has the grace to smile. "I heard all about her little leaving-home escapade. And I think I've been a good aunt to her."

"Agony aunt," I can't prevent myself saying.

"That too." She fixes me with her pebble eyes. "And she's been one to me. I don't think Stuart and I would be here together if she hadn't been."

"Oh."

This time I really am bug-eyed. I've forgotten all about burglars and squatters in the pursuit of more knowledge about Nell's budding career as an agony aunt for troubled elders, when I feel a tap on my shoulder.

"Hello, Jude." Stuart gives me a worried half-smile. He looks a little tired, almost what I might have called henpecked, except that I like his hen too much. "The constable here wants to speak to you. You've brought the keys, I take it."

I hand them to him and the two officers come over to interrogate me. Second time today, remember, so I'm pretty good at spelling my name and giving out my address.

"Could these keys have fallen into anyone else's hands?" the smaller policeman asks me, with a good Estuary whine.

"I don't think so," I lie. I know very well whose hands they didn't so much fall as were handed into. But my effrontery knows no bounds. I can't incriminate Toni when it was all my fault for offering up the temptation. After all, who wouldn't prefer to spend a night or three at Elizabeth's rather than heading home to the insalubrious dens of the Caledonian Road. Still, I am angry at him, internally angrier and angrier when I think of all those nights when I dropped him at the tube, only so that he could double back there. Though maybe he didn't then. Maybe it was only after I gave him his marching orders. No, no, he must have taken the keys on that very first night and presumably had them duplicated. Otherwise I wouldn't have the pair I'm now putting into Stuart's hands. Either that or he found a way in through the windows. Or maybe I'm suffering from premature paranoia — like my mother — and this has nothing to do with Toni at all.

"Were the keys with you at all times?" the second policeman asks. He's not very tall, not as tall as I think policeman were meant to be, and he looks straight into my eyes, so I look down.

"Well, I can't be absolutely certain."

"For example," Stuart asks, "might you have left them at home when you went off to work?"

I try to think back. "It's possible, yes. Sometimes I switch handbags and I don't transfer everything. There was the night I went to that do in Hampshire, for instance."

Elizabeth cuts me off. "That could be it, then. One of Nell's friends might have picked them up and . . ."

"That doesn't make sense. How would anyone know what house they belonged to?" I realize as I say this that I'm speaking against my own (and Toni's) best interests. But I can't very well have Nell bothered with all this. "Why couldn't the person simply have broken in, or climbed through a window? There are enough of them."

"There are no marks on the front door lock. Or on any of the windows," Stuart explains.

"Nell might have taken someone here." Elizabeth's face has

suddenly lit up. She won't let Nell's involvement go. Maybe she knows something I don't.

"Why on earth would she take anyone here? She's got a home."

"But you're there."

"What are you saying?"

"Maybe just that she wanted some privacy." Elizabeth is beaming. She definitely knows something I don't. Or don't for certain. "So she brought her friend here. And then . . . well, he just decided to stay."

I cringe. It must be visible, for Elizabeth pats my shoulder in a "there, there" gesture. I'm cringing because she's got the wrong member of the family. And I don't dare say. Not now. Not in front of all these people.

"No harm done, if nothing's been stolen," she adds.

"You'll have to get yourselves a new lock," the taller officer intervenes. "You can't be certain he won't come back."

"Yes, yes. First thing tomorrow." Stuart doesn't look pleased. I suspect he doesn't approve of Elizabeth's theory one little jot. His Nell is definitely an innocent. No friend of hers would do anything as louche as squat in someone else's house.

I'd like to pat him with a "there, there" gesture, but there's something else I have to ask first.

"I don't really understand why you think someone's been staying here at all."

"Oh, didn't I say?" Elizabeth gives me her kind face, the one which assumes I'm undergoing maternal anguish because my daughter has been sleeping with a man and hiding it from me, though apparently telling my best friend all about it without necessarily indicating the location of the great event. "It was the bed."

"The bed?" I'm aghast.

"Yes, yes. You haven't been paying attention, Jude. I was trying to phone you after I'd found the warm kettle. And Stuart was doing a prowl through the house. Then he shouted and I looked up. I was at the back window. And there, jumping down from the beech into the little lane which goes along the side of the house, was this youth. He was carrying a bag. Just there, look." Elizabeth points through the window and it's as if I can see Toni jumping.

"He must have hurt himself." I shudder.

"Well, that's what I thought, too, but by the time we went out to look, there was no one there. So it must have been a clean jump. That's why I was certain he was a *young* man."

"Then," Stuart takes up the story, "I went upstairs to check on the damage. And the bed in Nikki's old room, the small one at the top, was unmade. It had been slept in."

"At least he chose a small room for himself," Elizabeth says.

"Yes, that was considerate of him." There is more irony than I intend in my voice. I'm feeling deeply betrayed. Toni has taken terrible advantage.

"If you have any ideas about the identity of the man, Mrs. Brautigan . . . or if your daughter . . ." The small policeman is giving me the benefit of his slit-eyed suspicion.

"Ms. . . ." I say. "And yes, of course, if I think of anything or discover anything, I'll be sure to tell you."

"Thank you, officers." Elizabeth ushers the two out of the door. It has occurred to her that she might be getting her favourite teenager into trouble. "We'll let you know if anything has been taken. But it may . . . well, it may just all have been a misunderstanding."

197

As soon as they've gone, Elizabeth turns to me. "I'm so sorry. I only just worked all that out while we were talking. Silly me. I should have guessed."

"What did he look like?"

"I didn't really see properly."

"He was dark."

"You don't mean black, Stuart?"

"I said dark. I didn't say black."

I don't know why, but it's in the tone of that assertion that I suddenly know for certain that things are not altogether right for Elizabeth and Stuart. But I can't really think about them now. I can only think about Toni and this unsuspected betrayal. I stare out at the beech in Elizabeth's garden and I want to scream at him. But there's no one there to scream at. It's as if . . . well, yes, it really feels like that, but maybe it's because I'm so exhausted by all this and already dreaming. It's as if he's dropped a big, smelly turd right at the centre of our relationship. Maybe it's what I deserve for harbouring illusions.

There's more, Celia, but it's late and it'll keep. And I must stop going on and going over . . . You'll forgive me for being a little incoherent in the circumstances.

My love,

Jude

MONDAY, 18 JUNE

Dearest Celia,

This morning's post brought an odd little card from a Minneapolis post office. From the multiple-choice exam presented by its ticked and unticked boxes, I think I now know that you have moved again. Moved to San Francisco. The lure of the Pacific, I guess. You have truly become North American in the way you bustle across those vast distances as if it were a question of the fifty miles that separate London and Cambridge. We Europeans are so staid in comparison. We just can't keep up. I wonder if my letters have.

Never mind. I very much hope that this new address has caught up with the present you. Otherwise I'll be sixty by the time you get my letters. And, you know, I'm still hoping that we can spend our fiftieth together, somewhere, somehow. Seeing you seems to be the only thing I can manage to look forward to in these bleak days. I'm leaning towards Paris — for old times' sake? Or would that be a bad idea, given our last meeting there? I still don't like to think about that.

I saw an ad in the *New Yorker* this morning which made me think of Jim. "Hitting fifty?" a man who was meant to be asked in bold letters, though he looked so fit he was certainly younger than yours truly. He was trying to sell me an investment plan. He also looked not unlike Jim and I remembered that Jim had something to do with pensions and financial plans, though we were so uninterested back in those days that I never found out quite what. So I thought of Jim and I wondered again whether all these moves of yours are to do with him. And then — this is really strange, Celia — for the first time it came to me that I, too, had married an American. I never really thought about it before because Robert has always lived here in Britain, but today, after all these years, not to mention a divorce, I wondered whether I married him in some kind of twinning operation — or as a way of following in your footsteps.

I almost wish I had someone in whose footsteps to follow now, though I know it's high time my own were being followed. Perhaps luckily, my daughter has decided they aren't quite right for her.

Needless to say, I've been treating Nell like a fragile flower that needs constant watering and tending, on tiptoe, of course. Exams are in full swing. Nothing must disturb her, as she has repeated over and over. So for days I said nothing about Elizabeth's purported squatter. I even rang Elizabeth to alert her to Nell's delicate state and begged her to say nothing for the next few weeks.

Yesterday I don't know what took hold of me. Maybe it's just that I've heard nothing at all from Toni and I waver between blaming him for everything, including my sleeplessness, my drinking, my smoking and my expanding waistline, and exculpating him utterly of any offences (which is better for my sense of self, but still has no effect on my waistline). Whatever the case, at lunchtime I suddenly heard myself saying to Nell, "Darling. you didn't by any chance borrow Elizabeth's keys from my bag while she was away?"

"Why? Did you lose them?" Nell mumbles, her gaze glued to her biology text.

"No, no."

I shouldn't have bothered with the disclaimer. Nell's question should have alerted me to the fact that she hadn't borrowed the keys. But I uttered my no nonetheless, at which point she looked up at me.

"So, what's happened?"

"Oh, nothing. It's just that they seem to have had a burglar or a squatter in the place."

Nell stares at me, then leaps up, her eyes wider than the saucers she'd like to chuck at me. "And you think I . . .? MUM, how could you?"

"I don't think anything," I mumble. "It's just that Elizabeth . . ."

"You old women!" Nell rages. "Just 'cause I mention a guy . . . so you and Elizabeth think I took Damian . . . I don't believe it. I really don't believe it. Besides, Damian's got his own place."

She storms out of the room and I shout after her, shame-faced because I was testing the waters, though I knew in my heart of hearts that hers were hardly as muddy as my own.

"That's what I told her, Nell. She just thought, maybe . . . Because you'd been talking to her about him. It doesn't matter. Everything's okay. Come back and have lunch. You have to eat."

The admonishing "MUUUUMM" that issues from her this time is the one that contains nine and a half syllables. I know this mum well. She's the one who's always blindly intruding on Nell's bodily being. This mum has no sense of the limits which mark her daughter off as a physical other. She knows when Nell is hungry and needs to eat. She knows when she's tired and needs to rest. She knows when she's ill and should stay tucked up in bed. She knows when she's cold and needs a coat and scarf. She'll probably soon know whether Damian or A. N. Other is good for those parts mothers cannot reach.

This is a MUUUUUUUMM that makes Nell rage (one of the many), rightly so, I acknowledge, though I find it hard to hold her back, since in fact I do know all of these things about Nell, however hard she protests. They're written on her face as clearly as they were when she was a bumbling toddler. Yet I also know that I mustn't say these things. I can still remember how my mother, well into her dementia, would stoke uncontrollable ire in me by saying, "You're tired. You're nervous." And I was middle-aged (my youthful middle-age, of course).

Maybe one of the reasons both children and parents find adolescence so difficult is that we can still remember it, unlike so much of those empty stretches of childhood, which are, as a result, easy to romanticize (or demonize) precisely because they're so empty and so long. Whereas the moments of adolescence are etched in stone by flashes of Technicolor lightning. I suspect I panic about Nell and young men because I remember my own devil-may-care wildness all too vividly. One of the reasons I don't worry overmuch about her exams is probably because mine occasioned an almost pleasurable nervousness indistinguishable from excitement, then took place in an oblivious haze, which seemed to obtain the desired results.

Nell eventually does come back, but only after Francesca has arrived and the odour of a particularly creamy lasagna (I've outdone myself because it's exam Sunday) acts as pied piper.

Francesca isn't looking well. Phone calls aside, I've seen her only once in the last month and that very briefly. She's been busy with the father of her soon-to-be child, which is probably what's given her this slightly sallow colour. The babe, I mean, not the father. But I can't very well ask about all that in front of Nell and Ollie. Francesca's only picking at her food and I wonder whether she'd really rather be off in the toilet puking.

There was a point at which my morning sickness seemed to last all day, no matter how model a bearer of the next generation I liked to pretend I was. Maybe it's partly why I didn't leap right in and have another. Or maybe it's because I then lived under the illusion that time was infinitely elastic. Alas, alack. But enough of that or this page will be drenched with great gobs of self-pity.

At Nell's insistence and despite protests from Ollie and myself about leaving her alone, the three of us trundled off to watch a late-afternoon film Francesca wanted to see. It was at the ICA of all places. (You remember, down in the Mall, a stone's throw from Buckingham Palace, though I don't imagine Queenie visits a lot. The pictures on the walls don't altogether resemble hers, though I rather liked their garish exuberance.)

The film was Taiwanese and despite or because of its slowness was utterly wonderful. It had the randomness of everyday life; its edge of boredom, too, as if the director had no plot to rush us all along with or had lost it when the characters took over. And they were ordinary middle-class characters! Yes, middle-class — that category which has become anathema for anything that isn't romantic comedy. Funny how in the West there's been this long-time consensus that the only classes worth portraying are either criminal and inhabit the gutter or its nearest kin, or are outrageously rich and perverse and exotic. Yet there we were, shut in with a middle-aged business executive and his family, not so unlike any bourgeois family in the West, and they were proving themselves riveting. I wept so much I ran out of tissues.

It begins with this old granny who has a stroke just after her renegade younger son's wedding to his pregnant fiancée. Her granddaughter, a moody adolescent, thinks the stroke is all her fault because she forgot to take the rubbish out and granny strained herself doing it for her. The executive's wife, whose mother it is, is thrown into a crisis when the granny is sent home from hospital still in coma. The doctor tells them they must all take turns talking to the silent, sleeping body, even if there is no response. Summing up her days for her speechless mother, the executive's wife is confronted by the emptiness of her life. She cracks and goes off to a Buddhist retreat. Meanwhile her husband meets his first love again and savours a possible repetition of the affair; her daughter becomes passionately infatuated, first with the racy single mother and teenage daughter next door and then with the latter's rejected boyfriend. The eight-year-old son, who is edible, wants to know how we know what we can't see and starts taking photographs of the backs of people's heads, to help them know that invisible half of their world (maybe that's where the coma up and grabbed his granny when she wasn't looking).

The extraordinary thing is that what would be the core subject of the Hollywood film is what happens as an aside. Murder, rampant sex — that's all just next door, and somehow of secondary importance to the dying grandmother, the crisis in the executive's electronics firm, the little boy's attempts to understand the world and the girls who pick on him — the mundane yet crucial events of all our lives. It's only the adolescent daughter who's really moved by passion, by murder. Teenagers again. They inhabit a world of excess, whereas the rest of us have grown out of it, either to regret its passing or to forget all about it. Or both.

I'm going on again. I don't know why. You've probably seen the movie anyhow. But you know how those rare films can take you over. It made me think. Made me think that maybe Toni was my Hollywood action next door. And that not once in these last meetings with Robert have I had a serious conversation with him about how his work is going; how it feels to grow older in a high-powered job, particularly with all the takeovers of recent years.

Enough of that. What I really wanted to tell you about was Francesca. Ollie insisted that we go off and have a drink together while he went back to Nell, so I took him up on his offer because I really did want to talk to Francesca about the pregnancy. The film had done nothing to lift her colour or even her spirits. There was none of the usual bubble in her. In fact, as Ollie left she shot him a longing glance which made me realize she didn't really want to be with me alone. Didn't want to talk. At first I thought it might be hormones, those nasty little chemical messengers which seem to stimulate or inhibit just about everything that makes life life. But then it turned out my chemical explanation was not only too simple, but downright wrong.

We ended up in a brasserie on St. Martin's Lane, not as noisy as one might expect, because it was Sunday evening, the time when the rich are probably on their way home from country houses, whereas the young are still recovering from the night before. The trouble is, without the noise, I could hear Francesca clearly, and neither of us much liked what she eventually came out with.

It turns out that she isn't pregnant. Not altogether surprising, if one thinks of the instantaneity with which she thought it had happened, but a great disappointment to her because

205

she'd so convinced herself she was. The lateness of her cycle, the doctor told her, could be due to a hundred things, including — and this was apparently uttered with a meaningful stare — exhaustion or desire or even, heaven forbid, a premature judder of the menopause.

"I'm only thirty-eight," Francesca wailed.

"I'm sure it isn't that. He's just scaring you. Your GP sounds as if he enjoys scaring you."

"Sadist," Francesca mumbles, then bursts into tears for which we have no more tissues, so have to use her starched pink napkin.

What she really thinks is something the doctor even in his sadism wouldn't confirm. Maybe he's not as sadistic as she is towards herself. Francesca is convinced that fertilization did take place, but for one reason or another, mostly age, she miscarried very early in the cycle. She tells me that apparently there are hundreds of thousands of such undiagnosed miscarriages, which women just think of as late periods. So she concludes that she lost the one baby that destiny had recently offered her. That really is the pits.

"There'll be many more where that one came from," I try to console her.

"No, there won't."

Her face has grown so bleak that I daren't ask why she's so certain. Our plates of peppery rocket and Parmesan sit in front of us, fashionably untouched. I finally dig into mine with a large chunk of olive-oiled bread. It's too late for fashion where I'm concerned and I have to do something or I'll be weeping, too, and there won't be anyone there to take care of things.

At last Francesca murmurs, "It's over."

"Over?"

"Yes, over. *Kaput*. Finished. *Finito. Terminado. Konec.* And whatever other languages you can think of. Lover boy and I are through."

I wait. The sudden stridency in her voice, the theatrical blaze in her eyes would leap at any comment and mangle its maker. I tell myself this nascent rage is better than her earlier flatness. Francesca is not one of those women who gain in soulfulness when depressed.

"Through, I said. Are you going to ask why?"

"Why?" I squeak on command, though I know she's now going to tell me anyhow.

"Because he's a shit. A rich, ungrateful, untrustworthy, unloving, unlovely, unprepossessing, unfaithful shit."

"Oh," I manage. "What happened?"

She's crying again, though now, like me, she's stuffing leaves into her mouth.

"He betrayed me. Even before we found out I wasn't pregnant. Betrayed me with a man," she howls through green.

I make soothing noises and wait for her to control herself. I want to say that fidelity, when she last told me about this ultramodern partnership, was hardly part of the deal. I want to tell her that she's being unreasonable and that she's probably well out of it because it never would have worked anyway, and better to find out now than later, but suddenly I'm thinking about Toni and I bolt my mouth, because I know, in all those secret parts of myself, that irrationality is just the name of the game we call love, never mind whether the L is big or little.

"I know what you're going to say," Francesca says at last, pushing away her plate. "You're going to say he never promised anything. You're going to defend him. Well, don't."

"I'm not."

"Good. He doesn't deserve it."

"Did you tell him you weren't pregnant?"

"Did I tell him? Did I tell him? You bet I told him. I told him loud and clear. I told him he was incapable of it. Inadequate. Infertile. Insubstantial."

"But you just told me . . ." I stop myself. I had been going to point out that she was certain she had miscarried.

"I know what I just told you," Francesca sobs. Suddenly the cry turns into a laugh. "I'm being stoopid. Can't help it. Hate him. Hate myself. Hate everything."

"Degree zero is always a good place to start. Start again, I mean."

Francesca stares at me. "And how do you suggest we get the start-up engine going? Is there a government package aimed at new amorous start-ups? A special tax rebate? Help with plans?"

I don't really have an answer. I don't have an answer for much these days. I'm beginning to think it's the stars. The stars have been against new partnerships these last months. When you have no answers, superstition is always a good place to turn.

Let's hope the stars are better for our fiftieth.

Love,
Jude

Dearest Celia,

I left work early yesterday. It's been so quiet. My sixth-formers are busy with exams and everyone else seems to be just too plain busy for books. Particularly on a Monday. Anyhow, I took off early and I did what I thought I wouldn't do. I went to Toni's place, or at least to the address he gave me when he first came to work for me. Given that his phone didn't answer, I thought someone there might be able to help.

The place turned out to be a narrow (and as I had feared, insalubrious) terrace not far from Pentonville prison. The windows were peeling. The net curtains were a shade of grey. The door was a deeper shade, not just the colour of dirt, but the colour of historical grit, the kind that won't come off with a rub of Jif. There was no bell. I pounded on a boarded-up window and sincerely hoped that Toni no longer lived there. I quickly calculated what I had been paying him and cursed myself for providing too little. Rents in London are astronomical.

From inside I heard voices — a woman's, I thought, but no one came to the door, so I pounded again. At last a child appeared. A child of about eight, or perhaps more. He had those dark, liquid Mediterranean eyes, which always look so wise, with their slight pucker at the edge.

When I found my voice, I asked, "Is your mother home? Or your father?"

The child shook his curly head.

I peered behind him into a darkened hall and up some stairs. I had distinctly heard a woman's voice. The inside looked a lot cleaner than the outside, even the corner of a kitchen sink I could make out below the square of a back window.

"I thought I heard your mother," I said.

The boy shook his head again. "Not home."

I was somehow surprised by the English. It sounded distinctly North London.

"Never mind," I smiled. "I'm really looking for Toni. He lives here, doesn't he? Or at least he used to."

The child examined me. "You're a new social worker, innit?"

"No, no. Just a friend of Toni's."

He shuffled from foot to foot and I heard a slight noise behind him. From the side of my eye I thought I saw the net curtain move and the outline of a kerchiefed face, but it all happened so quickly I couldn't be sure.

"Toni's moved," said the boy, perhaps to distract me.

"Do you know where?" I asked, though I knew I wouldn't get an answer.

The child shrugged. "Nah. Outta London, maybe."

"Did he leave a phone number?" I persisted stupidly.

The boy folded his arms across his chest in imitation of some patient elder and shook his head again. "Nah. No number."

"Well, if he calls or anything, you tell him Jude came by."

"Sure, Jude."

He moved to close the door before I could think of anything else to say. I went back to my car. I could feel eyes watching me, but when I looked back at the windows, there was no one there.

It came to me on the way home that maybe what was uncanny about the little boy was that he reminded me of Toni. For a split second I even wondered if he might be Toni's son. It made me shiver. I discounted the idea as ludicrous.

I might have brooded over it all rather more, but when I got home to Nell, guess who was sitting with her discussing the day's exams? You got it in one. Robert.

Since Nell's been staying home to study on weekends, he's taken to dropping in rather more than is seemly for an ex. I try not to let it bother me, since I've got quite enough to be bothered by at the moment. But it's hard. Particularly when he more or less invites himself to dinner. Yesterday I caught him staring at me in a way that made me distinctly uncomfortable, as if he'd noticed the latest spread in my backside. I lit up out of spite and to remind him who was in charge in this house. And then Nell let out one of her MUUU-UMs, the kind that tell you there's a firing squad to face in an hour unless you behave, and I quickly stubbed out the barely puffed-at cigarette. I swear Nell takes secret lessons from some cloned or virtual Nero. And Ollie watches this performance with the bemused air of a young man who'd like to replay his childhood, now that he sees what one can get away with.

By the way, I've worked out that your Thomas must be over twenty-one now. What has he turned out like?

I so hope I'm going to hear from you soon now.

My love,

Jude

Oh, Celia,

It's very, very late and I feel ghastly. But I had to write this down. Just to ground it and myself in the real. Well, the written real, in any case.

Toni rang today, rang while I was in the midst of a chat with a regular client about the Orange Prize and its merits and demerits, and why it's called Orange anyhow when it should be Femina, and would it become One-2-One or Virgin when Orange money ran out. Yes, Virgin, my client decided, would be best for a prize for women. I didn't quite grimace, since that's not how you behave with regular clients, but I was about to object when Kate said I had to come to the phone.

So I bumped and squeezed past her (Kate has suddenly grown wondrously large and taut, a veritable drum; she claims the babe is going to become a drummer, so boisterous is the inner activity now). And there at the other end of the receiver was this strangled voice I didn't at first recognize until the proverbial penny dropped with a clang. Whereupon I started to stammer.

"Where are you? Where are you?"

"Doesn't matter."

"I need to see you." (I think I may have whined, despite myself.)

"Yes, tonight. You bring money. You owe money."

"Yes. Yes. But tonight is difficult. Nell's in the midst of exams. I mustn't leave her. You . . . you come to me." A vision of Nell's face confronting Toni rose before me and I regretted my words even before they'd left my mouth.

"No. Can't. You meet me. In Hoxton Square."

"In Hoxton Square?" My voice rose. "No, no . . ."

"Yes. Must." He cut me off, then added, "Please." Whereupon I knew I'd go.

I did just manage to blurt out something about Elizabeth's keys, but he didn't seem to understand and then said something like "No have." I didn't want to press him over the phone, so I left it and arranged the meeting for ten. To give Nell enough time to ask me any questions she might need to ask, you understand, and to storm and to wail, if that was necessary after today's trial.

So at ten o'clock I'm standing in Hoxton Square in front of the Lux, as instructed. Hoxton Square, you probably don't realize, is no longer the slum of Shoreditch, but as trendy as Tracey Emin's unmade bed, and far fuller. The young, in all manifestations of cool, parade through it, making me feel distinctly conspicuous as I wait for Toni in my clanging shades of beige.

He's late and I have plenty of time to mull things over while I wait. I'm not good at waiting. After fifteen minutes, my burning desire to see him turns into restless anticipation. After twenty, my firm intention to ask him to come back, at least to the shop if not immediately to me, is rumbled by all those doubts I had about his betraying me. Illusion is only one step ahead of disillusion and then no step at all. The passionate lover I so miss is transformed into the man who's been taking advantage of an aging dupe, pilfering keys, camping out at Elizabeth's behind my back.

Since Toni's telephone call, I had, of course, put all suspicions to one side. In fact, they'd all but disintegrated in some

213

remote corner of my mind. But on Hoxton Square they're re-embodied and become more substantial than the passing young with their shining eyes. Half an hour into my wait, I'm angry — nay, furious — and I get into my car and tell myself that in five minutes I'm off, Toni or no Toni. Which is, of course, just when he slips in beside me.

He takes my hand and squeezes it, and I might as well be a pudding as a woman with some serious questions to ask. It doesn't help that he isn't looking his best. That animal sleekness has gone from his face and his eyes don't glisten. His hair has been cut punishingly short, in prison inmate's style. In fact, if I had the ability to be objective I'd say he might even have been suffering . . . as I have.

I think I already have tears in my eyes when I ask him how he's been. He shrugs, then, with no small talk (it was never, I should point out, his strong suit), asks if I've brought his wages. While I take the money out of my bag, he shifts in his seat like an impatient or unhappy man — I really don't know which. I pass the envelope to him and hear myself praying that he isn't going to open it and count the bills. I have always paid Toni in cash.

He doesn't. He stuffs it into his inside jacket pocket and then, before I have the chance to say anything at all, he grunts a thank you and is already out of the car with the door slammed behind him and is racing towards the far side of the square. I get out and call after him. To my eternal shame, he doesn't turn. Not once. And yes, now the tears have spilled over. But for a different reason. I am a terminally foolish woman.

I find myself back in the car, tailing him towards the northern side of the square. Suddenly he disappears. I suspect he's vanished up a crack of a lane where the car can't go. So I drive around the square. Then I drive around again. I don't quite know why, except that I really have little else to do other than go home and wash my wounds, which isn't easy in front of my Amazonian daughter. So going around in circles is more tempting.

Well, I don't know quite how many of these I've done when I see Toni again. He's come out of the same lane and is now heading in the opposite direction. He doesn't see me. And I don't call out. But I watch him. His gestures are, to say the least, furtive. He keeps looking over his shoulder. Now that I think of it, he looked over his shoulder once or twice while we were together in the car as well. It comes to me that Toni has needed his salary money to pay someone off. That someone can only be a dealer. Which explains why he was in such a hurry, why he had to rush off to meet him in a darkened lane. Why he didn't want me to know. I think back and try to discover whether Toni took drugs while he worked for me. Was the brightness in his eyes cocaine? Were there needle marks on his arms? Would I be able to recognize such things even if they took on the prominence of a rhinoceros in my front room — I who daily and blindly monitor Nell's state of being?

I see Toni go into the Lux. I wait. He doesn't come out again. I get tired of waiting and I leave my car on a double yellow line. I want to see who he's with. I just want to know, I tell myself. I am not a stalker.

The bar is so crowded and so noisy and so full of chrome and mirror it's hard to make out anything — except that the clientele is half my age. But then I see him. He's behind the bar. He's working. I want to rush over and kiss him. I don't. Enough foolishness is enough. Even for yours truly.

When I get back to the car, a traffic warden has just taken out his ticket pad. I beg. I plead. I weep all the tears that I haven't quite managed to weep before and he lets me off. I know he thinks I'm demented and that if he doesn't I may start hitting him with my bag or run under a passing car. And he'll have to take the pieces to hospital.

This last minor triumph is the only positive note in my day.
My love
Jude

FRIDAY

Dear Celia,
The story continues. But I really don't know what to make of it. I'm beginning to feel like a character who thought she was the heroine of a movie, only to find she's a powerless extra somewhere on the periphery of the action.

This afternoon I was at the front desk of the shop when a tall, rather rugged man walked in. He was in his forties, I'd say, dark, shiny suit, receding hairline, bulbous nose, an unremarkable face. After a moment he picked up one of the biographies which this week are on a front table. He picked it up, but he didn't really look at it. He looked at me. It was an unblinking gaze which gave the impression that he knew me, though I didn't think I'd met him before.

I put on my best "May I help you?" expression and he began to walk towards me.

"Jude Brautigan," he said. It was a statement, not a question. I wracked my brain for a memory, but the senior grip was too strong. I smiled instead and managed a noncommittal yes. He pulled something from his pocket and flashed it before my eyes. The picture told me it was an ID, but his speed certainly didn't allow me to see any print. It came to me that he must be police. I had an instant anxiety attack.

"Nell. My daughter. Is something wrong?"

"No, no. Not your daughter," he assured me. His smile never reached his eyes. "Is there somewhere we can talk privately?"

"My mother? Is my mother all right?"

"I'm sure she is. It's nothing like that. Please. Is there somewhere we can talk?"

Two customers had just arrived at the desk and I gestured to Kate, who was at the rear of the shop, and she began to make her way regally towards us. Meanwhile my mind raced. I really had no idea before this that I was such a guilty person. It must be the Scots line. I thought of unpaid parking fines, council arrears, then worse — taxes. The Inland Revenue had found a huge gap in my return. No, no. It was the VAT man. That's who he was. I had heard horror stories from friends about the descent of the VAT man. But books aren't VATable. Had I failed to declare something else?

By this time we were upstairs and I was stupidly asking the man if he'd like a cappuccino or a latte. He refused, always a bad sign. Luckily it wasn't one of Ollie's days. It had just occurred to me that the man was here because of something to do with Robert.

At last we sat down at the far table, the same one where I had sat with Robert the day he appeared on his motorbike.

I was about to mention Robert when the man began to speak.

"I believe you know a Mr. Abaz Laco."

I stare at him. "No."

"He sometimes goes by the name of Toni Cellini."

I swallow hard. "Sometimes goes by . . ."

"Yes." The man looks down at a small black notebook. "Also Gianni Melacosta."

"Gianni Melacosta," I repeat idiotically.

"Yes. As Toni Cellini, I believe, Mr. Laco worked for you. Did odd jobs."

I hesitate, only finally to mumble something like, "You could say that."

"So he did or he didn't work for you?"

I nod.

"Does he still?"

I shake my head, and the words tumble out. "What has he done? He seemed altogether honest to me." An image of Toni bolting out of Elizabeth's window and scrambling and sliding down the beech leaps into my mind, so that I can feel myself beginning to flush. It's swiftly followed by an image of him in some dark lane off Hoxton Square.

"When did he stop working for you?"

"Oh, I'd say three, four weeks ago or so."

"Why did he stop?"

"No particular reason," I mumble. "Perhaps he found something better paid."

The man whose name I didn't manage to read from his ID and who hasn't pronounced it clears his throat.

I'm suddenly angry. This is a very unequal situation. He knows about me. He knows about Toni. I know nothing about him. "What exactly is it that you want from me," I ask a little aggressively, "Mr. . . . ?"

"Carton. Michael Carton. Do you know where I can find Mr. Laco — Toni Cellini to you?"

"No, I'm afraid I don't. And I still don't know why you want to find him. What's he done?" I insist on an answer this time.

"Really, Mrs. Brautigan. That should be clear. I work for immigration, after all."

"Immigration?" The loudness of my voice startles me.

"Yes. Calm yourself, Mrs. Brautigan. As I'm sure you know, Mr. Laco is an Albanian who arrived here under the banner of an asylum-seeker and then, like so many illegal immigrants, decided to disappear."

"What are you talking about? Toni is Italian."

This Michael Carton stares at me. "You became good friends, did you?"

"I don't know what you mean."

"Mrs. Brautigan, I'm not here to make trouble for you. I know you've hired an illegal immigrant. I know you've been paying him under the table, so to speak. I'm prepared to turn a blind eye on all that. All I want to know is where Mr. Laco is. So that we can send him home, you understand."

I'm beginning to hate this man. I have the feeling that if he says much more, I may just bop him one. "I have no idea where Toni is," I state with final emphasis and get up. I see Heather coming up the stairs and I wave her over.

"Are you certain of that?"

"Of course I'm certain. I hardly keep track of casual employees once they're gone."

Carton peers at me from narrowed eyes. He doesn't believe a word I'm saying.

"You will, of course, let me know if you do happen to see him." He takes a card and puts it on the table just as Heather reaches us. "I'll be waiting for your call, Mrs. Brautigan. Expecting it. All you have to do is leave a message. I wouldn't like to have to report you to . . ."

I cut him off. "Is that a threat, Mr. Carton? Because if it is, you can just take it home with you and smoke it. I've done nothing illegal. All my part-timers are paid appropriate wages and paid in cash. Most of them aren't Brits. Have you ever run a business, Mr. Carton? Do you know anything about the paucity of potential employees these days? No, of course you don't. Now as for Toni Cellini, as far as I knew and continue to know, he comes from Italy. A country which is a member of the EU. He is perfectly entitled to work here. And the name is Ms. Brautigan." I give him my back and turn towards Heather. "You'll have a coffee, won't you?"

Immigration Cop Carton, or whatever he is, doesn't insult easily. He presses his card into my hand now. "You'll remember what I said, Ms. Brautigan. You wouldn't want to be obstructing the laws of the land."

"My friend Jude is utterly incapable of obstructing any laws," Heather interrupts. She's been listening and she has her hoity-toitiest voice on, the kind she used to use in Cambridge seminars with that don we all loathed — you remember, Christopher Pringle. She also seems to have grown a head taller, so that she meets the Carton man's shit-coloured eyes head on.

"I used to chat to Toni now and again when I came in. His Italian was fluent. We both assumed . . . As for where he might be . . . I remember we once talked about Manchester. He showed a distinct interest. Perhaps he's moved north."

Carton slowly looks from one to the other of us as if he'd like to string us on a rope and hear us scream. Finally, with a shrug, he mutters an "I'll be in touch soon" and is off.

"I need a coffee," I mumble as he disappears from view. "A double. Actually I need a double whisky, only it's too early."

Heather pats me on the shoulder, but we don't speak until we've got our coffees in hand and are outside. I bring out the cigarettes I had promised myself I would throw out by the end of today.

"Did you take all that on board?" I ask Heather.

"More or less."

"I'm gobsmacked. Can the horrible slimeball be telling the truth? Toni always said he was from Bari."

"Well, he probably spent a little time there on his travels. It's just a stretch of water away to Albania."

I study her. I can feel my face fall. "You know something."

"Oh Jude, you're such an innocent. Where have you been living all these years?"

"In North London," I mutter.

"Did you ever try and speak Italian to Toni?"

"I don't speak Italian."

"Well, it's just as well, 'cause he hardly does either."

I stare at her and then my mouth drops as if someone's just given me a ball of concrete to chew. "That's why he wanted to marry me."

Heather chuckles. "Wouldn't you want to marry you? In the circumstances? And you're not even too bad to look at."

"Thanks. You knew all along?"

"Not exactly. But I guessed. I assumed, I'm afraid, that you did, too. I was full of admiration."

"For what exactly?"

She looks at me and shrugs. Then after a minute she says, "Don't take it like that. Just think that his desire to be with you was probably greater and for better reason than any man you've been with before."

"Did you know he was squatting at a friend of mine's without our knowing?"

"Did he do any damage?"

"I guess not," I say after a moment.

"He was probably desperate. On the run. It's hard for us to understand what we might do in that situation. He had probably convinced himself that you really would marry him. Because he was so useful in the café. So it didn't matter if he stayed at your friend's house."

It comes to me in a flash. "You've seen him. Seen him since he gave up the job."

She nods once. "He waited for me outside the museum. He thought I might be able to put him up. I did for a night. And then I put him onto a lawyer. He can't keep running."

"You think he won't go home?"

"I think he doesn't quite know what home is. In fact, he's a Kosovar and his parents sent him to some distant relatives in Albania when he was in his early teens. That didn't work out too happily, from what I can gather. He might have got caught up with some liberation group doing border skirmishes. I'm not sure about that, but it's clear that he couldn't go home. And then his family vanished during the war and he got on to one of those deathtrap boats bound for Italy. And now he's here. I don't know much more than that. Though I can imagine." Her face looks grim.

"Poor Toni," I breathe. In my mind's eye I see steep hills and machine guns and burnt-out houses and acrid smoke rising, while kerchiefed women holding babes file through a desolate landscape. "Poor Toni. If only he'd told me, I might have been able to help him."

"I guess he didn't know whether to trust you or not. After all, as his employer . . ."

"Of course." I think of that Carton man with his threatening voice and I want to hit out. I want to kick myself, too. How could I have been so close to Toni and known next to nothing about him? It's extraordinary that one can reach the age of just-about-fifty and be so dumb.

"How about you cut out early and let me take you for a drink. And dinner. Stop blaming yourself, Jude. That's not what it's about." Heather is so comforting, I know I must look dreadful.

"But if I'd known, I might have . . ."

"What?"

"Nothing." I'm thinking that I might have married him, but there's still Nell to put into that equation. I'm also thinking that if Toni had announced to me on day one that he could only work illegally, I might not have taken him on. I might have been too frightened.

"Come on, Jude. It's not that bad. He'll manage. He's tough. And clever."

"I think we should go and see him now, warn him."

Heather glances around us, as if the Carton man might still be there. She lowers her voice. "I don't really think that would be wise. That could be just what they're waiting for. So you know where he is?"

223

"Do you really think they'd tail me? Me? An upstanding citizen? A property owner? Winner of the Independent Bookshop of the Year Award?"

Heather raises her eyebrows and rolls her eyes so that she looks like nothing so much as a world-weary blues singer. "You better believe it, girl," she whispers. "You just better believe it."

A little while later we're sitting in my kitchen with Nell and Ollie, a vast Thai takeaway spread before us like Herod's feast (I wonder if I said that because I'm expecting Toni's head to arrive suddenly on a platter). We talk to Nell about her exams and cheer her along until she says she's due to go over to her friend Julia's for a couple of hours. It's the only night this weekend she's having off. They're going to watch a baaad video, she tells me, and veg out.

I don't know why, but I haven't blurted Toni's story to her. I haven't quite worked it out in my head. But once she's gone, I do tell Ollie just a little of it. That's because I want him to do me a favour. I want him to take a note to the Hoxton bar for me and give it to Toni. Ollie looks right for that place, and even if assiduous old Carton is hanging around outside, he's not going to follow Ollie anywhere.

Ollie is only too eager to help. Cloak and dagger, he tells me, is right up his street. The only problem is that he's never met Toni, a fact I've managed to overlook, so we'll have to describe him carefully.

I start in and Heather helps. After a few minutes, Ollie shakes his head and gives us a perplexed look. "I'm sure I'll find the guy, but apart from learning that he's got dark hair, now mostly gone, and is good-looking, you've told me nothing, ladies."

"I'll come with you," Heather says.

I'm about to protest, but she shushes me. "You head off first in your car, and if our friend is about, he'll tail you. Ollie and I will head off some fifteen minutes later in my car."

"Sounds good to me," Ollie says.

So that's what we do. I don't quite know where I'm heading because I've got my eyes glued to my rear-view mirror. There's the usual amount of traffic behind me and it's dusky now, so I can't really see properly into anyone's car. I find myself close to Francesca's house, so I decide to pop in on her. She's very low and is grateful for the visit. To stop her thinking about her own problems, I tell her about Toni (not the whole story, since I've never told her about him and me, but there's a story there about someone who's worked for me, and that one is quite ghastly enough on its own terms). Francesca promises to come around the next day in case I need her help with anything.

Later I pick up Nell from her friend's and come home. While I wait for Ollie's return (he's taking a long time), I write to you.

Oh Celia, isn't it bizarre what happens when history enters your life? I mean those big things — wars, uprisings, movements of peoples. Everything else seems so petty in comparison. We really must help Toni.

Without naming names just yet, I'm about to zap my MP with a ton of e-mails. After all, now that elections are over, they can just stop pretending to be righter than the Tories. I

225

just hope it was a pretence. And Kosovars are on some okay list for asylum, I remember. All Toni will have to do is tell them he's not really Albanian. It's all just a mad question of geography.

Fingers crossed, yours ever,
Jude

SUNDAY

Dear Celia,
I'm not sleeping. It's the middle of the night and I'm not sleeping. I haven't slept through the middle of the night, come to think of it, for weeks. Tonight (or to-morning), at least I'm doing something useful and writing to you. Usually I just lie there and get more and more depressed about life, to the point where I think well, Nell only needs me for two more years, three at the utmost, and then . . .

It's not that I don't fall asleep. I drink enough wine to avalanche into sleep at any moment after ten. I tumble into bed and probably snore or wheeze like some old barrel whose tap leaks slightly. And then *pow*, I'm awake. And miserable. Francesca says I need calcium, not to mention ginseng, omega-3 and a health food shop full of tablets to restore, beautify, condition, prevent. *Harper's*, or whatever I was browsing through at the newsagent's, said I needed calcium, too. Exhorted me to take calcium, now that my body has paused, and apparently paused most particularly on the calcium. Some doctor on Radio Four dittoed. Calcium, it seems, has become the plastic of the noughties. It's the answer to everything, including the plasticity of my brain cells. Invest in calcium. Oh yes, and gingko biloba. They keep the brain cells healthy.

Well, I took some this week, not only in pill form but today also in the form of three lattes and two bowls of ice cream, my preferred intake by far, and I'm still awake in the middle of the night and wish I could wave a little wand and turn the calcium into something a tad stronger. Or maybe I should just swallow the whole bottle. Can one OD on calcium?

Come to think of it, my mother took calcium. Maybe she still does, for all I know. It obviously didn't help her either, judging from the way our conversation went today:

"Hello." (me)

"Who are you?" (her)

"I'm your daughter."

"Who?"

"Yes, I'm your daughter, Jude."

"Jude. Oh . . . My daughter? I have a daughter? Who are you?"

Now, an expert in semantics would tell you that this is an utterly meaningless conversation, rendered even more meaningless by the gestures which accompany it. My mother clearly doesn't believe that I'm her daughter, which renders my daughterhood problematic, to say the least. Maybe daughters are not supposed to grow older than say, twenty, after which they become something else. Toadstools, from my mother's expression. There is no way, her look tells me, that this ageing bit of plush furniture which has parked itself in her line of vision can be anything called a child of hers.

So be it. One more relationship has been erased from my map. Not wife, not daughter, not lover, which leaves, for only a little while longer, mother.

"Only connect." So goes E. M. Forster's injunction, according to Nell's English notes, which we went over today. Nell has taken this to heart and is almost always connected. Forster, whom I suspect the girls imagine worked on the side for a mobile phone company, is therefore cool. Not that they're doing anything as ambitious as reading *Passage to India* and *Howard's End*, but they know of him because he's quoted in *To Kill a Mockingbird*, a novel they do read for months and months on end, as I think I already told you, presumably because its message on race is a little clearer than E. M.'s.

"Only connect." Well, I've been trying. But it's not altogether evident whom there's left to connect to. Presumably E. M. in his old days could connect to all the King's College undergraduates. (Do you remember? He was a bit of a wispy legend when we were there. I think he died the very year we went up.) As for those of us without a college . . .

Ollie tells me he's given up seeing his mother altogether. He can't bear her newest husband, who can't bear him. And his mother has made her choice clear. She wants peace with her new husband at all costs. When Ollie tells me this, he says it in a joking voice, but he looks like a small boy, smaller than I ever knew him, and somehow vulnerable. In his imagination his mother must above all be his (even if he hasn't seen her for more than a few days a year for some fifteen years).

My imagination is pretty demanding, too. It wants Nell to be completely happy (and Ollie, too, of course, but I'm not central to either his reality or his imagination), but it would also like to spend time with Toni and feel alive rather than calcium-deprived. But there is no Toni. He's vanished. When Ollie and Heather went to look for him, he wasn't at the Hoxton Square bar. Nor has he turned up since, as far as we know.

Heather tried to question some of the characters who worked there, but none of them had anything useful to convey.

Nor has that ratfink of an immigration cop been back, but I feel him looking over my shoulder. How must poor, poor Toni feel? If he asked me now, I'd say yes. Yes, straight away. But he's not here. And I'm just your old Jude, alone in the night.

J.

P.S. I read somewhere that according to the latest bit of neuro-scientific calculation, the brain is 100,000 times more powerful than the usual hard disk, which has 10 gigabytes of memory. Now that sounds like quite a lot in the abstract, but given that my hard drive announces it's running out whenever I try to download a dozen pics or so from the net, this really can't be quite enough to be getting on with. Only a hundred terabytes — that's what they call them. The human brain's total capacity is a hundred terabytes! More like terrorbites. No wonder my mum, who watched a lot of television latterly, has lost it. We should probably stick to print, which takes up less space. Do you think I can use this little fact to advertise the bookshop? Do terrorbites get used up by dreams? Help!

27 JUNE

Dear Celia,
I had lunch with Elizabeth today. We splurged and went to a newish Marco Pierre White, only cause we're both feeling a bit down. (A bit down! I feel as if I've been dragged, kicking and screaming, 40,000 leagues under the sea, and there's no Captain Nemo about to save me.)

You know the reasons for my current state, though I can't remember whether I told you that I had a second visit from slimeball Carton. I'm not sure it was a visit exactly. I caught him lurking outside the bookshop talking to one of the café's regulars and flashing a very bad mug shot of Toni. I gave him a piece of my mind, I can tell you. It landed on him like a ton of concrete. He had to slither away legless. A small crowd gathered to hear my screams.

I accused him of harassing my clientele, of persecuting innocents, of driving poor asylum-seekers to suicide. I told him that since a reading was to begin in an hour by a high-ranking QC well-known in the human rights field, he might just as well come in and explain to my public the hounding tactics he felt sanctioned to undertake in pursuit of his duties. I did go on rather. Oh well.

Not that it'll help poor Toni, of whom neither Heather nor I have heard anything.

As for Elizabeth's not altogether euphoric state, it has something to do with the way Stuart is responding to their newly re-bonded condition. She told me all about it over the glass of Chardonnay we thought we deserved, before we deserved another. Apparently Stuart is behaving like a little boy who's had his sweets taken away. He mopes about looking hard done by, subtly punished, but if asked what's wrong, claims everything's fine. As fine as it can be in London.

According to Elizabeth, he was happy enough to come back. Or so he said. But he's not behaving "happy enough."

I brashly point out to her that she has indeed taken away his candy. She gives me a sour look, but after a moment she acknowledges that I am right, even though that bit of candy, with her plunging neckline, tasted like poison to her. The trouble is, Elizabeth says, that sex was never the great thing between her and Stuart. They had hardly got together in their first youth, after all. And now Stuart was pretending it was something he missed. NOW!

Over the bass fillet, she confessed that, much as she was fond of him, she found it pretty hard work having him around all the time. He never stopped gardening, and on top of it all he'd taken up golf, so that she saw him from her study window all day long, rain or shine, pottering and potting or taking aim with his clubs. It was deeply distracting. She wished he'd take up committees instead. He'd be good at them and he's the right sort of age.

"So he's altogether given up the idea of divorce?" I ask.

Elizabeth scowls at me. "Of course. What do you think I was doing down in Carcassonne?"

"Maybe he misses the house down there and the south as well as . . . as . . ."

"His candy," she finishes for me. 'I don't doubt it. But I don't trust him there alone and I can't be there all the time."

"Funny," I say, probably because the wine I shouldn't have had has gone straight to my head and is battling with the calcium, or some weaker substance, "but you were perfectly happy until you knew. I mean, until he actually mentioned the divorce. Knowledge is a ghastly thing. Is it possible to un-know, do you think?"

"What are you trying to say, Jude? Be clear."

"I'm not sure. Maybe you could compromise. Not be too exacting. We're all getting on. There isn't that much time left. You know, the compromise of an old-fashioned marriage which is big enough for an old-fashioned mistress, the nine-teenth-century kind who never seemed to demand more than mistressing."

"We're in the twenty-first century."

"I know," I moan. "Maybe it's all too modern for me. Maybe for Stuart, too."

"So now you're advocating hypocrisy. Well, it's a Victorian value, I guess." Elizabeth doesn't approve of my musings and changes the subject. Something in the conversation reminds me of one with Francesca, where she too was harking back to an older and unsentimental idea of marriage, but that didn't work either. I tune back in to Elizabeth.

"Oh, I forgot to tell you. Stuart's obsession with the garden has accomplished one thing. He's found the keys. The keys our squatter must have used."

I choke on my polenta, which is too dry in any case.

"Did Nell ever say anything about it?" Elizabeth asks innocently. "Oh, I know she'll tell me eventually, after her exams."

"No, she won't," I say, too loudly.

"Why not?" Elizabeth looks hurt.

"It was my squatter, not hers."

Elizabeth's face moves from incomprehension to distaste to worry, and back again.

So I tell her the whole sorry tale, complete with the hideous Carton. As I speak, I realize that the little boy who opened the door at Toni's former address must, like his family, be from Albania or Kosovo, too — though perhaps they are here more legally than Toni; otherwise he would probably not have given out their address.

To do Elizabeth credit, she comes up trumps. "Oh, if only I'd known," she moans. "If only you'd said, or he'd said. Of course we would have put him up. There's plenty of room. He could have stayed there the whole time we were away. Oh, what a shame. I suppose he can't possibly come back now. He must know they're on his tail."

I think of my last meeting with Toni and I nod slowly. I have this deep and terrible knowledge that I'll never see him again.

My love,
Jude

1 JULY

(Already. Where does time go these days? I'm awake more than ever and still the hours hurtle past as if they were driving piggyback on a Harley-Davidson and making straight for you know where.)

Dear Celia,
You've probably already guessed where my imagery comes from. Robert was around this morning. Again. Nell's last exam is tomorrow. And he stayed for lunch.

To tell you the truth, if I were Emma I'd be just a tad concerned about his constant need to be with his daughter. It wasn't always thus. Emma really should start checking on the clingability of her tops, the sweetness of her breath . . . maybe even have a little review of the subjects she can use words about. "Black is this year's black" may not be quite good enough. Followed by an update of the goings on in *Big Brother*, it might actually send old Robert into a reverie we would have called sleep in the old days.

Sorry, sorry, just a little passing bout of spite. My own subjects of conversation these days leave something to be desired. In fact, I've got rather good on *Big Brother*, not to mention its Robinson Crusoe kin *Survivor* and the latest soaps, though I'm still a little stumped about what the big difference is between reality TV and ordinary soaps or game shows. They all seem to be about popularity in one way or another, or the uncelebrateds' version of celebrity. I guess the reality shows give an impression of unfolding in real time 'cause they have fewer cuts. The yawn quotient is therefore far, far higher. But then there's probably some deep biological link between boredom, repetition and the thrills of voyeurism. Just think of porn. (You assume I know nothing at all about porn, Celia, but you're only partly right. I have spent many nights in hotel rooms in various countries, and all hotel rooms have porn channels. One doesn't want to be ignorant about such a major industry.)

I'm rambling again. The other deep similarity between the realities and the soaps is that both help the rump grow. Luckily we don't have any scales in the house. Didn't want Nell weighing herself every day and becoming anorexic, so I chucked them when we moved in here. But I am going to have to take myself in hand. And soon. My will, however, these days matches the calcium-deficient jelly which comprises the rest of me.

Whoops. Another clang of self-pity.

What I really wanted to say was that Robert had a second reason for coming around. A letter had arrived for Ollie. The letter, says Robert, who knows about these things, bears the logo of one of New York's top headhunting agencies. Robert is desperate to see what's inside (if he'd still been with me, he would probably have asked me to steam it open) and he instructs Ollie, who toys with it, to open it straight away.

"I think I'll take it upstairs, Dad."

"Don't make your father wait too long," I intervene. "That would be cruel."

Ollie, who hasn't been in a good mood so far today, suddenly grins. "Gee, gosh, ma'am," he parodies. "I believe Sir can deal with just a little cruelty."

So Robert and I watch Ollie lope upstairs. Then I make more coffee while he quizzes Nell on her Spanish.

Have I mentioned yet that I think Ollie is sweet on Francesca, and vice versa? Actually, I don't "think" — I know. Francesca has told me. I haven't said this to either of them, but secretly I don't approve. And it really isn't because Toni is no longer on the scene. It's just that Ollie is so young and somehow so innocent, whereas Francesca is, well, my friend. I'm being ageist, obviously. But somehow I feel that if they really get involved, they'll both suffer.

There I go again. Ridiculous. Are there any relations that don't entail suffering at some point down the line? Not in my experience. Not even when we were children. So how can I rationalize this disapproval to myself? I've got it. It's a question of at what *point* down the line. With Ollie and Francesca, I suspect it'll be sooner rather than later. Or maybe I'm just being a maternal prude. (Funny thing is, I'm certain Nell, who has a nose for these things which is as acute as that of a mouse for cheese, doesn't approve either. She was unusually rude to Francesca when she came around the other day, and I know she's sniffed out something. I just hope it won't provide a reason for her making a dash for Damian the minute exams are over.)

Ollie doesn't appear again until I call him down for lunch. I'm not sure what this act of rebellion against his father has to do with. Maybe Robert gave him one too many lectures about picking himself up by the bootstraps and returning into the fray. But both of them are visibly twitchy. Ollie whistles from time to time and stares at the table. Meanwhile Robert keeps giving me looks I can't decipher, but he debones the salmon I've cooked with his customary skill and he arranges each plate with an aesthete's consideration, the basil mayonnaise providing a finishing touch of pale green.

"You're looking tired," he says to me. "You need a break."

He says it kindly enough, but I take it as a criticism. "Do I?"

"Yes, you do," Ollie chips in. "You're working too hard. And you're always cooking for us and taking care of your friends. Not to mention my madly demanding kid sister."

"Yes, you are looking tired, Mum," Nell echoes, grinning as Ollie ruffles her hair. "You'd think you'd been the one doing the GCSEs."

"Why don't you have a week off? I'll lend you the studio in Paris, if you like."

"What studio in Paris?"

"Hasn't Nell told you? Well, it's true, we haven't had it very long. It really only became habitable last summer. Emma's idea. Though we haven't had time to use it much. It's small. But it's central. Do you good. It's yours if you fancy it." Robert's smile is gracious, yet contains a perplexing hint of mischief.

"I can't leave the shop."

"Sure you can," Ollie chips in again. "I'll look after things. With Kate. She knows everything. And you should go now, before she's off on maternity leave."

I look from one to the other of them. They've ganged up on me. Apparently for my own good. I must look even worse than I feel. Now there's a consoling thought.

Nell throws in for good measure, "After Tuesday, when exams are over, I can come in and help, too. We'll manage just fine."

"I'll think about it," I say.

Then Robert starts reminding me how much I adore Paris, so that, by the time dessert arrives, I've succumbed, though still insist that I have to sort out possible dates. (Oh, if only you'd write, Celia, this would be perfect. We could meet up in Paris.)

As if my decision to go to Paris, at least in principle, is a cue, Ollie, with a magician's flourish, now hands the disputed letter to his father.

"What's in it?" Nell asks.

"I'm being asked to come for an interview. In New York, of all places. This big company wants me to manage three smaller ones they've bought up and intend to merge."

Robert lets out a low whistle. "Good salary. You'd be catching up to the old man in no time."

Ollie chews his salmon slowly and swallows. "I'm not going."

"You're not going? But it's a brilliant offer."

"I can't go," says Ollie. "I have to stay here and help out with the bookshop while Jude's away in Paris. And then when Kate goes on maternity leave, too, if Jude will have me."

I choke on a salmon bone, though I don't think there's actually one there.

"You don't *have* to help me out with anything." I take the letter from Robert and read it through.

"They want you to come for the interview next week."

"That's right."

"I won't be ready to go to Paris by next week. I have to sort things first."

"I don't want to go any week." Ollie is definitive. "It's not a firm I'm interested in. And I'm happy here."

"Ollie." Robert glares at him from icy eyes, yet his voice is low, melodious. "A little over a month ago — or was it two? — you were in a terrible state. You said to me you might never earn a penny again. You were unemployable. Now you get this offer out of the blue, a miracle of an offer, and you won't even consider it. That doesn't seem reasonable to me."

"I was exaggerating. I am employable."

"Ollie." I hand the letter back to him. "I think even if you don't want this job, you should go for the interview. These headhunters, if they're as high-powered as Robert says, probably have other things on offer, if not now, soon. More than likely they work with the British, too, and the Europeans, the whole lot. It's a global market, as everybody keeps repeating."

"Now you're all ganging up on me."

"But Mum's right," Nell throws in her penny's worth. She meets my eyes and I have a strange sense that she's thinking about Francesca. She'd rather have Ollie in the States than have him here with Francesca. "And maybe I could come to New York with you, Ollie. To keep you company. As a treat after my exams. That would be so random." She looks up at Robert for confirmation.

"Of course you can. A treat's in order. Particularly if Ollie thinks it's a good idea to have his little sister along."

"Hey. Slow down, you lot. I haven't decided I'm going yet."

"Oh please, Ollie. It would be great."

"Well, think about it until tomorrow. And when you're there," Robert chuckles, "tell them you can't start any job just yet because you're sorting out a small chain of bookshops in London and their Web site."

"Small chain of bookshops?" I look at Robert, aghast.

"Well, it might become one, mightn't it?"

"Not if I'm as tired as you all say," I grumble.

"You won't be after you've been to Paris," Robert promises, his dimple twitching so fetchingly that, for a moment, I'd like to invite him to come along.

"Okay. It's a deal. I'll go to Paris if Ollie goes to New York. In fact, I'll leave as soon as he's back."

"As soon as we're both back," Nell adds. "You'd better get that note ready for my teacher."

And so decisions are made in this strange little unit of ours, which is and isn't what the politicians might call a family.

Yours — in anticipation,
Jude

PART FOUR

Celia is coming closer. I know it. I can feel it. And now that she comes close, I'm just a little afraid. Why do I really want to see her after all this time? Do I need to know that she's forgiven me? And if she hasn't . . . Or is it simply that I feel I need all the friends I can find at this stage of my life — as if we had to huddle together and shelter against the great beyond.

To be honest, I've always been a little afraid of Celia. She knows how to be hard. Before that summer break when we were at school together, she never told me she wasn't coming back. I found out inadvertently from my mother. One August morning she caught me at a loose end and said wasn't it time I stopped moping about and took up with some of my old friends again, now that Celia had left?

Celia had chosen to tell her she was leaving for good, but not me. I couldn't understand why. I suffered. I had expected her to return. I suffered doubly because, in order to cement my friendship with Celia, I had abandoned older friends. Celia demanded exclusivity.

The girls were cold to me, huffy. They said I was weird now, contaminated by the gypsy with the strange eyes. They asked me where Celia had been taken. I couldn't tell them. They asked me to read them her letters. But apart from the one card, Celia never wrote. I fabricated letters from her and read them out in a choked voice. I invented escapades for my lost sister. I declared over and over again that she missed me.

Maybe it was Celia's ability to make me suffer that made her so important to me, truly turned her into the sister I had only a ghost of. Maybe only children need to invent the cruelty of siblings so as to get by in the world later.

When we met up again at university, I asked Celia why she hadn't forewarned me of her departure, had only written that once. She looked at me innocently, her eyes as round as an animal's transfixed by the headlights of an oncoming car. "It never occurred to me," she said. "I had so much on my plate once I reached my parents'."

I let the lame excuse pass. Now that Celia was there again, the past didn't matter. The joy was to be carried into her electrically charged sphere, where everything took on greater significance, whatever the cost. Celia breathed an air that was somehow denser than for the rest of us mundane souls.

While we talked about it, I really did believe that an overwhelming destiny had propelled her into Patrick's arms. It was only later that I understood I might be one of the components of *that destiny. Each of us acted on the other like a force field. Yes, sisters. Envy, in our case, wasn't a one-way business.*

Then, too, I urged myself on to give Celia things to envy me for. Celia transformed a timorous soul into an adventurer. That's probably why I started writing to her and carried on throughout these last months. Celia allowed me to re-enter the world of desire I thought I'd left behind. She gave me Toni — whether for better or worse.

I remember now that it was also Celia who gave me a taste for humour. Making Celia laugh was a consummate pleasure. It was as if I was repairing some deep, impenetrable hurt she had once mysteriously suffered. I'd like her to come back and laugh with me again.

3 JULY

Dear, dear Celia,
Only connect! YES.

I can hardly believe it. I've had a letter at last. Not from you exactly, and probably not from your very favourite person anymore, but at least I've had a reply and I know where you are. More or less. And there's time, Celia, there's just about time to plan that fiftieth birthday reunion . . .

Jim wrote to me. It's Jim who lives at that San Francisco address I've been sending letters to most recently and he suddenly clocked that the letters he'd been stacking up with the "J. B." and a London address on the back were from me. Maybe he secretly opened one. In any case, he's told me. He's told me that for the last year you've been living and teaching in Ghent.

Ghent! Why, it's just a stone's throw away. You should have got in touch, Celia. Or maybe you haven't bothered coming to London. You never did like this place much. Never really lived here, did you, except for those six months or so just after Cambridge, when we shared a place. You preferred Paris. And now, after the great North American trajectory, you're in Ghent.

Jim didn't say whether it was a man who'd brought you there or the temptation of setting up your own university department. He did tell me you'd divorced some three years ago and had lived apart a little before that. He pointed out it was a perfectly friendly split. What he said, in fact, was that you'd both realized for quite a while that you'd been together long enough, and you finally did something about it.

He also mentioned a big book of yours that came out some four years ago. About nuns, he said, nuns in European and American literature. I don't know how I missed it — except that I don't really keep up with American academic publishing, and it sounds as if it appeared just when I was in the midst of the turmoil with Robert. Nor did I know that you'd done a late-ish PhD in Minneapolis. You always were fiercely clever.

Jim said he'd forwarded all my letters to you, but he didn't know whether you'd get them immediately, since he thought you were probably still travelling. He knew this from your son, Thomas, who's now doing a law degree at Berkeley. Extraordinary. In the last picture you sent of him, atop a Christmas card, he looked like nothing so much as a plump putto in a Renaissance painting.

Anyhow, Jim said he thought you'd joined some archaeological dig in southern Turkey as soon as your term finished, or maybe even before. He was very sweet, Celia, quite in awe of you, as he always was. I can't imagine Robert being quite so respectful about me.

He also kindly invited me to come and stay anytime I fancied the West Coast. I suspect he might have opened one or two of my letters and was feeling sorry for me. But maybe I'll just take him up on it in any case. Things are so ghastly here. Would you mind?

I know I've kept silent about it, Celia, but all this time I've been writing to you I've been wondering about it. Wondering whether the real reason I've heard nothing from you is that you haven't yet altogether forgiven me my little escapade with Jim. I'm so relieved to know it isn't that. And yes, I do acknowledge, with the distance of hindsight, that it was one of the sillier, less pardonable things I've done. But we were still in the seventies then. And very drunk. And it was only one weekend. And you were off god-only-knows-where and Jim was feeling a little sorry for himself. I think I was probably paying you back for Patrick, too. Not that it was clear to me at the time.

The relations aren't exactly parallel, I know, since Jim was husband material and Patrick was only that in my wildest fantasies. But emotionally there was a resonance, which is probably why I did it. And it really was my doing, not Jim's, as I'm sure he must have told you.

In retrospect I realize, of course, that it was all about you and me, not Jim at all. I don't think I intended to hurt you in any way. Not really. It felt like a settling of accounts with *myself*, in the first instance. Then Jim went and said something which made you suspicious, so I confessed. I guess I really did want you to know how betrayal felt. But most of all, I think I wanted you to notice that I was still there. I didn't want Jim to take you away from me altogether.

It wasn't, I agree, the wisest way to make my presence a loveable one.

You didn't seem to take it too badly, Celia. You were miffed, of course, and astonished. And you went icy cold for a bit. But you shrugged it off after I insisted over and over that it was just a passing aberration and meant nothing significant either to Jim or to me. You must have understood that it could hardly be counted as a serious event; you did marry Jim pretty speedily afterwards. And you couldn't have been catapulted into marriage only because I'd slept with him. The legacy of passing girlhood rivalries doesn't stretch that far, surely?

All water under the bridge now, in any case. All so long ago. Though, writing these letters, I've started to feel newly guilty. I know our friendship cooled after that. I always preferred to think of the cooling as circumstantial. You and Jim got married quietly in Paris. You had a brief stay in London a little while after. We all met up for dinner a couple of times, do you remember? It was early in my life with Robert. And then you went off to Canada. Our correspondence continued, too. For a while. I was all excited when you announced Thomas's arrival. I still remember the blue dolphin mobile I picked out to send him.

Oh, Celia! Now that I know for certain where you are, I'm going to wait to hear from you before sending off any more instalments in the ongoing saga of my diminished life. I suddenly feel shy. And I may be the very last person you want to connect with once you've read my mad letters.
Yours,
J.

Dear Celia,
Wanted you to know — just in case you're back in Ghent and feel like a trip to Paris . . . It's all arranged. I shall be there from Sunday the 8th for about a week. I'll be staying at 35, rue de Lille in the VIth. Fifth floor. Door code 039 4B. Tel. 01 46339375. Still hope we can catch up with each other for the Big 5-0.
Much love,
Jude

PARIS, 20 JULY

Dearest Celia,
Yes, I'm still in Paris and, yes, I spent my fiftieth here. And no, I haven't started dictating my letters to a spider. That's just the way handwriting begins to look when you're propped on cushions on the floor and have painkiller rather than blood in your veins, not to mention a certain whooshiness in the area of those so-sadly-depleted brain cells. In fact, I think I can hear my billions of dendrites dancing a Zimmer samba to the sound of the sea, though I'm a little far above sea level here.

No, Celia, I'm not drunk. It's just that I've taken something of a "turn" — I think that's the way my mother would have put it in the days that she put things one way or another. The turn was wholly unexpected, as turns often are, and it's left me something of a basket case — though the basket, which is Robert's studio flat, is a nice one. In fact, if I edge my eyes just a little above this sheet of paper I can see a stretch of pale beech flooring, the patterns of an Afghan rug or two and the legs of what I noted when I first arrived was an attractive rectangular table.

I don't like lifting my eyes too high, since it generally means I lift my head as well and, who knows, perhaps even my shoulders, all of which engenders a start of pain (happily distanced by drugs, but nonetheless OH-SO-ACUTELY there) in my back and my left leg — which are the source of my current misery and mean I can't water the cactus (chosen by Emma for its frugal aquatic needs) in its giant terracotta pot, nor the window boxes with their rampant geraniums. Nor can I stand at the window terraces and gaze out on distant steeple and roofs, as dazzling as mirrors in the sunlight, and the delicious little oasis of a courtyard with its verdant green. Nor can I sit on the plush cerise sofa, with its lovely sink-into cushions which would envelop me like steel prongs so that I could never get out again. Nor can I climb the ten stairs which lead to the mezzanine, with its bed and skylight.

But, but . . . I can now shuffle to the loo without crawling on all fours, which has got to be a blessing. No, I'm not going mad, Celia, though I have thought I might be at various points in this last week. It's a very good thing you never came to join me here, because I would undoubtedly have ruined your fiftieth, too. And now I'm writing because it's one of the very few things I can actually do, apart from listening to Emma's collection of music, which is not altogether stacked with my favourites.

Here's what happened. I left London as planned a week ago Sunday, just overlapping with a tired but ecstatic Nell and an

Ollie whose spirits had indeed been boosted by the New York headhunting experience. (He didn't take the job, but did give the excuse Robert had suggested and they said they'd be in touch again soon.) Everything was in order in the bookshop with the ever-brilliant Kate in charge. I confess I was very glad to board the Eurostar — no need to daily confront Toni's absence from his position behind the counter; no need to be solicitous of clients; no need to talk to wholesalers or accountants or indeed anyone, if I didn't feel like it. Freedom — plus the knowledge that Nell was safe with her responsible older brother. What more could a woman ask? — despite the fact that she's always asking for more.

And then, there I was in Paris. I'd forgotten what a glorious city it is. Oh, it's not that I'd forgotten the sights or the cafés or the streets, but in the mind's eye it's never quite as exhilarating as it actually is. There's never that slight edge of danger, the rifling gaze of a passerby, the reckless hoot of a motorist. Nor are the colours and the smells ever as intense. Anyhow, I had a wonderful time just walking and walking, reacquainting myself with the streets, the quais and the lanes, visiting the Tuileries and the Cimetière Montparnasse, lazing over the breakfast café au lait while pretending to read *Libé*, strolling through the Beaubourg and the Musée d'Orsay. And shopping. Yes. But there's no need to recount all this. You know it all far better than I do.

What was interesting was that I got used to being alone — I mean eating in restaurants alone, sitting in cafés. I rarely do that in London and I've always rather feared it. But it's not so hard in Paris . . . By the second time you go into a café or the baker's or visit the fruit or cheese stall in the market, everyone greets you and asks how you are as if you were a long-lost friend. It quite satisfies one's need for human contact. I can even imagine that if you actually lived here, some friendly shopkeeper would notice when ageing and decrepit Ms. Brautigan failed to turn up two days in a row and would send someone around to investigate before her body putrefied.

Whoops. Sorry. What I was saying was that I was having a great time. I was even building myself up to phoning some distant acquaintances. I thought I might arrange to see somebody on my birthday. I didn't feel this was essential, but in preparation I carted some extra wine bottles up to Robert's place. It's on the fifth floor and there's no lift. The trek isn't quite Himalayan, but if you're as wondrously unfit as I am, it can be a Herculean achievement to reach the door with all packages intact and your breathing not quite loud enough to disturb the neighbours or make the walls tremble. Amazing, really, that they've held up four times longer than I have already.

Anyhow, on the morning of my birthday, after Nell sweetly rang to wish me a happy one and the sun was still shining, I coughed. Not a ferocious cough. Not even a heaving smoker's cough or a bronchial hack. Just a rather ladylike dry cough, probably brought on by fifty years of swallowing, so that the muscle had got a little tired and decided to fight back over that crumb of baguette.

Well, in the wake of this little ladylike cough, a savage pain the like of which I have never, never, never experienced — not even in the ardours of unladylike labour, which brought altogether un-Home-Counties-like screams to my throat — cuts through me, pierces my back and legs, so that suddenly I'm writhing on the floor like some serpent who's been slashed in two but whose nervous system is still heinously sensitive and all too wonderfully intact. I scream. I cry. I shout. And I scream again. I don't know for how long, except that I'm certain I'm about to pass out from the agony of it and then die. In fact I want to die. All I want to do is die, so that the pain will stop.

I don't die, 'cause the pain is still there and still as intense, and I realize I have to do something. Ring an ambulance. Ring the police. The minor hitch is that I can't move. Every motion engenders a screech of agony. I can't get up. I'm flat on the floor on my butt and the telephone is a desert away in some unreachable oasis. A panic of helplessness overcomes me. Like an idiot, I whimper into the void, "Help me. *Sauvez-moi.*"

Then, since amongst my father's many useless proverbs there was that sterling "God helps those who help themselves," I start to inch my way across the floor. I push and prod myself along, still on my back, my useless, agonizing back which has decided to give up on me. I feel like some ancient upended turtle catapulted onto land and into helplessness by an angry sea. Or a beetle. Or a worm. No. I have arms, sort of. A worm with arms.

I don't know how long it takes me to wriggle across the room, but by the time I reach the telephone, I'm sobbing so hard I can't quite remember why I've got there. Nor can I reach the phone. It's on the table, high, high above the world of upside-down turtles and beetles.

I pull on the wire and the whole thing comes toppling down. Slowly, agonizingly, I reach for the parts, and at last I have a receiver to my ear making a buzzing tone. Only problem is, I haven't got a clue about how one calls the operator or emergency or anything useful. I try 999 and nothing happens. I try 100. Nothing. Ha. They tell us Europe is federalized, that individual cultures are melting into a global soup spawned by the marriage of MacDonald's and Hollywood. Well, I want everyone to know that, useful as this little bit of globalization would be, emergency telephone numbers are not standardized.

I try various permutations on three digits and get nowhere. I now know for certain I'm going to die alone and in paroxysms on my fiftieth birthday. You'll read my obit in some briefly noted column. My poor Nell will have to go and live with Robert and Emma. My wonderful bookshop will be sold off to some uncaring chain that will auction off prime space to the highest-paying publisher.

I haven't even left any plans for my funeral. No matter. Hardly anyone would come. Luckily I told my mother's carers I was going away and left them Ollie's name.

At last, whether by design or accident, I realize I've pressed the memory button on the phone, followed by a one. Isn't memory miraculous, even in objects? I now rue my fulminations against the way our technologies of memory (telephones, computers, psions, etc. etc. etc.) have meant that we rid ourselves of our own. I'm grateful to the telephone's memory. I thank it as I listen to the bleeps and buzz. And when I hear a voice saying "hello" in what sounds like it might even be English, I would kowtow to it, if I could. But then I'm already flat on the floor.

"Hello," says the voice again.

"Hello," I sob. "Hello. This is Jude Brautigan. I'm in Paris and I can't move. Can you help me?"

"Jude," the voice says. "Jude? What's the matter?"

I recognize Robert and I know I'm hallucinating, though I don't know quite why I should hallucinate him at this juncture, except that it is his rotten flat that I'm about to die in.

"Jude, are you drunk?"

I splutter a no which comes out as a wince and a moan. This is no time for repartee. You can't stand up for yourself when you can't stand. I stop wondering why Robert should be at the other end of the phone and try to say something coherent between howls of agony. Like how the hell does one get an ambulance?

Robert's voice now seems to come from a great distance. It's muffled by the Channel. Or maybe it's that the phone has slipped from my ear. But I hear him say something calming. I'm not to worry about anything. He'll organize help. He'll try and reach the concierge, friends. Someone. Meanwhile I'm to lie very still and take deep breaths. Very still and take deep breaths.

I'm already taking them when I hear him shout, "Jude, Jude. Put the receiver back."

I think I do as I'm told. I'm trying to lie so still that no breath will rattle any of my vertebrae, let alone any bit of me from the waist down, where the pain blazes away as fierce as a forest fire consuming parched needles of pine. Obviously the calcium hasn't worked, I think amidst it all. Obviously everything has grown as brittle as a cheese cracker. One little cough and the entire structure crumbles.

I don't know how long I lie there or whether I've passed out, but suddenly I hear a buzzing sound which isn't coming from inside my brain. The doorbell, I tell some bit of me I hope is listening, the bit that usually propels my legs. But my legs aren't functioning. I can still only inch along on my back. I scream something which I hope sounds like "wait." The only response is a second buzz, then a third. By the time I reach a door which has moved further away than Timbuktu, everything has grown quiet. As silent and echoing as an abandoned chapel in remote countryside.

No matter, I tell myself. I couldn't have reached the door handle in any case, let alone the lock. Both float above me as inaccessible as the top floor of a Hong Kong banking tower. I clench my teeth, an action which sends judders along my spine, and stretch upwards. I know just how Tantalus felt in his circle of Hell, condemned never to be able to reach the object of his burning desire though the fire licked at his nether parts. I force myself onto my knees and try to reach up from this new excruciating position. I'm a dog whose front paws haven't been made to grip. I imagine firemen in luminous yellow taking an axe to the door. I imagine Robert's look of dismay. And then I'm there. I've reached the lock. I twist it and fall back, but my hand is already on the latch and I give that a pull before collapsing back on the floor.

The door is open. But there's no one behind it. I lie there yelping. Then I hear footsteps on the stairs.

Moments later the concierge is standing above me. She's a tiny woman. But now she looms like Goliath, her dark head clutched in her hands. "*Ah, Madame, pauvre Madame,*" she moans in her Portuguese-accented French. She says something I don't grasp, but I see that she's dangling keys in front of her, which must be the keys to Robert's place. I needn't have moved. I want to laugh. Laugh at myself. Laugh in relief.

Because someone has come. Because I'm not alone. I won't die in agony alone.

Soon a second person arrives to diminish my solitude further. This person wears a brown suit, is neat and quick in his movements and carries a capacious black bag. The kind doctors used to have in my childhood. My eyes fix on that black bag as if it were Lourdes, and Bernadette herself were in attendance.

"SOS Médecins," the small suited man announces. He asks me what the problem is.

"SOS. Yes! I can't move," I tell him.

"*Anglaise*," he replies. "I speak a little English."

He listens to me babble something, takes my pulse, runs his hand along my spine and then reaches into his bag, which I see is replete with bottles and packets and gleaming implements. He's saying something I can't quite make out. It sounds like sciatic nerve, but I'm not up to asking questions. And then he winches me onto my side and, a moment later, I have a glimmering sensation of a needle travelling into my buttock.

"You lie on floor. Don't move," he says, as if he thought I was about to attempt some parachuting expedition.

"The pain," I mumble.

"The pain gets better with injection. I send nurse. Twice a day."

"How long before . . . before I can move?"

He gives me the benefit of a full Gallic shrug.

"But I will move?"

"Oh yes. Slowly. A week. Two . . . four. When you are a little better, you go to specialist."

"That long . . ." I'm already protesting. Even though I'm relieved. So relieved.

257

"You rest. No move. No get excited." He suddenly grins. "No stairs."

The man is a fantasist! I try to take in what he's now saying to Madame the concierge. She's already begun to move. Lucky woman. She's taking cushions from the sofa and the bed, pulling the rug towards the wall, bringing down the duvet.

It seems I'm to live on the floor.

At least I'm indoors, I tell myself. Not homeless, just legless.
Yours,
Jude

LATER

Dear Celia,
That same evening, Robert arrived with the nurse.

At first I thought I was dreaming. Reality is such a strange place when you're in pain and floating on top of it. Then, too, I'd been moving seamlessly in and out of sleep for hours. (I suspect that legit drugs these days may be weirder and more potent than any of the hallucinogenics that made the rounds in our youth.)

Anyhow, I opened my eyes and saw this stunningly pretty woman, dark, sylphlike, with those full, naturally red lips that only the French seem to have. Behind her, I saw Robert. So, needless to say, I thought "that two-timing bastard," though it wasn't quite clear to me whom exactly he was two-timing. Then, from beneath or beside this bewitching little cape-like jacket, the woman brought out a hypodermic, and in a flash it made straight for my butt while she smiled and uttered a polite "*Bonsoir, Madame.*" All the while Robert stared out the window and babbled something about my needing looking after and him feeling responsible, and those blasted stairs and backs and their fragility and poor Jude, and how fortuitously he'd met Mlle. Derain ringing the concierge's bell and how they'd all soon get me shipshape.

The arrival felt like a miracle. I think I only then realized how frightened I'd been and how, now that Robert was here, I felt safe, despite the pain and the paralyzed immobility. Maybe all those years of living together count for something after all.

When Robert rushed off, I didn't allow myself to protest, though I wanted to. I was terrified of being alone.

He came back carrying a huge bouquet, champagne and a Vietnamese takeaway. He wished me happy birthday. I hope I managed to smile graciously before the tears spilled over.

Later still, when I floated out of sleep, I heard the sound of snoring above me. I listened for a moment and recognized the snores as his. He was asleep upstairs on the mezzanine. When we lived together, his snoring would wake me into a murderous rage. Now I found the sound and the rhythms of his breathing reassuring. Breathing is, isn't it? You have to be alive to hear it, as well as do it.

I found myself thinking about all those years ago when Robert had his op, when breathing was a precarious business for him. It occurred to me that, in part, he was here with me because he felt he had a debt to pay. He might have left me because of the burden of that debt. And now, well, now we'd be quits. One has odd thoughts in the middle of the night.

I'm telling you all this now as if I remember it clearly. But I don't. I certainly don't know when I had which thoughts. I spent so much time in a slumberous state. At one point I remember thinking about Patrick, but he'd turned into this big fluffy cloud or Cheshire cat or something and he was grinning unstoppably as he tried to seduce me into joining him. Another time I think I said to Robert that he'd got so thin it was worrying, and he grinned, too. But maybe it's just that everything looks strange from this angle on the floor. I don't know how toddlers make it through. No wonder they're impatient about getting bigger.

At various points in the week I thought about Toni. I wondered whether this sudden collapse of my back and that splodgy cartilage they call discs and the billions of nerves round them, which is where the pain flames from, was my punishment. A double or triple punishment. Punishment 'cause I was really too old for the kinds of exercise I was asking my body to take. Punishment for deluding myself and thinking that a youth like Toni could see anything in me but advantage. Punishment for the secondary delusion of not allowing myself to confront that and drowning my humiliation in nice liberal compassion for Toni's plight. Now my back was torching the truth into me. Toni never wanted me for myself, only for the legitimating documents I might provide. And quite rightly, too, from his point of view.

Sorry about the note of self-pity. It keeps catching me unawares. And it's a ridiculous puritan habit to look on illness as a form of punishment. Toni no more wanted me for myself than I wanted him for himself. After all, I didn't even know his name, let alone all the rest. Strange to think, too, that if he had been able to tell me the truth, not at the moment I took him on in the bookshop, but once he had proved himself, I would probably have been prepared to help him more than I was because he was my lover. What perverse creatures we are.

But I was going to tell you that, on the Saturday after my back took me over and I was metamorphosed into a cockroach and Robert arrived like Sir Galahad, I had another surprise. Nell suddenly appeared in the apartment. She had travelled by Eurostar alone and was glowing with a sense of accomplishment as she strode in ahead of Robert and all but threw herself down on the floor beside me.

"Mum, you poor thing." Nell hugs me awkwardly. Her hair is gleaming and smells of warm almonds.

"She insisted," Robert says, evidently proud of his daughter, yet not sure how I will take this surprise arrival.

"I've come to help. And look, I've brought you these. Dad said you'd be getting bored." From her rucksack, like some Santa's helper, she pulls out a pile of my favourite CDs, followed by a small heap of books. "They've just come in."

"You're an angel." I hold back my tears. The ducts are in overdrive these days.

"And you're not to worry. Ollie and Kate both say you're not to worry. Everything is absolutely fine at the shop. Everything."

"I'm glad to hear it."

Nell examines me, her look that of an anxious eight-year-old who's trying to behave like a grown-up, even though she's lost in the department store and wants to cry. "You will be able to walk, won't you, Mum, like before?"

"Of course she will," Robert answers for me. "It's an incredibly painful business, but there shouldn't be any lasting damage."

Nell waits for my reassurance, which I give. After which she behaves as if it isn't at all peculiar for me to be lying in a heap on the floor while she's the one who fetches and carries. Maybe it takes only a little tilt of the see-saw, a little passing incapacity on the parental side to bring out the best in otherwise overweeningly self-interested teenagers. It would have to be passing, though . . .

Robert leaves us that evening to stay in a local hotel while Nell occupies the bed on the mezzanine. But she doesn't actually go to bed until late. She stays with me. From the window we still see the occasional spread of a firework and hear the bangs of the fourteenth of July celebrations. Above their noise Nell reads to me. She's extraordinarily solicitous. I think it's my wince at changing positions that brings on the tremulous query, "Was it me, Mum? Did I get you too overwrought?"

At first I don't know what she's talking about.

"When I ran away. I didn't really mean all that much by it. I didn't think it could . . . you know." She gestures at my supine form.

"And I'm sorry about Toni, too," she rattles on, just as I begin to realize that she thinks she's responsible for my condition. "Elizabeth was going on about him when Ollie and I went around for dinner. I had no idea he was in such a fix. Me and Stuart and Elizabeth went to his old address to leave a note for him. Just in case he came by. But Stuart said he wouldn't. He said he'd probably left London. I told Damian about it anyhow, 'cause Damian has an Albanian friend he works with and he said he would ask about Toni . . . He also said maybe Toni needed to run away 'cause he was being pursued by the Albanian Mafia, which controls some of the Soho vice rings. So, like, you mustn't feel bad, Mum, really."

I can't keep up with Nell's flow of intelligence, and store it away for future reflection. What I do see is that she's beseeching me from a face grown wretched.

"This bloody back has nothing to do with you, darling. Really not. The stairs did it. Too many of them. And I guess I was tired and out of condition."

"Only they said on the Net."

"Who said what on the Net?"

"These back-pain sites I went to visit. You know. To find out. They said stress could cause . . ."

"They say stress can cause anything. Everything. You might as well say life causes things. 'Cause there isn't one without stress."

Nell stares at me.

"It's not to do with you."

I stretch out my hand to clasp hers. I am so touched by her need to apologize and her concern that I want to cry again.

She comes close to me for a cuddle. Then she murmurs, "Maybe you could take up meditation."

I imagine myself cross-legged and start to laugh. So does she. But it hurts. Laughing hurts. That's the worst of it, Celia.

Robert goes back to London on Monday evening and Nell stays behind as my principal carer. We make a funny old team. Every morning, almost as early as if it were a school day, just after she's let the nurse in for my first injection, she races off to the *boulangerie* and the market and comes home triumphantly with supplies. Both of us are practising French, and before she heads off anywhere we rehearse the conversations she's going to have. I send her off to buy me a dressing gown and a couple of nighties. Pyjamas, let alone clothes, are too hard to put on. I send her off on an expedition to the

Louvre with specific instructions about the pictures I want reports on. She comes back exhausted, but her sketch pad is packed. Her chat is full of stories of the men who tried to pick her up in front of Canova or da Vinci. Galleries, it seems, are still sites of amorous play. Some things haven't changed.

The one plus in all this hideous business — apart from this wonderful new closeness with Nell — is that I've stopped smoking. I think it's the drugs and all that half-sleep. The cigarettes don't agree with them. Then, too, I can't ask Nell for supplies, nor Robert. So the promise I'd made to myself that I'd stop on the Big 5-0 has come true. Despite myself, I'm a smoke-free zone.

Yesterday we have a surprise visit. Elizabeth and Stuart have decided on a day trip to Paris. Burdened with gourmet food, they're panting by the time they reach my eyrie and ring the doorbell. I'm touched by their visit, equally touched by the feast they prepare for us. I try to eat to please them, but with all these drugs and lying about, my appetite isn't what it was just a short few weeks ago. Elizabeth is full of advice. She's had back problems in her time, too, though nothing quite like this. As soon as I manage to get back to England, she tells me, I have to go to her osteopath, and he'll advise me as to whether a scan is necessary or whether traditional therapies will see me through. Elizabeth sounds like an expert as she talks up a storm about spines and sciatic nerves and L3s and epidurals and operations. My mind goes blanker than it already is.

After lunch she sends Stuart off with Nell and I know we're going to have a chat about him. Things are going better between them, it seems. Elizabeth's face has a trace of caginess. Yes, soon Stuart is heading off for a stint at the Carcassonne house, where she'll join him in August. Elizabeth winks at me boldly and laughs. "He misses the place. And I . . . well, I suddenly feel up to a little adventure."

I wish I could say the same for myself. My adventure consists of taking a shower. Have you ever tried getting into a bathtub when you can raise your foot only some six inches off the floor? Scott of the Antarctic had nothing on this.
Love,
Jude

MONDAY

Dear, dear Celia,
I can barely believe it. It's happened. A word from you. A word that, judging by the postmark on the change-of-address card, left Ghent several months ago, maybe not so far from the time when I started to write to you. And you ask me to get in touch, since you're just across the Channel. Oh, Celia, you were trying to find me, just as I was trying to find you. The card arrived at home this week and Ollie gave it to Robert, who brought it here. I don't quite know what trajectory it went on before that, whether it lay in some dead-letter office or simply gathered dust at my former address until someone remembered where to post it on. No matter. Serendipity.

You know, I never altogether believed those stories of telepathy or coincidences. Like this young woman Francesca knows, who was kicked out of boarding school because of a boy she was seeing clandestinely and then moved by her parents to another city. Fifteen years later she and the boy both set out at the same time to find each other by e-mail and, lo and behold, they do. And now they're living together.

Or my one-time neighbour years ago whose husband died, and a month later she hears from her first-ever high-school boyfriend in America, whose wife has left him, and he's been trying to track my neighbour down, and . . . well, I won't bore you with happy endings.

And now, you and me . . . Could it be that you'd read Patrick's obituary, too, and our thoughts moved towards each other?

Whatever the case, I'm so glad to hear from you, Celia, because I really had promised myself I wouldn't write to you any more and bore you with my misadventures. But here I am, still on the floor and with little to do. So it's a pleasure to be given permission to succumb to my only remaining addiction, rather than vowing to wean myself as soon as I'm up.

I now actually believe I will be up. Yesterday, with Robert's help, I not only stood relatively straight, but I did several turns round the room and stepped out on the tiny rectangle of a terrace to look up at the sky and breathe in the outdoors. Bliss. Everything is so extraordinary when you're convalescing — colours, scents, shapes, tastes. I could wax lyrical, but I'd need a poet to help.

It occurred to me as I stood on the terrace with Robert at my side that maybe my back had struck on my fiftieth to provide me with an initiation rite into life on the other side — to remind me that it was a privilege to be alive, that small things could be just as significant as the supposedly big ones.

One of the legs hasn't quite made it back from the dead, though. Feel a bit like a marionette whose strings aren't quite pulling the appropriate limbs. A doctor whom one of Robert's friends recommended came to tap and tug and said it was all just a matter of time, with a little help from the kines-therapies (that's what he called them). Time and motion therapy — just what a BIG 5-0er needs for her birthday. At least he didn't tell me to start on a longer book to pass the hours. I've all but finished *Madame Bovary* in French. No, I didn't choose it because of the suicide. It just happened to be in the studio. Maybe Emma identifies with her namesake and harbours fantasies of lords in country mansions vs. dull-as-dishwater husbands.

Not that Robert felt dull to me over this last weekend. Downright exciting, in fact. But then, the distractions a floor offers aren't all that many. Seriously, it really was wonderful to have him here. In my vulnerable state he makes me feel secure — to the point that I think my back relaxes more when he's here.

He's being so sweet and generous, too; I even told him so. I have, after all, despite myself, taken over his and Emma's place, so that he has to go off to a hotel while Nell and I are in occupation. I was glad that at least this weekend he took some time in the evenings to see friends.

He's been with us so much these last weeks, not only here in Paris, but at home as well, that I finally built up my courage yesterday while Nell was out, and said something. I said, "I hope Emma doesn't mind my being here in the studio too, too much."

Robert gave me a blank stare, then gazed out the window. I thought he might start whistling the way he always used to when he didn't feel like talking about something. Instead he cleared his throat and said, "You might as well know."

The rest of the sentence was a long time in coming. "Emma and I aren't exactly together anymore."

"Oh?"

"Yeah. It's been building up for quite a while." His eyes are fixed on the house opposite as if he were Jimmy Stewart in *Rear Window*.

"You mean . . ."

"I mean Em's been seeing someone else. We've more or less split up."

If I weren't on the floor and grateful and an up-and-coming icon of born-again goodness (which is the effect that gratitude can have on you unless it acts in perverse ways), I might at this juncture have said, "I could have told you so. Did you really think a young and sexy woman would spend all her days being faithful to an old codger like . . ." But I didn't. I had only just thought it before I chased the thought away. But what popped out was almost as bad.

"Well, it can't be because of Nell and me. We never managed to keep you apart before."

"Ouch. Guess you're feeling better."

"Sorry. Sorry. Didn't quite mean it that way. I'm really sorry."

Robert had the wit to laugh. "Inevitable, really. The parting, I mean. Strange thing is, apart from the wounded vanity, I don't mind all that much. I haven't been concentrating on her for some time."

At this point, he met my eyes. He had a little of that lost air which sometimes overtakes him when he isn't in full, determined control — like a dog who doesn't understand quite why he's suddenly been hit.

I was about to tell him that he looked tired, but I bit back my words. Those particular ones have the same effect on Robert as they do on Nell — which isn't good. And I was being mellow. (No, I wasn't crowing. I think I'd got quite used to the idea of Robert with Emma. It gave shape to my plight. A little like a defining identity with a ready-made solidarity group, which saves you the bother of having to find any others. You know, middle-aged woman with large chip on shoulder 'cause she's been thrown over for a trophy bimbette.)

"It's probably a good thing we didn't get married," Robert muses.

"Didn't you? I hadn't quite taken that on board."

"No, it didn't feel like the kind of thing one needed to do a third time."

I managed a laugh.

Robert didn't join me. Instead he said, "We went to visit your mother, Ollie and I."

"Did the home ring him? Was something wrong?" I try not to stiffen in nervousness 'cause it hurts.

"Apparently she kept telling the staff you were getting married and she had to get ready for the wedding. So they wanted to check."

His eyes quiz me as I mumble something about my mum's confusion.

"Ollie calmed her down." He pauses. "She really has deteriorated quickly, hasn't she?"

"Is it that quick?"

"Maybe not." Robert is kind to my defensiveness. He looks out the window again. We both seem to be listening to the passing of time.

"Jude," he says at last, in a voice which makes me wish I'd put some makeup on. "I think by next weekend we should be able to get you back to London. The stairs are going to be difficult, though. If you can't manage it, we'll have to get someone else here to stay with you."

"I know. Nell's camp begins. We've talked about it. Francesca might come for a few days. But it should be okay. I'll do it. I'm almost ready now."

I say it with more certainty than I feel. The strange thing about not going out for so long is that you want to more than anything else, but you're also petrified. The world feels like a terrifying challenge.

So I'm building myself up to re-entry slowly. This morning I got dressed, with almost no help from Nell. Knickers are the worst. Tights are out of the question, as are trousers. But skirts and dresses are fine. Which means my wardrobe is useless. Guess the silver cloud in all this is that when I've had enough of the kines-therapie, I can take myself shopping. Maybe we can go together, Celia. If you don't turn against me after all these letters land on you.

Love,
Jude

WEDNESDAY, 25 JULY

Dearest Celia,
You rang!

So strange to hear you after all this time, and quite wonderful. If I hadn't been lying down, I might well have fallen over when Nell picked up the phone and called out, "It's for you, Mum. Celia someone."

Well, hello, Celia Someone.

I wouldn't have recognized you, you know, without the prompt of a name. Your voice has changed. It's moved down a notch or two. You've gone all sex and fags and Lauren Bacall-y. Or is it the effect of the years in America? Whichever, Celia, it was such a pleasure to hear you. It also made me trebly curious. Who are you now? What are you like? We have to meet. Soon. And you'll have to come to me, 'cause in my present state, the trek back to London is the only adventure I'll be able to manage for some months.

I was devastated to hear that you'd just got back to Ghent from Paris, where you'd come straight after your months in Turkey. To celebrate your birthday here. Just like me. We were a mere matter of streets away without realizing it. If my back hadn't given up, we probably would have bumped into each other at the market. Would we have recognized each other, I wonder?

You sounded shocked to hear about my back. True, it hasn't been a salutary experience, though it has kept my mind off wrinkles and sags. Still, shrieking pain aside, I don't like being reminded quite so graphically that mortality has taken a hold. A stranglehold. But everyone assures me it'll pass. Hope so. Don't think I can run a profitable bookshop from a reclining position. As far as I know, there are only two things you can do from this position. The first would hurt too much, and during the second you're unconscious, if not terminally laid out.

By the time you receive this, you'll probably have read a chunk of the letters which have pursued you from Canada to the US to Belgium. I'm so pleased that you opened my most recent letters first, so that you knew where to reach me straightaway, and left the packets from the US to one side. If by now you've read some of what Jim sent on from San Francisco, you may no longer be speaking to me. Being cornered by unexpected intimacy may feel like having a large dog slobbering all over you. An unpleasant imposition, to say the least.

Just chuck the letters, Celia. I'm already ashamed of them and there's no need to read them, as I said on the phone. After all, the habit of writing to you started because I wanted to tell you about Patrick's death. The rest is probably more than a friendship *interruptus* can bear. I hope Patrick's book arrived, by the way. I sent that on before I left London.

I have to confess, it feels odd writing to you now that we've spoken. You sounded a little timid over the phone, as if we hadn't shared so much. I know, it was all a quarter of a century ago. The Soviet Union still existed. Chairman Mao was alive (or so they told us) and the Sex Pistols were kicking. Maggie Thatcher was only a little-known milk snatcher. Sixty-seven per cent of Brits, prompted by yea-saying Tories (yes, Tories), voted to stay in the European Community. Mere bricks created a scandal at the Tate Gallery, which hadn't burgeoned into more and bigger and better Tates. The sex discrimination act had just come in and, love it or hate it, everyone seemed to know what feminism was for. And even I could manage without a bra.

The world has indeed changed. Now you're a stranger, Celia. Never mind, we'll get to know each other all over again. *My love,* *Jude*

Dear, dear Celia —
How kind of you. I'm so touched. There they were waiting for
me when I got back to London, the most beautiful assortment
of summer blooms, a whole cottage garden tied with ribbon.
Thank you. Thank you so very much. The get-well message
cheered me, too.

I needed the cheer, I can tell you. The journey home felt
like an Outward Bound expedition to the Hebrides, with me
starring as the rucksack. First there were the stairs. It's interesting how this technology for ascending and descending,
which I've never paid any attention to before, except for an
occasional groan after a glass too many, suddenly looms as the
invention of the devil himself. It took us half an hour to get
from the fifth floor. And that was going down. Robert is about
to be awarded the Florence Nightingale gold medal for
patience on crooked stairwells (with a sub-citation for sterling
imitation of a banister). It really would have been easier to
lower me from a window in one of those bread baskets pur-
veyors used in the more distant part of the twentieth century.
Or just to throw me out.

Stairs accomplished, getting into a taxi was easy-peasy and
took a mere ten minutes of clenched teeth while lowering rear
end into the seat, which I swear was far lower than what cars
had a mere two weeks ago. Luckily my rear end is now substantially shrunken, thanks to diminished appetite, so wasn't
pulled down with a thud by great weight. I won't bore you
with my grand entry onto the Eurostar. I succumbed to the
wheelchair I had initially refused, closed my eyes to make

myself as invisible as everyone seemed to assume I was anyhow, given that I found myself in one, and let myself be pushed.

I have never, never been so happy to reach home. The house felt like paradise.

Nell was pretty happy, too. She got straight on the phone, having stayed off her mobile for the entire journey from Waterloo, and was out the door an hour later, her navel once again in evidence, her trousers sweeping the floor. It was Saturday night, after all, and she was off to see Damian. She did cast me a second's glance and say, "You're all right, Mum, aren't you?" To which, of course, I nodded a reassuring yes. The order of the universe is restored.

During the week, Robert and Ollie had purchased a rock-hard divan with multiple cushions and had had it installed downstairs. I can now recline at my ease like some world-weary Mme. de Merteuil. I look out on the garden while I ponder the various tasks I can't do. Or I can entertain. I'm only an apple's throw from the kitchen. This is a real boon. On the way home I had been dreading that extra set of stairs up to the bedroom. Robert really has thought of everything, despite the fact that he's seemed just a teensy bit distracted.

I suspect that has to do with Emma, about whom I really can't in all fairness ask him too much, though I'm more curious than an alley cat looking in on the juicy remains of an interrupted feast. I'd like to sniff round all the broken plates.

Nell knows far more than I do, and inadvertently let a little drop in that time we had together. Needless to say, she's more than pleased at the thought that her dad and Emma are going their separate ways. Emma's, it seems, has taken her to the home of a well-known record producer (known to Nell, in any case, and she's rather impressed at that, but won't, I suspect, be invited over).

They didn't row much, Nell tells me, not that she heard, anyhow. The little she said made me conjure up scenes of a bored, slightly catty Emma occasionally attacking Robert just to get a rise out of him, or simply going off to pursue her own pleasures so that Nell could have her lovely dad all to herself. I imagine my mischief-making daughter may have been as responsible as Robert himself in throwing Em into the arms of another.

As for Robert, he looks a little dazed. Come to think of it, this is the first time he's been left, poor sod.

Well, it's given him more time to deal with yours truly and her now innumerable difficulties. He actually said to me after we'd got back and I was ensconced on my new divan, "You know, you really ought to talk to your neighbours and see if they're planning to sell at any point. You'd be better off down-stairs. And you'd have the garden. I know you love gardens."

My response was to glare at him, though he's right, of course. Backless fifty-somethings should live as close to the ground as possible. I'm just not too sure that my ex should be organizing my life. So I turned the tables on him and asked him what he was going to do with his ultra-cool loft now that his ultra-cool mate had run off. (I didn't put it like that, really I didn't. I was measured and contained and altogether lady-like, not to mention grateful.)

He just shrugged a "we'll see" and turned his attention back on me. It occurs to me that, in some ways, I'm rather useful to him at the moment. He can do things for me if not for Em, and Robert has always had that enviable quality of liking to do things for people.

Then, just as I heard Ollie and Francesca at the door, he actually said . . . "Maybe I'll just move back in with you and leave Em the loft."

I was about to rise to that when I saw the teasing grin on his face, and Ollie and Francesca were there, hugging me — well, not exactly hugging, but treating me like rather brittle china — while they explained that they'd met on the street. And while they explained, I had this thought that Ollie might now want to move back to his dad's place, just as I really needed him around here.

But now I've done far more than send you the planned thank-you note and have probably bored you to distraction. Why don't you just come and visit, Celia? There's plenty of space, what with Nell going off to her camp and me downstairs. You could even have my bedroom. I won't be great on the taking-you-out-for-dinner front, but we can giggle over Patrick's book and go for walks (I'm meant to be walking as much as I can without combusting into pain) and catch up on your life and . . . well, just take up friendship again. Ken Livingstone knows you might even like London now. It's a lot livelier than when you left it. (And I promise not to drag you to visit my mother.)

My love,
Jude

MONDAY

Dear, dear Celia,
I'm so, so pleased that you've decided to Eurostar over from Brussels. I enclose instructions on how to get here, in case you're stuck with a cabby whose knowledge leaves a little to be desired. I so look forward to seeing you.
Love,
Jude

5 SEPTEMBER

Dearest Celia,
I'm sorry I haven't written sooner, even to acknowledge your thank you, but life has just been — well, extraordinary. I don't know where to begin. But I know, I just know, that in some odd way everything that has happened has been precipitated by you — even if you're not aware of it.

But first of all, let me just say how wonderful it was to see you — and see you looking so amazing, too — all continental and impeccably groomed, yet still girlish despite the years. Did I manage to put into words that I thought in a way you had reached your ideal age — that mysterious one we're meant to carry within ourselves? (I think mine was unfortunately around twenty-eight and is sadly long gone.) Seriously, Celia. You seemed not only wiser, but kinder.

I'm rambling. I just want to underline how much I enjoyed catching up and hearing about all those years in your life that I'd missed. I was so glad that you'd forgiven me my mad weekend with Jim, and had decided to take it as a tribute to my wanting to be close to you (though that accommodation took a few years of wisdom to arrive at, I know). I was so glad to be able to talk about Patrick with you and to giggle over his rendition of us in his book. I was glad about the girl and body chat and the children chat and . . . well, about everything really, except that my parlous state didn't allow me to take you out and show you the town. So I was specially glad that before you left Robert was able to do a little of that in my place and then drive you to the station. I think all that gladness must have somehow prepared me for what happened next . . . And though it's difficult to put things in an exact order, I'm going to try, since I still haven't quite managed to make sense of it all.

You'll remember that on Sunday we were sitting chatting with Heather (whom I could feel you weren't all that keen to see, but I had invited her thinking you might like to . . .) when Robert arrived bearing flowers and a heap of groceries. He seemed a little nonplussed to find us all together. Conversation began to creak distinctly, so I had this idea that you and Robert might be happier with something else to do, and I sent you off on a sightseeing expedition, the long way around to Waterloo.

No sooner were you out the door than Heather says to me, "I don't know what you think you're doing."

"What do you mean?" I ask.

"I mean sending your distinctly delicious ex off with that Celia. She'll seduce him in no time."

"Heather! Robert's not . . . Celia's not like that." I was flabbergasted. "And . . . well, even if she did, it's none of my business."

"You're mad." Heather started to rant at me. "And he'd obviously come around to be with you. Do you really not give a damn? 'Cause if you don't . . ."

I won't bore you with a recap of this entire conversation, Celia, but I started wondering whether I did in fact give a damn. And whether you might just use some of your winning ways on a newly free Robert. All of which sent the fantasy channel swirling.

Not that I had much time for any channel, because the doorbell rang soon after and there, lo and behold, stood Toni.

I was sorry that you'd gone. I would have liked you to meet him, even though the poor, poor darling wasn't at his best. To be honest, he looked utterly wrecked, though how I dare even squeak that — given what he's going through, let alone what he must have thought of the newly backless yours truly — I don't know. In any case, to cut a longish story short, Toni sat down at table with us and ate ravenously. It was clear that he hadn't had a square meal in days. I didn't like to think why. It was clear, too, from his embarrassed hemming and hawing as he told us that he was hoping to go up to Edinburgh, where he'd heard there was work, that he was desperate for funds and wouldn't be able to cover his train fare if we didn't help.

I let him understand that I now knew about at least some of his difficulties and that I'd be happy to give him a loan to set him on his way. Heather dittoed. He looked at us with a mixture of shame and gratitude. It made me want to take him in my arms. I realized simultaneously that the desire was now purely maternal!

Anyhow, Heather went off to the bank with both our cards, since Toni needs his money in cash. Meanwhile I suggested to

Toni that he might like a shower, even a change of clothes (I was planning on raiding Ollie's room).

While he was showering, the doorbell rang. I couldn't work out who it might be. It was too soon for Heather to be back, and I just hoped, as I hobbled down the stairs, that it wouldn't be some god salesfolk, since I wasn't buying, and I was in no mood for being sweet just 'cause some sweet black child was in tow helping to spread the word.

The figure I saw when I opened the door would have made the Witnesses welcome. There, in all his bludgeoning shininess, stood Michael Carton, he of the immigration squad, and there, unsuspecting in my shower, stood poor Toni.

I won't bore you with the non-conversation that took place — with my insisting no knowledge, while Carton insisted otherwise. It was when he tried to push past me and my voice rose to a veritable shriek that things took a dramatic turn. 'Cause it was then that Robert chose to turn up and, imagining heaven only knows what, made a good show of lifting Carton by the lapels, exclaiming something like "If my wife says go, you go!" and shoving him out the door.

The man didn't know what had hit him. He squealed, "Your wife?" as he tried to reach into his pocket for his ID. I would have squealed too, but the thud of the door rather took my breath away.

As we made our way up to my living room, I attempted to thank Robert, but he was so busy asking me what all that was about that I don't think he heard me. Toni, on the other hand, must have heard something of the fuss at the door, because when we reached the living room, he was standing there, still damp, wrapped in a towel. I don't like to describe the look Robert gave me then, but it wasn't kind. Nor was his colour.

He had turned a purple his cardiologist would have attributed to an "episode." But he didn't clutch his heart, so I deduced it wasn't a heart attack he was suffering from, just a bit of overexertion coupled with surprise.

I told Toni to go and get dressed and explained as best I could to Robert who Carton was and why he'd been so insistent. Robert had decidedly lost his ability to speak, on top of which he refused to meet my eyes, so I hurried to make some tea, at which point the bell rang again and he raced down the stairs as if he were off into the boxing ring. I can't tell you how relieved I was to hear Heather's voice.

I started to catch her up on matters and she cut me off with, "So that's why he looked familiar." She had apparently seen Carton getting into his car and driving off.

"Right," Robert said as soon as he heard that. "We'll have to move your friend out of here while the opportunity presents itself."

"But, where can he . . . ?"

"He can't stay here." Robert flashed me a fierce look. "That snoop will be back."

Instead it was Toni who was back in the room, dressed now. He probed our faces with visible anxiety.

"You come with me," Robert ordered.

Toni cleared his throat, but before he could say anything Heather intervened. "Yes, I think that's a good idea, Toni. Robert here will take you somewhere safe." She managed to hand Toni the money with a totally inoffensive gesture and a murmur of "And here's what we owe you."

He gave us each a dignified little bow and a smile, so utterly charming, that I wanted again to hug him, but Robert was standing by, all but tapping his foot in impatience, so I just murmured "good luck" and prayed that Robert didn't dump him at the nearest tube station simply because he was young and fetching and therefore a threat to all womankind.

So off they went, and Heather and I poured ourselves some wine and paced and brooded over Toni's fate. She also kept repeating that she thought Robert was distinctly interested in me, and I have to say, to my surprise, my heart lurched; maybe, on top of everything else, the way he had handled that awful immigration cop had got to me.

But Robert didn't come back that evening, or the next or the next. Nor did he phone. I concluded that Heather had been a little wishful in her assumptions and that I had managed to fantasize myself into terminal delusion. Misery took me over, as did worry. Why didn't he tell me what he'd done with Toni? Why didn't he ring or come by, something he'd been doing with great regularity since my back gave up? I asked Ollie discreetly how his dad was, but he'd heard nothing either.

I can't tell you how slow and ghastly the passage of the days was. The back was still too delicate for work. Nor could I drive. In fact, the thing I could do best was pace. Or lie down. I paced. I didn't even have the energy to write to you.

By mid-week I rang Robert at the loft and, guess what, Emma was back. Needless to say, I hung up with a bang, something I'd never sunk to, not even in those first weeks. It all made me so furious that the next day, like some Hannibal crossing the Alps, I engaged in the unthinkable. I rang Robert at his office, only to be smartly told that he was in a meeting and did I want to leave a message. I didn't. The words of the message would have left his assistant blue and gasping, like a speared fish.

I think it was that day that our very own immigration snoop decided to come around again. I was pleased. Not so much by the male company as by what it implied. Carton hadn't got his hands on Toni yet, though he made such a good job of threatening me with all kinds of fines and tortures that I thought I'd invite him in and let him have a good look round. As a tease, really.

He didn't have the courtesy to say thank you.

By Saturday I had begun to worry about Nell's homecoming. Robert usually collects her from the train station on the Sunday after her camp weeks, but who knew where he'd gotten himself to this year? So I geared Ollie up to fetch her and on Sunday waited impatiently for her return. I miss Nell when she's away, even more so this year.

But guess what? It isn't Ollie who comes back with a wind- and sun-toasted Nell. It's Robert. I don't know how I could ever have imagined he would let his daughter down.

The post-camp routine involves putting everything Nell is carrying and wearing into the washing machine while she herself steps into a hot bath and scrubs the weeks of mud away. This happens before any debriefing.

So, after a cursory hug and an "It was great, Mum," Nell heads for the stairs. She's a quarter of the way up when she turns back and lobs a ball towards me. "Has he moved in yet?" she asks, with a smirk at the two of us.

She's upstairs before I can splutter anything in return, but I'm about to shout an emphatic no after her when I meet Robert's eyes at last. There's a plea in them which makes me go very still.

"I know. I should have rung."

"You've had other things on your mind. Emma's come back."

"What?" He looks at me uncomprehendingly, then swallows in that way men have when they're about to say something they haven't got words for.

I haven't got any either, for once. So we just look at each other, and finally I manage to blurt out, "What happened with Toni?"

"Toni. Yes, yes. Of course." Robert is searching for something. Maybe it's a chair. I've forgotten to ask him to sit down.

"Would you . . . would you like a glass of wine?" I gesture lamely towards the kitchen counter.

"Yes, yes. I'll get it. I've been thinking . . . We should talk."

But he doesn't talk straight away. He just uncorks a bottle and then looks around for glasses and, finding the dishwasher full ('cause I find it hard to bend to empty it), decides to empty that, and while he's tidying away some plates he says, as if in afterthought, "Yes, Toni. I drove him to Horsham. Set him up with a job at the warehouse."

"What?" I can't quite seem take this in.

"Yeah. They had some openings. And the manager's always pleased to rent out a room in his house. So the boy's okay. I had a word with a top immigration solicitor, too. Hope I got the story right. Nell's rendition was very dramatic."

I swallow. "That's very kind of you."

Robert suddenly meets my eyes head on. An icy blaze of blue. "Do you miss him?"

"Miss him?" I echo stupidly, and turn away to stand by the window. The street is deserted except for the tabby who lives opposite. He's perched like some forlorn china jug at the top of the steps and is staring at his front door.

Robert comes to stand beside me and I hear him say in a low voice, "Because I thought we might try again. Have another go. It's been on my mind for a while. Even before Em picked up and left. Sometimes it's unclear who's really done the leaving."

I look at him. His face is taut, serious. He's talking about me, too. All those years ago — when neither of us could get used to his having been on the verge.

He suddenly strokes my hair and I find myself shivering. I take a step towards him and he brushes my lips and suddenly I hear a wild yelp of laughter.

"Yo, you lot. Cut that out. I'm ravenous." Nell is grinning like some star conductor bowing to the audience at the end of an opera. Her cheeks are pink from scrubbing. Her hair shines, and she comes towards us to give us each a hug, so that a moment later, despite that precarious back of mine, we're all entwined.

So, Celia, this is my staggering announcement. Robert and I really are going to have another go. Maybe not wedding bells and cream-puff dresses straightaway, 'cause that might make Nell puke, whatever my mother's attraction to weddings, but some simpler arrangement that may eventually look quite a lot like a version of togetherness. We'll certainly have a big party, to which you will be duly invited. It is partly your doing, after all. I might not have been quite so amenable to Robert and his undeniable attractions — might even have been eternally barricaded against them — if you hadn't been there to help me through. All of us have grown kinder, I think. Gentler in our wants.

And you know what? It's strange, but I feel solid again — as if I've acquired some kind of inner heft and gravitas, despite the brittle bones and the tick-tock of Father Time. As if I'd left behind that slightly flimsy tumbleweed of a thing I'd become. I think Robert feels the same.

You and Robert — between you most of the years of my life are stored . . . We're all ballast for each other. No bad thing in these days that fling one around so much. Kicking fifty and coming out the other side has its pluses.

All my love,

Jude